MERCY
DOGS

ALSO BY TYLER DILTS
LONG BEACH HOMICIDE SERIES

for Karen,

3/17/18

MERCY
DOGS

Thank you for reading and supporting Book Carnival!

TYLER DILTS

[signature]

🐦 THOMAS & MERCER

Text copyright © 2018 by Tyler Dilts
All rights reserved.

Published by Thomas & Mercer, Seattle

www.apub.com

Amazon, the Amazon logo, and Thomas & Mercer are trademarks of Amazon.com, Inc., or its affiliates.

ISBN-13: 9781503951785
ISBN-10: 1503951782

Cover design by Scott Biel

Printed in the United States of America

For my mother, Sharon Dilts,
who never does bad things.

"The Krauts called them 'sanitary dogs,'" the old man said, shaking his head.

"But when I was lying there in the middle of all that stink and carnage, absolutely sure I was going to bleed to death from where I took the shrapnel in my leg, out of nowhere that collie came up to me with its Red Cross saddlebags and I remembered what they told us about the dogs and I got out the bandages and the tourniquet and I was able to fix myself well enough." Here he paused to tap the handle of his cane against his prosthetic leg, making a hollow, echoing thump. "I was still alive when the medics finally got to me. While I was waiting, and it was a long wait, I watched that dog.

"She had moved on. A few bodies to the south of me, she came upon that kid Etheridge, the one who'd only been with us a couple weeks. He was a lot worse off than me. That collie, she knew, I could see it." He paused for a long moment, as if lost in the memory, then continued. "She nuzzled her head up against his chest, and he took his arm—he just had the one at that point—and he wrapped it around her. I watched her head there on top of him, moving up and down with his breathing. When it stopped moving, she let out this low, sad moan. Then she moved on to the next soldier. And the next. And on and on like that.

"Fucking Krauts didn't know what they were talking about. We called them what they were. Mercy dogs."

—Peter Shepard, *Towards Our Distant Rest: World War I and Its Aftermaths*

ONE

Grace was gone.

"Where is she?" Peter asked. Usually by this time she'd be out on the back patio with him, coffee cups on the table in front of them, both of them bundled up against the morning chill as they waved at the early departures from Long Beach Airport jetting overhead.

"I don't know, Dad," Ben said.

Anxiety crept into Peter's voice. "She's not in her place?"

"No." Ben had already checked the studio out back. No sign of her. He'd even walked around the attached garage into the alley to see if her Prius was in the parking space along the back fence. It wasn't there.

"Did I do something bad?" Peter's hand started to shake. "Make her mad?"

"No way." Ben rubbed his father's bony shoulder. He still hadn't regained enough weight after the last surgery. "You never do bad things."

Peter looked up at him.

Ben took the notebook out of his pocket and checked it. Maybe Grace had mentioned something the day before and he'd forgotten. He thumbed back through the pages. A note about his insomnia, written after three that morning, his handwriting even more indecipherable than usual. Then the list of his evening meds with the time, 12:17 a.m., and four check marks to ensure he hadn't missed anything. Before that he'd watched that new show where everybody dies and Kiefer Sutherland becomes president. Didn't think it was very good, but watched the whole thing anyway. *Okay for Dad???* he'd scribbled. Then Peter's list of meds, with check marks that looked just like the ones he'd made above. He went back page by page.

Nothing about Grace.

"Does it say about her?" Peter asked with hopeful eyes.

Ben shook his head. "We'll figure it out. I'm sure it's okay."

"I hope so."

"She's just renting the studio from us. She doesn't have to tell us everything about where she goes or when she'll be home."

"She's nice," Peter said.

"I know she is, Dad. I know."

As Ben scribbled in his notebook, he heard the scream of jet engines rising in the east. He watched his father turn his eyes to the sky and wait for the plane to make itself visible beyond the edge of the roof. Peter's eyes widened when he saw it and he lifted his hand, but his wave was half-hearted and there was no smile on his face.

• • •

Peter lay back on the exam table and pulled up his flannel shirt.

Dr. Riyaz checked the scar on his stomach from the last surgery. "This looks good. How long has it been?"

Ben knew the question was directed at him. "Seven months." He watched the doctor palpate his father's abdomen. "We've finally gotten some weight back on him," he said. "But I know he still needs to gain more. The most we've been able to get down in a day is sixteen hundred calories."

"Does this hurt?" Riyaz asked.

"No," Peter said.

He pressed in more places and watched Peter's face. After the last one, he said, "Good. You can sit up."

Peter pulled his shirt down and winced as he pushed himself upright. The doctor was typing and didn't see his face.

"Did that hurt, Dad?" Ben asked.

"A little bit," Peter said.

The doctor looked back at him. "Where?"

Peter put his hand over the incision.

"The abdominal muscles take a long time to heal," Riyaz said. "How is your stool?"

Peter looked confused, so Ben answered for him. "Mostly loose and liquidy, but occasionally, maybe every third or fourth day, a little more solid with small, kind of curly pieces." Ben had double-checked his notes for the last few weeks to make sure he'd be able to answer correctly.

Riyaz looked both surprised and pleased by the degree of detail. He was always pleasant and unflappable, but seemed especially warm when he said, "You're a good son."

• • •

10:45 Dad Gastro Appt
Healing good, everything ok
Cont. Miralax daily, adjust dose as needed
Increase calories / GAIN MORE WEIGHT—Fruit, veg—smoothies, shakes
Come back three months

• • •

"How about a shake for lunch, Dad?"

Peter sat at the counter, facing Ben in the kitchen. "Could I have some more?" He held up his coffee cup.

"Sure. But we need something else, too. I'm going to make you a shake, okay?" Ben took the cup and filled it halfway with vanilla Boost Plus, then topped it off from the fresh pot of decaf and added a tablespoon of sugar. That was good for another 190 calories. He'd have to check to be sure, but with the breakfast coffee and oatmeal, that should be around 580 so far. Ben blended berries, apple slices, yogurt, milk, and sugar in the NutriBullet. If Peter could get it all down, they'd be well over 1,000 and might be able to get to 1,600 by bedtime.

"Is she back yet?"

"I don't know, Dad. She probably just got called in to work an extra shift or something. I'm sure it's okay."

"Did you look to see?"

"No."

Peter looked down at his hands.

"I will, okay?" Ben poured the smoothie into a cup and put it on the woven blue placemat in front of his father. "Drink that and I'll go outside and check on Grace."

"Okay." Peter made a sour face as he took another sip.

"Alexa." Ben waited for the blue ring on top of the black cylinder on the counter to light up. "Play Willie Nelson."

"Shuffling songs by Willie Nelson," she answered. As he walked out the patio door on the other side of the dining table, he heard the opening chords of "Always on My Mind" fading behind him.

He stepped off the concrete and crossed the large back lawn to the small second patio in the back, along the alley. When he'd grown up in the house, all that was attached to the garage was an unfinished bonus room the family used for storage. His mom had always wanted to turn it into a small studio guesthouse so Grandma or Aunt Marilyn could stay there when they came to visit. Maybe they could even rent it out someday. But work on the bathroom and kitchenette had barely been finished when she got her diagnosis. No one had ever stayed there for more than a night or two until five years later, when Ben was released from rehab and moved in so Peter could take care of him.

It didn't happen often anymore, but as Ben got closer to the studio, he felt the familiar surge of uncontrollable memories assault him.

You wake to the sound of your own screams, middle of the night, shaking, sweating, the cold cutting down to your bones. The dream, the nightmare, is almost there, you can almost touch it, but as you begin to realize where you are, it recedes, and the faster you chase it, the more swiftly it retreats. You know only that it terrified you, but somehow you think—no, you're certain—that the terror you're so desperately trying to reach is the truth of what you lost and that no matter how horrific it is, if you could just reach it, catch even a fleeting glimpse of it, you would be able to shine a light into the darkness of the vast empty chasm of your memory and that you'd be able to see, to understand, to know—

"Ben!"

The voice sounds far away.

But you recognize it.

"Dad?"

"I'm here, son, I'm here." You feel his arms around you. The cold begins to recede. You're hardly even shaking anymore.

But it's gone.

You almost saw it.

You almost knew.

You feel the darkness but you also feel the warmth.

Your father holds you, rubs your back like he did when you were a child, and you can't understand how you got from there to here.

There was still no sign of Grace. But if she'd been called in to work a breakfast-to-lunch shift, she wouldn't be back yet. She almost always worked nights. At least in the five months she'd been here. Tuesday, Wednesday, Thursday. She didn't like weekends. Too busy, she'd told him. She did okay on the weeknights. Okay enough, anyway. They were giving her a great deal on the rent. Probably only about two-thirds of what they could have gotten for the place. But they'd only been half-serious about taking on a tenant when Rob Kessler, Ben's old partner from his first plainclothes assignment in Narcotics, called out of the blue and asked for a favor.

• • •

"Q-E-D?"

"Yeah," Ben said, stirring a purple capful of Miralax into a blue Solo cup of water. Had to be blue. The red ones didn't work for Peter. "Q-E-D."

Quetiapine fumarate 50 mg. Escitalopram 20 mg. Donepezil 10 mg.

Ben lined up the three pills and the cup of laxative on the small wooden TV tray next to Peter's worn armchair in the living room, just as the *Jeopardy!* theme song finished on the TV. Peter couldn't answer the questions anymore, but they still watched every night before he went to bed.

"Quod," Peter said as Alex Trebek read off the categories for the first round. He put the first pill in his mouth, squinted, and swallowed. He couldn't go too fast or his stomach would start to hurt.

After the break in the first round, when Alex chatted with the contestants, Peter said *"Erat"* and took pill number two. He waited until the end of the next commercial break, and as Alex read off the categories for Double Jeopardy, Peter looked over at Ben, who smiled and nodded.

"Demonstration." He took the last pill and sipped the remaining Miralax over the rest of the round. During the last commercial, he held the cup out so Ben could see it was empty.

"Good job, Dad." Between Peter's second and third intestinal-obstruction surgeries, he'd started having hallucinations—paranoid fantasies about the neighbors trying to break in the house in the middle of the night and things like that. His doctor added the quetiapine to the mix with his antidepressant and dementia meds. Ben had been surprised when his father saw the abbreviations for his medications on the notepad and blurted out the old Latin phrase he'd taught his son decades ago. *Quod erat demonstrandum. Thus it has been demonstrated.*

Peter got up and went back to his bedroom to brush his teeth and change for bed. Ben was surprised he didn't ask about Grace again, but after he thought about it, he supposed there was some sense to it. They never saw her at this time of night, so there wasn't a pattern for Peter to miss. Or maybe he just forgot.

Ben made the normal evening med notes and added *Stomach seemed pretty good.* When Peter was feeling more stomach pain, Ben would add an Advil PM and maybe a lorazepam to the mix, but he was glad that wasn't needed tonight.

He knew he had another fifteen minutes before Peter would be ready to turn in, so he went outside and checked the studio again. The lights were off and Grace's Prius still wasn't in its spot. A hint of anxiety feathered its way into his abdomen. For the first time that day, he began to think something might really be wrong.

Back inside, as Peter pulled the blankets over himself, he looked up at his son's face. "Is something the matter?"

"No, Dad. Nothing."

"You look like something's the matter."

"I've just got a little bit of a headache is all."

"Did you take your medicine?"

"I'm going to right now."

"Good." Peter rested his head on the pillow. "Let me know if you need something." He squeezed Ben's hand and checked to make sure the old AM/FM Walkman radio was on the side of the bed in case he couldn't sleep. "Good night, Ben."

"Good night, Dad."

"I love you."

"I love you, too." Ben turned off the lamp on the dresser, looked at his father in the soft glow of the night-light, and eased the door shut behind him.

He sat on the sofa in the living room with his phone in his hand and thought about texting Grace. What were the boundaries? Would it be appropriate to ask if she was okay? Was he her friend or still just her landlord?

His Fitbit said he'd only done 8,272 steps so far that day. Dr. Okada said to try for ten thousand every day. Ben always pushed for at least twelve. When he had still been a cop, he'd always prided himself on exceeding expectations. No one expected much from him anymore. Most nights when he found himself short, he would do laps, either out in the backyard if it was warm enough or inside if it wasn't. Starting at the fireplace on the far end of the living room and looping around the table in the dining room on the way to the refrigerator was good for seventy-five steps. Some nights he would repeat the circuit for an hour or more.

When Ben hit his goal, he'd worked off a lot of the nervous energy he'd been feeling earlier. He sat on the sofa in the living room and looked at his old detective's badge on the mantel over the fireplace. When he'd come home from the rehab facility, it had been waiting for him, bubble-wrapped in a shipping box: his shield, encased in a brick of Lucite. To remind him of who he used to be. And that's just what it did, every time he looked at it.

That's what it was doing now.

You used to be someone else.

For six years you wore a Long Beach Police Department uniform, for two you worked plainclothes Narcotics, and for eight more after that you wore a suit and tie in the Violent Crimes Detail. Then you got shot in the head. And, more or less, you survived. Except for the dent in the back of your skull where the bullet went in, which you can't really see unless you get your hair cut too short, and the scar under your right eye where the bullet came out, you look pretty much the same. A bit thicker, maybe, a little shaggier, older. But pretty much the same.

Sometimes, though, people you've known for years, people the old Ben Shepard knew, will walk right past you without a hint of recognition.

You understand.

You get it.

Because sometimes you'll look in the mirror and even you won't see who you used to be.

Those are the good days.

TWO

Ben didn't know what woke him. A noise. It must have been a noise. But it was quiet now. One moment he'd been asleep, the next sitting up in his California king, alert and awake.

He listened to the darkness.

Maybe his father was up—Peter went to the bathroom two or three times most nights. Ben knew the sounds. The shuffle-scrape of slippers on the hardwood floor. The running faucet. The whoosh of the toilet followed by the low hiss of the tank refilling. But he heard none of those. Not even the spinning rattle of the paper rolling into his father's shaky hand.

Nothing.

He waited.

Nothing.

Just as he decided to lower himself back down, the creaking sound made him open his eyes again.

It could have just been the sound of the old house settling. It was built in '45. Thirty years before he was even born. When was the last night he hadn't heard it settling half a dozen times?

The noise came again.

He recognized the sound. The low, long moan of floorboards inside the front door. Whenever he came in after his dad had gone to bed and eased the deadbolt into place behind himself, he'd always walk as lightly as possible, but he could never be completely silent, no matter how hard he tried. Sometimes, if he took a big-enough step, he could almost make it across, but there would always be something, some sound. And even though it might be louder or quieter depending on how careful he managed to be, it was never completely silent.

There it was again.

Someone was inside. Ben was sure of it.

He wished he still kept a gun in the nightstand.

Instead, he had the big old Maglite in his hand as he inched open the bedroom door. It hadn't quite been closed all the way. He always kept it cracked in case his father needed him in the night.

He didn't see anything. It wasn't completely dark in the house—there was a lamp on in the living room ahead of him, and the light over the stove dimly illuminated the kitchen and dining room to the right.

There was no movement.

Ben listened.

No sound other than the furnace blowing warm air through the vents and the muffled hiss of the refrigerator.

He stepped through the door.

Just moments ago, he'd been sure someone was in the house. But now, he didn't know. He clicked on the flashlight and lit up the living room.

Nothing.

He moved cautiously through the dining room and kitchen.

Nothing.

The hallway.

Nothing.

Ben stood on the balls of his feet outside Peter's bedroom door and listened to the heavy in-and-out of his father's breath. Almost—but not quite—snoring.

There was no one else here.

Back in the living room, Ben looked through the window across the backyard. He couldn't quite see the studio from there, but he could tell there were no lights on. When Grace worked nights at the restaurant, she'd get home at eleven or twelve and wouldn't go to bed for a while.

It was close to two now, though, so he couldn't know for sure if she was back unless he went outside and looked for her Prius.

The nervous tension and the adrenaline rush were fading, but he didn't want to unlock the back door and go outside.

Would waiting until morning to check for Grace be more anxiety provoking or would it be worse to check on her now? If she was back, it would be better to know. He'd be able to stop worrying and sleep. But what if she wasn't? Would he ever get to sleep at all?

He looked at his badge on the mantel again, opened the door, and went outside. It was quiet and chilly, but there was more than enough moonlight to see by, so he didn't have to turn on the flashlight. The studio was still dark, but as he got closer he heard something in the alley on the other side of the fence. A scuffling sound.

As he neared the small back patio outside the studio, a car door slammed shut and an engine turned over.

Ben's old instincts kicked in and he ran for the gate. He made it through in time to see a red Camaro run into his neighbor's trash cans, slowing just long enough for him to read the license plate. As it sped up the alley, Ben reached for his notebook to scribble *2CDG720* but realized he'd left it inside. When he'd been a cop, memorizing plate numbers was second nature, but now he wasn't sure, so he repeated the number over and over again under his breath like a mantra, hoping to hold on to it long enough to write it down when he got back inside.

He stood there, trying to catch his breath and thinking about what he had just seen.

Judging by the sounds he heard and the position of the moving car when he came through the gate, the Camaro must have been in or close to Grace's parking spot next to the garage door.

As he was trying to figure out the implications of what had just happened, something occurred to him.

He'd forgotten.

Just for a few seconds.

But he had forgotten.

He hadn't stopped to think.

He hadn't hesitated.

He had acted.

Was that who he used to be?

• • •

Of course sleep never came. He took a lorazepam and that helped tame the anxiety to a small degree. There was Ambien in the cabinet, too, and Ben knew it would probably work. It almost always did. But what if Peter woke up and needed something? And if he took it now, he wouldn't be able to get up in time to make breakfast.

Usually when insomnia hit, he would turn on the white-noise machine or the radio or listen to music. Sometimes, if it was really bad, he'd get up and do more steps. Those things helped him focus and calm the cascading thoughts that made him anxious. But he didn't do any of them. That night, his wandering mind wasn't the problem—no, it was the inescapable question of what to do in the morning that kept him awake.

Grace hadn't come home in more than eighteen hours, and someone had been parked in the alley. Was the driver of the Camaro looking for her, too? He must have been. There was no other reasonable explanation for why he would have been there at that time of night. Was he just looking, or would he have tried to get into Grace's apartment if Ben hadn't come outside?

But the real question he kept asking himself was whether or not to call the police the next day. Did he have a good-enough reason for them to open a missing-persons case? Would the car in the alley be enough to convince them? With his history, would they even take him seriously?

He wouldn't let himself ask the next question that needed to be answered: Should he take himself seriously? It had been more than three years since he'd had any significant issues with paranoia. Once they'd found the right meds and he'd started the sessions with Emma, things had settled down and he'd made a lot of progress.

But how many times had he called in false reports in those early days? That was before his father's first surgery, so Peter headed a lot of them off, but still, how many were there? Six? Eight? And how many times did he see the pity and fear in the responders' eyes when they recognized him and let him off the hook again? He felt the embarrassment and humiliation just thinking about it.

Could he even bring himself to call again?

Then he had an idea. Maybe not a good one, and he'd still probably embarrass himself, but it might not be quite as bad.

He turned on the lamp on the nightstand and opened his notebook. The license-plate number, 2CDG729, stared back at him while he wrote. He hoped he had gotten it right.

2:58am Still awake
Call J?

Ben didn't feel like he'd slept at all. But he must have, because when he'd closed his eyes it was dark, and when he opened them again, the morning light was streaming in through the slats of the shutters.

Before he made his morning notes and before he turned on the coffee maker and before he put the kettle on to boil the water for Peter's breakfast oatmeal, he went outside and checked the alley, the cold morning biting through his T-shirt and shorts.

There was no sign of Grace.

And no sign of the Camaro in the alley.

What did he expect? Skid marks? A pile of cigarette butts like in some stupid movie?

Shit.

Had he even really seen the car last night? Could he have imagined it? He'd never really had hallucinations except for when he took that one medication, and that was years ago, wasn't it? Things had been better lately. Good, even. He wasn't filling the notebooks like he used to, one or two every day, trying to hold on to everything. His memory wasn't quite normal, it probably wouldn't ever be again. But it was better. It was good now. And he wasn't the only one who thought so. Dr. Bolinger confirmed it. Emma did, too.

He had seen the Camaro. He was sure of it. Wasn't he?

When he went back inside, his first step on the floor squealed and he looked down at his feet. His Tevas were covered in wet grass from his trek across the back lawn. He took them off and left them by the door. In his bedroom, he put on a thick pair of socks and a sweatshirt. Ben hadn't even realized he was shivering until the shaking began to subside.

Still gone, he wrote.

The call from Kessler was a surprise. You hadn't seen him since the hospital. He was on one of the first lists you made. Early on, when you were still using those spiral-bound steno pads. THE ONES WHO CAME. *Jennifer and her partner from Homicide, what was his name? Becker? They were right up at the top. Only the lieutenant was there before them. Everybody from Violent Crimes showed up eventually. Even a few from your uniform days. But not as many as you'd expected. Not as many as you'd hoped. You never made the other list, the ones who didn't come, but it was always there, no matter how hard you tried to push it out of your head.*

But you didn't expect to hear from Kessler. Not then. He'd moved to San Bernardino three or four years ago, worked for the sheriff's department now. Lateral hire.

When you call him back, he says, "Hey, Ben, how are you?" He used to call you Shepard. Everybody did. Now they call you Ben.

"I'm good, Rob," you say. It's easier that way.

"How's your dad?"

"It's been rough since the last surgery, but he's doing better now."

"That was his second?"

"Third."

"Shit. Sorry to hear that."

You want to say something, but you don't know what. You used to be good at it, talking to people, making conversation. That was your thing. It made you a good cop. A good detective. Now, though, not so much. You're always worried about saying the wrong thing, embarrassing yourself. Making it weird or awkward for the person you're talking to, the way it always is for you.

"Listen," he says. "Are you still looking for someone to rent your guesthouse?"

You don't say anything.

Because for a moment, you don't know what he's talking about.

Then it comes back to you. You told some people at the LBPD that you were hoping to take on a tenant, hoping a cop referral might help you find someone reliable. How long ago was that? Three months? Four? You make a note to check your notes. How did he hear about it all the way in San Bernardino?

"I guess so," you say.

"Good," he says. "I think I might have somebody for you."

Ben waited, but his father still hadn't asked about Grace.

Peter held up his coffee cup. "Can I have some more?"

"How's your stomach feeling?"

"All right." He'd only been to the bathroom once so far, and he'd usually have gone twice by his second cup. But calories were calories. As Ben stirred the coffee, Boost, and sugar, Peter asked, "Outside?"

"It's pretty cold this morning, Dad. Why don't we wait until it warms up a bit?" Ben put the cup down on the place mat.

"Okay." Peter seemed to be thinking about something. "Is the girl here today?"

"I'm not sure," Ben said. "I haven't seen her, but I'll check in a little while."

That seemed to satisfy him. At least for now.

• • •

1/9 9:50 am
560 calories, good bm, stomach not too bad
no Grace—text? Call? Missing person rpt.? Not sure, but camaro
Don't know what to do
Anxiety/stomach hurts (ME not dad)

• • •

After lunch, Ben sent the text. He spent way too long composing it, but he was still worried that he was overstepping his bounds as a landlord. Maybe she met someone and stayed at their house. Maybe she went away with a friend or relative for a few days. Maybe she went someplace by herself. Why was it any business of his? Grace was friendly and generous, sure, especially with his father. It was only two or three weeks after she moved in that she was spending an hour most days on the patio with Peter. She was good with him and he certainly liked her. *At what point do you consider a tenant a friend?*

Hi, Grace, the text message said. We haven't seen you for a while and we wanted to make sure everything is okay. My dad is asking about you. Please let me know if you need anything. He added a ☺ for good measure, but regretted it as soon as he sent the message.

Peter was finishing up on his exercise mat in the living room. He had a stretching routine he did a few times a day. It was a combination of a couple of old stretches from his long-ago running days and a set of yoga positions and exercises he'd been taught ten years ago by a physical therapist when he'd first started having gastrointestinal problems.

Ben couldn't figure out how his father remembered the whole routine. But Peter, for some reason, did very well with physical tasks. He still did the laundry, kept the kitchen clean, dusted and swept every day. He couldn't remember what the laundry soap was called, but he knew exactly how much to use. The neurologist diagnosed him with vascular dementia, though it never seemed that simple to Ben. Before the first surgery, almost five years ago now, Peter was having some mild difficulty with names and paying bills and things. That seemed to be as much due to his macular degeneration as to his memory. When he had the colonoscopy, though, and they'd had to schedule a major procedure to remove a polyp that was too big for Dr. Riyaz to take out with the scope, the real trouble began. The recovery was harder than anyone expected, and Peter was never the same. His cognitive decline was so significant that even Ben, who was still mired in his own recovery, knew they were in trouble. Then the first emergency surgery for an obstructed intestine hit him hard again and the second, a year and a half later, did the same. It seemed to Ben that Peter only lost more of his words and memories after each surgery. He didn't think his father had slipped much between the procedures or since he'd come home from the last one. Ben was keeping track in his notebooks along with everything else. He lived in constant fear of another trip to the ER, because he knew if Peter had to go under again he'd lose what little he had left.

An hour after Ben sent the text message, Grace hadn't responded. He checked out back again. She hadn't returned. He went through the gate and stood in the spot where he'd seen the Camaro and looked up and down the alley. Then a memory triggered a thought and he began to scan the backs of the houses across from him.

There it was, right where he remembered it, about a foot from the top of the redwood gate two houses down, across the alley. "WARNING," the sign said in white letters on a red banner, over an image of an old-school wall-mounted video camera. "VIDEO SURVEILLANCE IN USE ON THE PREMISES."

The camera itself was still there, too, up under the eave above the top-right corner of the garage door. It was rectangular and bigger than most of the newer cameras he'd seen lately. It had been there for a long time. Probably since he'd moved back in with Peter. So a few years at least. Ben wondered if it even still worked. Maybe, if it was compatible with all the new video-security apps everyone seemed to be getting these days.

He walked out of the alley and around the block to the front of the house on Gaviota Avenue. Even though he walked past it almost every night with his father, he wasn't sure who lived there. It was a pale-green house with a red-orange door. He felt a knot twist in his stomach as he stepped onto the porch and hesitated. *Jesus.* Even knocking on a neighbor's door made him nervous these days. After a few deep breaths, he rang the bell.

An older woman with short silver hair, who he recognized but couldn't name, answered. "Oh, hi, Ben. How are you?"

"Pretty good," he said, feeling awkward.

"How's Peter?"

Shit, he should know her name. Why couldn't he remember it? "He's doing well."

"That's good. I'm happy to hear it."

She waited for him to speak.

After what felt like a very long pause, Ben remembered why he was there. "That video camera in the alley? Does that still work, by any chance?"

"That old thing?" She let out a sound like a polite snort. "Fred put that up years ago. It never really worked at all. It's fake."

"It is?" Ben felt the small bit of hope he'd been holding on to flicker out.

"I told him it was dumb, but he said no one would know and it would be just as good as a real one. Why? Did something happen back there?"

"There was a strange car parked by our garage last night. They took off when they saw me coming. I was hoping you might have gotten them on camera."

"Oh dear. I'm afraid not. Do you think they were burglars?"

"I hope not."

"Me too," she said. "Tell your dad hi for me, okay?"

"I will," Ben said. *If I ever remember your name.*

It came to him much quicker than he expected, as soon as he stepped onto the sidewalk. "Kelley Hall," he whispered. She'd been one of his mother's best friends. Brought casseroles every couple of days when she was sick. Held her hand near the end.

He should have remembered.

• • •

Back at home, he wondered what to do.

His gut told him something was wrong, but these days his gut was always telling him something was wrong. Could he trust it? He didn't think so. The spare key was hanging on its hook in the kitchen. Maybe if he took a look around inside, that would give him something to go on. That wasn't right, though. One Camaro wasn't enough probable cause to go into Grace's apartment.

Probable cause. Thinking like a cop again. He had to stop that.

Maybe he should call the police, though. Make a missing-persons report. Was it too soon for that? You didn't have to wait forty-eight hours like on all the TV shows. That was bullshit. You didn't have to wait at all. At least not in California. He couldn't remember if it was the same in other states, though he was certain he used to know.

He wondered if it was the same for his father. If Peter knew how much he couldn't remember, how much was lost. Ben didn't think his father was as aware of the vast ocean of the past now forever lost as he himself was. Oh, Peter knew he forgot things—of course he did—but, Ben thought, he didn't really know how very much was gone.

The LBPD would take his report and at least run the plate of the Camaro. Maybe they'd come up with something. And it had to have been four years since he made the last inappropriate call—back when the paranoia was still a problem and the anxiety poorly managed. Still, though, he knew they'd have him flagged. Half a dozen false alarms, imagined home invasions, break-ins, and prowlers. Nothing too serious, but more than enough for him to be considered a nuisance. And they always recognized him. Always. He wondered if everyone would still know who he was. The reporters never called anymore. Maybe the cops had forgotten, too.

He thought about the boundaries again, and almost managed to convince himself he was overreacting. Almost.

A few more hours, he thought. *I'll wait a few more hours.*

You thought it was odd, Rob wanting to check the place out himself before he told you anything about the prospective tenant. Especially since he lived more than an hour away. But, you told yourself, what did you know about renting apartments? Besides, if he was being this careful, wasn't that a good thing for you, too?

You told Peter that Rob was coming, that you thought he'd met him a long time ago, but it was okay if he didn't remember.

When you let Rob in, he shakes your hand, smiles at you. He looks older than you expect him to. Grayer. Still has the old-school mustache. More tan. Must be the desert, *you think.*

"How you doing, Ben?" he asks.

Before you can answer, he looks at your father, smiles at him, too. "Peter. It's good to see you again."

"I'm sorry." Peter lowers his eyes, looks down at the floor. "I don't remember."

"That's okay. It's been a very long time." Rob looks at you. "How long ago was the wedding?"

"You want something to drink?" you ask. "Just made a fresh pot of coffee."

"Sure," he says. "Sounds good."

You sit at the patio table with him and catch up, which mostly involves him telling you in detail about San Bernardino and how working for the sheriff's department is much worse than working for the LBPD. It's not that he's trying to dominate the conversation, he asks about you and how you're doing, but you stutter and have trouble getting the words out. Like you always used to. You feel your stomach churn. You don't know why. You do a little better when you tell him about Peter. It's easier to talk when it's not about you.

"It's good to see you, Ben. To see how good you're doing," he says.

You know what you want to say. It's easy—It's good to see you, too—you can hear the words in your head. But you can't seem to remember how to make your mouth form the It's *sound. So you nod.*

After what seems like a long time, you say, "W-want to see the studio?"

"Yeah," Rob says. "Let's take a look."

You take him in the back. Show him the little porch, the walkway to the gate that opens onto the single parking space.

"People have trouble with cars getting stolen, broken into, in the alley here?" he asks.

You show him the light with the sensor that comes on at dusk. "Not much more than on the street in front."

He looks at the back of the house across the alley. Points up at the eaves on the side of the garage door. "That a real video camera?"

You shrug. "Not sure."

"Could she park in front of the house on the street if she wanted to?"

"Of course."

Rob nods, as if that answer quells his concerns.

Back inside the gate, you hand him the key, let him open the door. He examines the deadbolt, the heavy-duty strike plate. Nods again, steps inside.

You follow him.

He looks around, sees one decent-sized room, sixteen by eighteen, with the three-quarter bath and kitchenette alcove to the left along the alley side. "It's nice. Pretty small, but nice."

It is nice. Hardly been used at all. It's almost the same as it was when your mother remodeled it. Before everything turned around.

Rob looks up at the two skylights, nods in approval, then starts testing the appliances. The water pressure. The garbage disposal.

"Everything works . . . great," you say, hoping he didn't hear the pause. You should have just let yourself stutter. The pause made it sound like you didn't really mean it. You might as well have held up your fingers and made ironic air quotes around "great."

He looks at you and you know you were wrong, that he didn't take it that way at all. "How much?" he asks.

"A thousand?" You know you could get more. The other guesthouses in Bixby Knolls—even some of the studios—are going for twelve or thirteen now.

Rob grins. "You cutting me a break?"

"Yeah."

"Thanks." He sounds sincere.

You wonder if he's ever going to say anything about the tenant.

It felt wrong. As soon as Ben was inside her studio apartment, he knew he'd made a mistake and crossed a line he shouldn't have. But what should he do now? He was already inside. Maybe he should just take a quick look around and see if he could discover anything that might ease his anxiety.

Grace hadn't brought much furniture with her. She was happy to keep the small dining table and the daybed. The one thing he'd added before she moved in was the TV. He'd gotten a new fifty-five-inch in the living room so Peter could see it better, and had put the old one out here. It wasn't really *that* old, though. A forty-two-inch with Netflix built in. Ben had had a guy come in and mount it on the wall to give her more room.

All she'd brought in, though, were a small upholstered chair and a bookcase filled with books. She'd put a few framed photos on top—of her family, she said. An older woman, who Ben thought must be Grace's mom, was in two of them. One with Grace herself, and the other with another young woman, mid to late twenties. Grace's sister, maybe?

Now the sleeper sofa she'd bought a few weeks after she moved in, to replace the old daybed, was folded up, the cushions tucked neatly in place and the coffee table slid back in front. She didn't always do that. It seemed like the few times when he'd come back here during the day, the bed was left folded out. Did that mean anything?

Ben wondered if there was any contact information for the women from the pictures, anywhere in the studio. Probably not. Everybody had everything in their phones now. Or on their computer. He looked around. Saw her MacBook on the table. It was closed. He thought about opening it but quickly dismissed the idea. That would be too much of an intrusion.

This felt wrong. But he couldn't be sure if it was just his own sense of inquisitiveness or if something seemed out of place. He took a quick look around. Checked the bathroom. Nothing seemed wrong. Nothing obvious, anyway. He had to remind himself that was good, that signs of a struggle or blood on the floor would have made deciding whether or not to call the police easy for him, but would have meant very bad news for Grace.

When she'd moved in, Ben remembered, she had most of her personal belongings in a rolling suitcase and a backpack. He didn't see the backpack anywhere, but he knew she used it fairly regularly, so that didn't tell him much. What about the suitcase?

If it was in the closet, that would mean she probably hadn't planned on going anywhere for any length of time.

Ben decided he'd take a quick peek and see if it was in there. Just to be sure. His hand twitched as he reached for the knob.

"What are you doing?"

Ben felt fear cut into him as his whole body tensed. The sun seemed to grow brighter in the skylights. Something smelled bad. Like burning plastic. A guttural noise, half-scream and half-moan, burst out of him.

"Oh no!" Peter rushed across the room.

Ben was hunched over, hands on his thighs, trying to breathe, as if he'd been punched in the gut. His father put an arm around his shoulders. "I'm sorry," Peter said. "It's okay, it's okay, it's okay." When Ben began to calm down, Peter pulled him into a hug. "Shhhh," he said. "It's all right."

They stood like that as the cloudy winter sky spilled light down on them from the skylights over their heads.

FOUR

They went for their evening walk a little early. It was only about four. The city was replacing some sections of the sidewalk on their usual route, so they cut over an extra block to Walnut. Halfway up the block, Ben heard the rumble of a jet taking off, so he paused as Peter turned toward the sound and watched to see where the plane would emerge over the rooflines of the houses. His father pointed when he saw it and then waved as it flew over them. They were only half a mile away from the end of the runway, so they had a good view. Ben watched his father's outstretched hand as Peter spun with the passing plane.

"What kind was it?" Peter asked.

"JetBlue."

"JetBlue," Peter repeated as if trying to make sure he wouldn't forget. "Is that the good one?"

"Yeah, Dad. It is." Ben wasn't sure how long he'd be able to keep saying that. The airline was behind a push to add international flights to Long Beach Airport. No one in the community around the airport wanted that, but most of the city council didn't seem to give a shit what the community wanted. They just saw money. Peter was probably the only one in the whole neighborhood who'd be happy with more departing flights.

"Do you think they saw us?" Peter said, still watching as the plane continued beyond the treetops, out of view.

When Ben didn't answer, he asked, "Are you okay?"

"Yeah, why?"

"I'm sorry from before," Peter said. "Sorry I scared you."

"That's all right, Dad. You don't have anything to be sorry for."

"I know, but I'm sorry."

As they approached the corner, Peter stopped to gaze at the purpling sunset. "Look at that," he said. Ben marveled at his father's capacity for simple wonder, the way he would stop to run his hand along the bark of a tree or examine a flower. Maybe he even envied it a little. As he looked up to the west, he was impressed by the colors—they really were unusually pretty—but he saw the clouds rolling in, too. The weather report said rain overnight and into tomorrow.

They were almost home when Ben saw Bernie, a few houses down the block, walking toward them with Sriracha on her leash. They'd known Bernie for decades. The Bellos had lived up and across the street when the Shepards moved in. Ben was just a few years ahead of their oldest son in elementary school. He still saw Jorge, who took over the family welding business when Bernie retired, once in a while when he brought his family over to visit.

Peter was about to turn and go up the front step, so Ben tugged on his elbow, pointed, and watched his father's face light up again. The little terrier tugged at her leash when she saw him, and Bernie pressed the button on the plastic handle to let out more slack.

"Hi, girl! Hi," Peter said as she jumped up on his shins and he bent over to pet her.

Bernie nodded and said to Ben, "You look worried. How you guys doing?"

"We're hanging in there. Some days are just a little rougher than others."

"I know what you mean," he said. "You know if you need anything, all you gotta do is ask."

"I do know. Thank you."

They watched Peter, still bent over and scratching Sriracha's belly, say "Good girl" over and over.

"I wonder if I should get a dog for him," Ben said.

"Might be good."

"I'm just not sure about adding to the load, you know?"

"Yeah," Bernie said. "I do. Why don't I bring her over more? Maybe let you guys dog sit a bit, see what you think."

"That would be good. Thanks."

"No sweat."

Ben had a thought. Bernie was out walking Sriracha at least three times a day, and he talked to everybody. If there was anything happening in the neighborhood, they either heard it from him or they didn't hear it at all. "You don't know anybody around here with a red Camaro, do you?"

"I don't think so. The old kind or one of the new ones?" Bernie asked.

"One of the new ones. Somebody was parked in the alley last night, but they took off when they saw me."

"That doesn't sound good. Any idea what they were doing?"

Ben thought about mentioning Grace, but he didn't want Bernie to think he was being paranoid and jumping to conclusions, so he just shook his head.

Bernie said, "I'll keep an eye out. Ask around."

"Thanks."

"No sweat." He looked at Peter with the dog, then said, "Hey, you two. Either break it up or get a room."

Peter laughed, and Ben wondered if he really got the joke. Just as they were about to move on, Ben saw something black buzzing along over the roofs of the houses ahead of them. At first he thought it was some kind of bird, gliding low, but as it came closer, he realized it was a drone. He turned back to Bernie and said, "You see that?"

"Oh," Bernie said. "You know Tim over on Gardenia?" He gestured toward the next block over.

Ben nodded, even though he wasn't sure who Bernie meant.

"He got a new toy. Saw him playing with it in the alley the other day."

"I didn't think people were supposed to fly those things so close to the airport."

"That's what I said. Tim just shrugged his shoulders and kept at it."

Great, Ben thought. *One more thing to worry about.*

•   •   •

When he'd been a detective, Ben would spend hours on the phone without a second thought. But now, even the simplest of calls made him uncomfortable, even anxious. He had to take a few deep breaths to steady himself. Why hadn't he called earlier? They'd be changing shifts now. By the time they sent a patrol car out and someone took a report with Grace's information, it would probably be too late for them to do anything until the morning. Without a reason to suspect foul play, unless something significant came back on the Camaro—an arrest warrant or something else relevant on the registered owner of the car—beginning the investigation probably wouldn't be urgent enough for anyone working an overnight shift.

He cleared the LBPD number from his phone and went out in the back again. Just as he expected, nothing had changed.

Then it occurred to him. Maybe Rob would know what to do. Before Ben let himself think of a reason not to, he found the number in his contacts and made the call. It started ringing and he didn't know what to say. How should he start? But it just kept ringing. Finally, the voicemail kicked in and he heard Rob's voice. "This is Robert Kessler. Please leave a detailed and specific message and I'll get back to you as soon as possible."

Detailed and specific? Shit. Okay. "H-hi, Rob. This is Ben Shepard. I wanted to talk to you about something. Grace, uh, Grace. She hasn't been home in almost two days and I'm starting to worry? Thinking about filing a missing-persons report and—uh, should I do that? Call me back as soon as you can, okay? Thanks. This is Ben."

God. He hadn't felt this awkward and incompetent since the early days when he had to learn how to talk again, how to walk, how to feed himself and go to the bathroom. The helplessness he'd felt then was the worst thing he'd ever experienced. Worse than the pain. Worse than the nausea. Worse than the loneliness.

He was afraid, and not just for himself—for his father, too, and most of all for Grace. Could something horrible have happened? After eight years in Violent Crimes, how could anyone not imagine all the horrible things that could have happened. Dozens of horrible things happened literally every day in Long Beach.

Ben sat in one of the blue plastic chairs by the back fence, rubbing his fingertips across the indentation in the back of his head, and waited for Rob to return his call.

He was still waiting when it got dark and he had to go inside to give Peter his medicine.

The first thing you think is that she's really cute. The warm smile, the brown eyes, the shoulder-length curly hair. The second thing you think is that you're a douchebag, because you're going to be her landlord and you're probably old enough to be her father.

"This is my dad, Peter," you say.

She shakes his hand with both of hers and holds on to it while she speaks. "It's really nice to meet you, Peter. Thank you so much for letting me rent the studio."

"You're so nice and pretty," he says.

She smiles again, and you lead her through the patio doors and back along the narrow concrete sidewalk to the studio. "This is it."

"Wow," she says as you unlock the door. "This looks great."

"We haven't rented it to anyone before, so you'll be the first person to live here."

She turns and looks at you, and for a moment the smile disappears from her face. "I've never been the first person to live anyplace," she says.

Sometimes they called it the office, sometimes the den. It was in the back of the house, next to the master bedroom. The same bedroom his father had shared with his mother from the time Ben was in elementary school. The same room she died in. The same room Peter now slept in alone. Ben could hear him snoring through the closed door.

He checked his phone again. Rob hadn't called back, and the text message he'd sent to Grace had been delivered but not read.

The last thing Peter had said to him before he told him good night was, "Will she be back tomorrow?"

Ben made a decision. If he hadn't heard from either of them by morning, he would call the LBPD and file a missing-persons report.

The desk lamp was the only illumination in the room, but it gave him enough light to go through his notebook and review the day. He wanted to be sure he remembered everything from today, and, honestly, he would probably need to clarify some things, because if he had to look at them in a few days or weeks, they might not make any sense. That happened sometimes. So he did this most nights. He might let it go if nothing significant had happened on a given day, but he knew the more careful he was now, the better off he would be down the road. For a while, he had tried rewriting everything into a journal on the computer, but he'd found that writing by hand was much more effective in helping him remember.

He went through everything, and his notes seemed clear and specific. Peter's morning meds, his breakfast, the first round of his stretching routine, all the normal things, were sandwiched between Ben's worries and the time at which he'd gone to see if there was evidence of Grace returning. There were notes about lunch, calorie counts, their early walk, Bernie and Sriracha. Even about Peter clapping when Ben knew the right answer to Final Jeopardy! Everything was there. It was clear he'd gone out of his way to be thorough. He asked himself if there was anything he needed to add and he couldn't come up with anything.

Sometimes, despite his best efforts, things would slip through the cracks. He wouldn't get a chance to make a note and then he'd forget to do it afterward. In some instances, he'd only realize later, when he got a phone call about a missed appointment or a message about refilling a prescription. Maybe Bernie would say something that triggered a memory. Once or twice that had even happened with Grace.

His anxiety twitched more forcefully than it had in a long time. Was it all about Grace? Or was there something else? Maybe something he forgot or something he should have been able to figure out. He wished Rob would call him back. Maybe he still might. It was only a little after nine. Or, god, maybe Grace would just come home. That would be the best thing. Tell him she'd gone to see someone for a visit. A friend, maybe, or family.

In the living room, he flipped the channels around on the TV. He had some things stacked up on the DVR. A few movies. Several episodes of *Drunk History. Westworld.* Stuff he always waited until after Peter's bedtime to watch because it was too hard for him to follow or he just didn't like it. Ben didn't want to commit to any of those, though. He knew he'd be too distracted to pay attention, and he didn't want to waste something good by watching it that way. One of the channels was showing *The Shawshank Redemption*, which he'd seen dozens of times, more than enough to pick up the story and follow along no matter how often his racing mind pulled his focus away from the screen. It had started half an hour earlier, and it distracted him for a while. Just after the sequence in which Brooks, the old man who has been in prison all his life and can't adjust to life outside in the real world, gives in and hangs himself, Ben got up and went over to the mantel. He picked up his Lucited badge, took it to the shelf in the corner, and slid it out of sight behind the photo of his mother. The one where she was wearing the new lieutenant's insignia on her LBPD uniform.

• • •

Instead of going to bed after taking his meds and making what he expected to be the day's last entry in his notebook, Ben went back into the living room and lay down on the couch. He thought about trying to find something else to watch, maybe the news and one of the late-night network shows. But that wouldn't be good tonight. The anxiety was already roiling in his gut, and all the doomsday political reporting would just make it worse. Not even one of the comedy shows would help, because it would only be rehashing the same exhausting headlines. So he just left it on the same channel he'd been watching earlier. They were showing a Robert De Niro movie he didn't recognize. It seemed like it was supposed to be funny.

The first time is after only a few days. An early storm blew through the day before, but now the sun is shining bright, the way it only does when the sky's been cleared by a good hard rain. Even though it's cold outside, Peter wants to have his second Boost and coffee on the patio. He isn't going to change his mind, so he bundles himself up in his warm fleece jacket and blue knit cap.

You give him an old towel in case any rain has blown up under the patio roof onto the table and chairs and tell him to go ahead, you'll be out in just a minute. It was a rough night and you are exhausted. Every time you managed to get to sleep, the bad dreams would come and you'd be up again. You went through five or six cycles, the agitation growing worse with each one. On your way into the bathroom, you pass your unmade bed and you're tempted to climb back in. Even just half an hour would help. Peter wouldn't mind. He likes it when you take naps or go out to run errands, because he knows it's a break for you, a bit of time when you don't have to worry about him. He hates that, how much you have to worry about him. But you know you'll have to go back outside to tell him so he won't just sit there waiting for you, and if you have to do that you might as well just sit down with him for a while. So you go to the bathroom, then put on long pants and a sweatshirt and head back.

As soon as you get out of your bedroom door, though, you realize the dining-room door is still cracked open, and you hear him outside, laughing. You're confused for a few seconds, then you hear Grace. She's laughing, too, more softly than your father, but still loud enough for you to hear. You stop where you are and listen.

Grace says something, then Peter does. You can't quite make out the words, so you tiptoe closer to the door.

"She died," Peter says, not laughing anymore.

"I'm so sorry." There's a tenderness in Grace's voice that you haven't heard before. You're glad it's there. You hadn't really thought about her

talking to him like this, without you to help facilitate the conversation.
"When did it happen?"

Peter doesn't answer. You know he's trying to figure out how long it has
been since your mother's death and that he has a hard time with things
like that.

"That's okay," she says. "You can tell me later."

You're surprised. And pleased. You wonder if she's cared for someone
with dementia or memory problems before or if it's just instinct. Usually
when someone is talking to Peter and he struggles to remember some per-
tinent detail, the person he's talking to will see he's having trouble and say
something like "It doesn't matter" or "It's not important" or "Don't worry
about it." They're trying to be kind. They don't realize that what they're
really witnessing is him showing them that it does matter and it is impor-
tant and he is worried. You know they're decent people just trying to be polite
and let your father off the hook, but every time someone does that to Peter,
you want to break their fucking jaw.

But "You can tell me later" is perfect. It says, What you're saying is
so important that I want to make a point of hearing it and I'm patient
enough for you to tell me when you can.

Peter says, "It was before."

"Before what?" You imagine you can hear Grace smiling.

"Before Ben got hurt." The tone in your father's whisper is so broken
that you don't have to imagine anything at all.

FIVE

It was still dark outside when Ben woke on the sofa to find Peter sitting in his worn easy chair, watching him.

"Hi." Peter reached over and patted his foot on the end of the couch.

"What time is it?"

"Early."

"You okay?" Ben asked. "Have trouble sleeping?"

"No. I wanted to get ready."

"Ready for what?"

"Is it today we go?" Peter raised his hand to his face and touched the edge of his eye.

Shit. Was dad's eye appointment today? Ben couldn't remember. He sat up on the couch and tried to focus. It couldn't be today, could it? He didn't even know what day it was, at least not the date. The appointment was on Friday. He knew because he'd been telling Peter that all week. Whenever his father knew an appointment was coming up, he would always start asking about it a few days before. Honestly, sometimes it got to be a little bit annoying, but the truth was that they would have missed more than a few if not for Peter's need to be reminded.

In the kitchen, Ben flipped on the light switch and squinted at the brightness. He looked at the calendar page taped up on the cupboard. In the square for Wednesday the eleventh, he had written in *Dr. Boswell*

1:45. Was that today? He didn't know. Where was his phone? He looked on the counter by the charger. Not there. He went into the bedroom and checked the nightstand. No. *Shit.* Where was it?

He went back into the kitchen and Peter was still standing there. "Are you mad at me?" he asked.

Ben stopped. Took a breath. "No, not at all."

"What's the matter?"

"I can't find my phone."

"Do you have to call someone?"

"No. I just wanted to see what today is. I'm not sure if it's the day of your appointment."

Peter's face lit up and he pointed at the Echo on the counter.

Ben sighed. "Alexa, what day is it?"

"Today is Tuesday," she said. "January tenth."

Peter smiled.

"Thanks, Dad." He tried to smile back, but couldn't quite manage it. "The appointment isn't until tomorrow. One more day."

"Okay. One more day."

The clock on the microwave said it was 5:40.

"What do you say we go back to bed for a while?" Ben said.

"That's good. You should sleep."

"What about you?"

"I think I'm up."

Ben went into the kitchen and got breakfast started.

• • •

His phone had been in the bathroom. He didn't find it until after he'd gone back outside and checked for Grace. Of course, he'd seen nothing that suggested she or anyone else had been back to the studio. And there were no new texts or phone calls. Sitting on the toilet, he heard the morning's first plane scream across the sky. He knew that meant it must be a few minutes after seven. The city's noise-abatement ordinances limited the scheduled departure and arrival times. If the morning sun didn't stir him enough to get out of bed, the first takeoff usually did. Now that he'd been up for an hour and a half, his anxiety had gotten a head start and was already trying to wrestle the morning out of his control.

He opened the medicine cabinet and took a lorazepam. He'd just give it a little while to kick in and then he'd make the call.

"I was a teacher," Peter says.

"Oh," Grace says, "what did you teach?"

Peter thinks about it, tries to come up with the words. You know you should give him more time before you say anything, that if he works for it he might be able to find the answer. "History," you say, unable to bear the silence.

This is the first time she's had coffee inside at the counter with the two of you. It's also the first time it's rained since she started having coffee with Peter. You were surprised that your father walked out in the drizzle and invited her to join you. Usually he asks about things like that before he does them.

The corners of her mouth turn up. "History was always one of my favorite subjects."

Peter smiles back at her.

You think about throwing out that famous quote your father used to joke about, years ago, before his first surgery, when he couldn't recall something, before either of you ever gave any serious thought to dementia as an everyday reality. Those who cannot remember the past are condemned to repeat it. *But you catch yourself before you speak. Without any context, you think, you'd just sound like an asshole.*

"Ben?" your father says. You realize that he asked you a question and you were lost in your own head for a second.

"I'm sorry. What did you ask?"

He looks at Grace.

She says, "Where did Peter teach?"

"Long Beach City College," you say, trying to hide your embarrassment. "Thirty years." You take your cup and walk back around the counter into the kitchen for a refill. Holding up the coffeepot, you say, "Anybody else?"

Peter nods.

"I'm fine, thanks," Grace says.

Ben breathed in, then out. Did it three more times. He had already keyed in the number. One more deep breath, and he sent the call. They picked up quickly, considering he was using the nonemergency number. When he said he needed to report a missing person and the dispatcher took his name, they transferred the call. They must have flagged him somehow. Or maybe the dispatcher recognized his name. Otherwise they would have just sent a patrol unit out.

He was on hold for a while, then a sergeant whose name he didn't recognize answered, and he said it again. "I need to report a missing person."

"Can I have your name, sir?" Ben figured the man on the other end of the line already had it, or he wouldn't even be talking to a sergeant at all.

"Benjamin Shepard." There was a pause. Why? Had he been wrong about them knowing who he was? He'd never had grandiose delusions before.

No.

The sergeant recognized his name. He'd almost surely been with the department long enough to remember. It took a long time to make that rank.

"I'm sorry for the delay. The computer's running slow today." He asked Ben a few questions and told him he'd have someone out to the house as soon as he could to make a full report.

After the call was finished, Ben wondered if the sergeant really had known his name. Everybody did for a while. It was a huge story, made the national news. Two detectives shot. One killed, the other survived an injury that should have been the end for him, too. Even if the sergeant didn't know his name off the top of his head, he must have figured it out. Missing-persons reports were usually only a high priority if they involved a child or someone with diminished capacity or if there was evidence of foul play. Not when a landlord hadn't seen a renter for a while.

But they were prioritizing this. Why else would they do that if not because of his past? Honestly, though, he was less worried about them remembering the incident and patronizing him than he was about them seeing the records for all the false reports he had called in when his meds weren't working, before the doctors figured out the particular cocktail of antidepressant and antianxiety and antiseizure and anti-mood-swing drugs that would stabilize him. For those first few months after he came home, he'd had manic episodes that filled him with paranoia. He'd also sometimes forgotten he wasn't a cop anymore. There were calls reporting prowlers. Calls about people stealing his identity. Calls requesting officer assistance. He even tried to have his father arrested once. For Ben, that was the worst part of the whole thing. It was the only time through all of the ordeal that he'd felt genuinely ashamed.

He just hoped they would send someone he didn't know. Someone who didn't know him.

"Dad?" he said, walking into the living room.

Peter was on the floor, doing his exercises. He stopped and looked up at Ben.

"Someone from the police department is going to be here soon."

"Is something wrong?" Peter got to his feet and started rolling up his exercise mat. His spryness was impressive. Physically, aside from stomach and eye problems, he was in great shape. The last time they'd been in for a primary-care visit, Dr. Matthews had asked him if he'd had any falls since the last time he came in. Ben told him he hadn't and tried to make a joke about the fact that he himself had fallen twice in that same time frame. But the doctor knew Ben's history, too. Nobody laughed.

"Well," Ben said, "I'm getting a little worried about Grace. They're going to help us figure out if she's okay."

"She's not okay?" The worry in Peter's voice raised it an octave.

"I'm sure she is, Dad. We just want to be certain." He could tell his father was getting anxious. So was he.

"His teeth are bad, too," you say.

"So that's why he eats so much yogurt and oatmeal?" Grace asks.

"Yeah. He has partial dentures. He only has his real teeth right up in front."

"I was wondering about that. He doesn't like to wear the fake ones?"

"They hurt him. He has to keep them in a couple of hours every day to support the ones he's still got. It stops them from shifting and getting worse. At least, that's what his dentist says."

"You take good care of him," Grace says.

You can't quite read her expression. It's almost as if there's a sense of wonder there, but some kind of sadness, too.

"You're a good son," she says.

"Do you know who I am?" Ben asked, regretting his choice of words even before they were out of his mouth.

"Yes, sir, I do," Detective Becerra said. He was shorter than Ben had expected.

"I'm sorry," he replied. "I didn't mean—there's not . . ." He could feel the words slipping out of his control. Deep breath. In. Out. "You can't really say that without sounding like an asshat, can you?"

"Most people can't." The detective raised his black eyebrows, then his expression fell and became more serious. "I was there that night."

"Oh. Wow." Ben didn't know what to say. A lot of cops were there that night. He never knew what to say to them. *Thank you? I'm sorry?* "That was a rough night for a lot of people. I'm probably lucky I can't remember any of it."

"We remember it."

Ben wanted to change the subject, to talk about Grace. This was exactly why he'd been hoping they'd just hand his call off to a routine-patrol unit. He should have known that wouldn't happen. He didn't try to shift the gears, though. It would go better if he let Becerra guide the conversation. Interviewing and interrogation had always been one of Ben's strengths as a detective. He didn't want Becerra to be concerned about how to handle him. The focus needed to be on Grace, not the cop who got shot in the head. And it had to be clear that this wasn't just another paranoid delusion. He knew he needed to be taken seriously.

Becerra was on the ball enough to sense that Ben didn't have much more to say about himself. "Tell me about her," he said.

"Do you know Rob Kessler?"

"Used to be in Narcotics? Yes. Not too well. Isn't he out in Riverside now?"

"San Bernardino." Ben told him the story of how Rob had heard about the rental and referred Grace, and how Ben and Peter had grown close to her.

"So you don't think of her as just a tenant. It's friendlier than that?"

"I'd call her a friend, yes."

"Do you know any of her family or other acquaintances?"

Ben thought about it. Grace didn't talk about her family very much. He told Becerra that.

"What about friends?"

"Not really. I just briefly met a woman from her work who came over two or three times."

"Did they seem like close friends?"

"Yeah, they did."

"Maybe something more?"

"I don't think so. She went through a bad breakup with a guy before she moved. But she didn't talk much about that."

"Do you know his name, by any chance?"

"No," Ben said. "Actually, I think it was Rob who told me about that."

"Have you tried to get a hold of Rob?"

"Left a message. Haven't heard back."

Becerra asked him a dozen more questions. Nothing that surprised him. Routine stuff. Trying to get an idea of who Grace was, what useful information Ben might have. All he had was the red Camaro. If that concerned Becerra, he didn't show it. "Did you check out her apartment?"

"Through the window," Ben said. "I wasn't sure if I should go in, if it was appropriate." He looked down at his hands. "I've never been a landlord before."

"Can we go take a look? You have a key?"

Ben got up, grabbed the key, and led him outside to the studio.

When you go out into the alley to bring in the trash cans, there's a U-Haul truck, one of those big Ford pickups, parked in front of the garage door. The front end is pointed at you, and someone is trying to unload something from the back. You take a few steps around it to see what's going on and see Grace, all by herself, standing behind the tailgate and trying to slide a sofa out of the truck bed.

She's surprised when she sees you, but her expression quickly turns to one of amused embarrassment. "Oh, hi," she says. "A friend of mine from work gave me this. It's a sleeper. I hope it's okay."

"Of course it is," you say. "Why wouldn't it be?"

There's a furniture dolly on the ground by her feet. "I know the daybed has sentimental value for you."

You haven't given much thought to that. Mom put it in the studio years ago, though, so Grace is right, even if you've never really considered it before. It makes you feel odd, Grace realizing something about you that you didn't realize yourself. "Don't even worry about it," you say. "Can I give you a hand?"

Shit, Ben thought as he followed the detective into the studio.

Oh fuck.

No.

His head was spinning. He'd decided not to let himself into Grace's room. He was sure of that. But now that he was inside, memories were popping into his head. Images, feelings, flashing brightly and then disappearing before he could catch hold of them.

"You okay?" Becerra asked.

"Yeah." But he wasn't okay. This wasn't how this was supposed to go. "I'm just worried."

"I know. It's natural. But statistically speaking, everything's probably going to be okay." He looked around, then turned back to Ben. "I don't need to tell you that, I'm sure. I'm sorry."

"For what?"

"Talking to you like a civilian."

That just made him feel worse. Was it more patronizing when someone admitted they were patronizing you or when they pretended like they weren't doing it at all?

Ben stood by the door and watched Becerra survey the apartment.

How could he have forgotten that he had been here and done the same thing himself? It was hazy in his head. Almost like trying to remember a dream. Had he seen something? The harder he tried to recall his actions, the more slippery and distant they became. For a moment, he tried to convince himself that he had not been in there at all. But he knew that wasn't true.

He had been.

What had happened?

It had been almost four years since the last seizure.

No.

If the seizures came back, he couldn't—
No.
Fuck.
Just no.
Stop, he told himself. *Focus.* He had another concern now. The lie he'd inadvertently told to Becerra.

• • •

When they got back inside the house, Peter was standing nervously by the table. When he found out the police were on the way, he'd gone into his bedroom to clean himself up and change his clothes. He still hadn't come out when they went back to the studio.

Ben had mentioned his father, the dementia, so Becerra was prepared when he shook Peter's hand. "Hello, Mr. Shepard. It's a pleasure to meet you."

"You too," Peter said. He looked uncertain and confused, but Ben was confident that he remembered the police were coming. "Is she there?"

"No, sir, I'm afraid not. But we're going to try to find her, okay?"

Peter nodded. "Okay."

Outside on the front porch, Becerra said to Ben, "I'll run the Camaro right away and start looking at a few more things. I really don't think there's any reason to worry yet."

"Thanks," Ben said.

Becerra was halfway to the sidewalk when Ben called after him. He turned around.

"They sent you because of me, right? Because of my history?"

Becerra came back and looked up at him standing on the porch. "Yes, Detective Shepard, they did. The watch commander asked for me specifically."

"Because he thought I was delusional again?"

"No. First off, Lieutenant Hinsley's a woman. But that's not it at all. She told me not to let you down."

"Why?" Ben asked.

"Because you're a hero."

Ben watched Becerra pull away from the curb. He couldn't tell if *hero* was just the lieutenant's word, or, because he managed to say it with a straight face, if it was something Becerra believed, too. Hinsley. Not a name Ben recalled. Had he ever met her? He didn't think so. Was she one of those high-ranking flacks who throw that word around every time they mention a cop, or did it really mean something to her?

Jesus. *Hero.* If that's what they really thought, it was worse than them thinking he was crazy.

SIX

Ben left his father with a cup of coffee and Boost and went to Ralphs. Peter was okay on his own for a few hours at a time. Really, all he needed Ben for was to help with fixing meals to keep his calories up and making sure he didn't eat too much at one time. Or if he needed extra medicine for his stomach or anxiety. Still, Ben worried when he had to be gone for more than two or three hours.

But he thought it would feel good to get out of the house for a while. It usually did. They only lived three blocks from the Ralphs on Cherry and Carson, but Ben usually drove the extra ten minutes to the one down on Lakewood off of the traffic circle. That store was smaller and had a crappy parking lot, but it was the closest location with self-checkout lanes. If anyone asked, which no one ever actually did, he would tell them that it was about convenience, that he hated waiting in line, which he almost always had to do at the closer location, and that he liked to bag the groceries himself. All of that was more or less true, and that was the rationale he used to justify the extra time and distance to himself. Really, though, he just preferred not to have to talk to anyone. Every interaction with anyone, even the smallest and most trivial, made him self-conscious and reminded him that he wasn't who he used to be. He didn't want anyone to see him now. The old Ben, the real Ben, had liked people. Liked to talk. Didn't worry about slurring his speech. Didn't have to write down everything he needed to remember. Didn't mind being seen.

He sat in the old Volvo XC with the two paper grocery bags on the floor in front of the passenger's seat, tracing the depression in the back of his head with his index finger, and worrying. About Grace, mostly, but also about his father and himself. They'd been doing pretty well. Renting out the studio had worked out better than he ever thought it would. The bone-deep fear he'd had of it irreparably upsetting their comfortable routine had proven to be unfounded, and they'd settled into something even better. He told everyone that it was really good to have Grace around for his father, because more interaction was good for him. It made him more alert and engaged. His stomach and his memory both worked better. But Grace was good for Ben, too. There were only a few people he could talk to and spend time with without worrying about embarrassing himself. There were Bernie, his father, and Emma. That was pretty much it. And Emma didn't even really count, because not embarrassing him was part of her job.

Peter wasn't the only one who needed Grace.

• • •

Bigmista's Morning Wood was a relatively recent addition to the neighborhood. It was a spinoff of Bigmista's Sammich Shop. The owner had gained a local following, selling ribs and brisket and anything else that came out of a smoker, before he finally opened his own shop. That did well, so he branched out. The city was chock-full of breakfast places, but as far as Ben knew, Morning Wood was the only place that specialized in breakfast barbecue. And the name still made him chuckle.

He didn't really like to eat out much, not like he used to. And he made a point of not going anyplace so often that the employees would get to know him well enough to stop treating him like a stranger. Morning Wood was the exception. Peter loved the biscuits and gravy. Ben had to admit they were good, but the reason he came to order them twice a week was the fact they were one of the only really calorie-dense foods his father could eat without his stomach hurting.

He didn't know the name of the big African American woman behind the counter, and he was pretty sure she didn't know his. All the same, she greeted him with a broad smile and a friendly hello. "How's your dad doing?"

"Pretty well."

"Oh, that's good. He's a sweetie."

Ben had brought Peter in a few times, but more often than not, they both preferred takeout. He smiled back at her. "Yeah, he is."

"The usual?"

Ben nodded. The usual was an order of biscuits and gravy for his father and a breakfast bowl with tater tots and brisket for him.

"Just give us a few minutes, okay?" she said, handing him his change.

At one of the tables, he checked his phone. No new messages from Grace or Rob. He wished he could remember what it had been like before, what normal was like. How worried should he be? It felt like he was close to Grace, like she was more a friend than a tenant. But was that true? Was it just his limited frame of reference? There wasn't really anyone in his life anymore except his father. Not in any significant way. Grace had people in her life. So he and Peter were surely much less central to her than she was to them. He thought of her as a friend, but she wouldn't be likely to think that way of him. He was her landlord. Maybe her neighbor. But that was the extent of it, right? If she went away for a few days, would she even feel obligated to tell him? He tried to remember the days when he'd been a renter, before he bought the house with—that was so long ago. It was hazy, but it didn't seem like he would have felt the need to tell anyone about his plans. Was this just all a massive overreaction?

"Here you go," the counter woman said.

It didn't register at first that she was speaking to him. But he looked around and realized he was the only one waiting for an order. "Thanks."

"Tell your dad hi for me." She smiled again.

"I will," he said.

On the way home, he circled around the block and then cut through the alley, looking for a red Camaro.

• • •

It was sunny and cold when he got back. "Hi, Dad," he called when he opened the door. There was no answer. Peter wasn't sitting in the living room watching TV, as Ben had expected. He wasn't in the kitchen or dining room, either. Ben went in back, past the office and the laundry closet to the rear bedroom. He wasn't there.

Ben felt a feathery twitch in his abdomen.

He checked the bathrooms. The patio. No sign of him.

Could he be outside?

He put a hand on the back of one of the chairs to steady himself. *Breathe,* he told himself, *breathe.*

When he was steady, Ben went out through the French doors and headed back toward the studio. It wasn't until he was halfway across the lawn that he saw his father in one of the blue Adirondack chairs and stopped as the relief swept over him. Hands on his hips, he let out a chestful of air. He hadn't seen him in the shadow of the cherry tree.

Peter waved and smiled.

Ben walked closer to his father. "What are you doing out here?" he said, his voice harsher than he meant it to be.

"I came out to look for her?" He'd clearly heard the edge in Ben's voice. "Did I do something bad?"

"No," Ben said, trying to sound reassuring. "You never do bad things. But how come you're still sitting out here?"

Peter pointed to the sky.

"A plane?"

His father nodded and the corners of his eyes crinkled. "Waiting for the next one."

"I brought you some biscuits and gravy."

"Oh, I like those." He pushed himself up on the arms of the chair.

"I know," Ben said. "Why don't we go inside to eat and then we'll come back out and watch?"

Peter nodded.

• • •

1/10 12:30
Couldn't find dad after store
He was outside by Grace's, watching for planes, FIRST TIME?
Ate Bigmista's
Lorazepam (me, not him)

• • •

Nothing happened all afternoon. Well, not nothing. Just the usual things. Peter watched TV. Ben sat with him when *Ellen* came on, trying to read the Springsteen autobiography, but he couldn't focus. Not with Grace missing. He checked his phone every ten minutes, vainly hoping for something from anyone.

It was a quarter to four when he got the text message.

Don't call the police.

He froze. It didn't feel like he could move.

There was no ID and the number wasn't one he recognized. It was from the 909 area code. Where was that? He should know. Why didn't he know that? *Nine-oh-nine,* he thought, over and over again. He used to know. He used to know all the area codes for California. Now, though, he didn't know shit.

He had already called the police. Did someone have Grace? Had she been kidnapped? Was this some kind of threat?

Ben was suddenly aware of his heart beating in his chest. It grew stronger and faster. He started to worry that his father could hear it, but Peter was just grinning at Ellen talking to some celebrity that neither of them recognized.

What should he do?

Text back?

Call?

His stomach knotted.

Then he got the second text.

This is Rob by the way

Then another.

Not sure if you have this number

Fuck.

No, Ben replied, I didn't have this number. I thought you were a fucking kidnapper or something.

Sorry

I already called. Filed a missing persons report.

Shit

Why? What's wrong?

ill explain later

Explain NOW

Ben waited for a reply, hoping he hadn't been too aggressive.

Rob?

Rob?

Please.

I'm sorry.

Rob?

???

Wherever Rob was and whatever he was doing, he wasn't respond-ing anymore.

Why shouldn't Ben have called the police? What did Rob know? What the hell was happening?

After he went into his bathroom and took another lorazepam, he called Emma's voicemail. "Hi," he said. "It's Ben Shepard. I've got kind of an urgent situation. Could we make an appointment? As soon as possible, if you can. Thanks. Uh, did I say this was Ben? It's Ben. Thank you. Um, have a good day?" He disconnected the call, cringing at his awkwardness.

• • •

After Peter went to bed, Ben made another call. To Jennifer Tanaka. She picked up on the first ring.

"Ben," she said. "Hi. How are you?"

"I need help."

"Where are you?"

"Home."

"I'm on the way."

SEVEN

Ben waited ten minutes, then tilted open the plantation shutters on the living-room window and watched the street outside. He turned off the TV and all the lights except the lamp next to the couch so he'd be able to see out into the darkness.

He tried to remember how long it had been since Jennifer had bought the house in Belmont Heights. She'd already been working Homicide a long time. A year? Two? Even though she'd invited him a few times, he still hadn't seen it. From what she'd told him over their last several lunches—they still got together every month or two—it was a nice place. She had a guesthouse, too, and was renting it out to a rookie cop. Was that where he got the idea? Maybe. He thought about it. It was possible that hearing about her tenant gave him the idea to look for renters through the LBPD. How long would it take to go through his notebooks and figure it out? Certainly too long to try now. He took the pen and the little Moleskine out of his pocket and jotted down a reminder to check later.

Outside, a car pulled up to the curb, but stopped before it was in front of the house. Could it be her? What did Jennifer drive now? She didn't have the 4Runner anymore. Ben knew that. Now she had one of those smaller SUVs. The car outside wasn't one of those. It was a sedan, and it didn't look like a department-issue plain-wrap cruiser. The driver got out and crossed the street. A lady, older, maybe. Not anyone he recognized.

Ben checked his watch and waited. It took eight more long minutes before he saw a RAV4 park across the street. Jennifer closed the car door behind her and crossed the street. He opened the front door for her before she had the chance to ring the bell or knock.

"Sorry," he said. "My dad's asleep. I didn't want the sound to wake him."

She stepped across the threshold, put her hand on his arm, and said, "Are you all right?"

Grace says, "This morning your dad asked me for another cup of coffee."

"Oh," you say. "I'm sorry."

"No, it's not that. I didn't know if it was okay. For me to get him another one?"

"You wouldn't mind that?"

"Not at all. I just wasn't sure if I should."

"It's definitely all right, if you don't mind."

"I don't. I like helping him."

You smile at her.

"I don't know exactly how to do it, though. Is it just Boost and coffee?"

You go into the kitchen and show her. "If it's his second cup or it hasn't been more than like an hour and a half or so, I always just do a small one."

"Okay," she says.

You reach up and get a cup out of the cabinet, then take a fresh bottle of Boost out of the box on the counter. "For a regular cup, it's pretty easy. You just pour half the Boost into the cup, then fill it up with coffee and add a tablespoon of sugar."

"Got it."

"I know that seems like a lot, but we're still trying to gain weight."

Grace nods.

"For a small one, I just eyeball it now, but if you want, you can use this." You open a drawer near the Mr. Coffee machine and take out a measuring cup. "This one's a quarter, so just do one of each, then a big teaspoon of sugar, and stir it up."

She smiles and nods again.

"You want to try one, for practice?"

"No, I'm good."

And you realize of course she's good. She probably pours a hundred cups of coffee every shift at work. You feel like a condescending idiot.

"Do you want some more coffee?" Ben asked.

Jennifer shook her head. "Not if I want to sleep tonight."

"I could make some decaf. There's herbal tea, too."

"It's okay, thanks."

They were sitting on the couch in the living room, where they had been for more than an hour while Ben told her everything he could think of about Grace and Rob and his confusion about what to do.

"You remember what you used to tell me when I started in Violent Crimes?"

"No," Ben said. "Not really."

Jennifer pressed her lips together and looked down at the coffee table, and Ben knew she regretted her choice of words.

"You used to tell me the hardest part of detective work was figuring out how to be patient in the most urgent circumstances."

He thought about that and he could almost feel the words coming out of his mouth. They felt right. Like something he would have said before. "So you're saying I shouldn't do anything?"

"No, I'm saying you should be patient. Let Henry do his job."

"Who's Henry?"

"Becerra. Sorry. I know him. He's a good cop."

Ben tried to remember reading Becerra's full name on the card he left. He had read it. He'd studied the damn thing. Typed the name and number into the contacts on his phone. Looked at it a hundred times. Was it Henry? He honestly couldn't say.

"What about Rob?" he asked.

Jennifer's brow furrowed. "I'm not sure. He was always solid, as far as I knew. But it sounds like something's going on with him. Wait for him to get back to you. See what he says."

"Should I tell him about Becerra?"

"Yeah. I'll check in with Becerra tomorrow, okay? See how it's going. And I'll reach out to Rob, too."

"You'd do that for me?" Ben asked.

She looked sad, but he didn't know why. "Of course I would."

Outside, as she was getting into her RAV4, Ben said, "Could you do one more thing for me?"

"Sure. What?"

"Find out who owns the red Camaro?"

She studied his eyes, then tilted her head and said, "I'll see what I can do."

• • •

For about an hour, Ben felt better. Calm. Reassured. Jennifer was one of the few people who could make him feel that way. He'd partnered with her on her first permanent detective assignment in Violent Crimes. Showed her the ropes. They'd worked together for two years, until she transferred to Homicide. On their last day together she'd given him an expensive silk tie—he still cared about ties then—and a card in which she called him the best mentor she could have hoped for. He remembered reading it and trying to recall the last time he'd actually cried.

The tie was in a box on his closet shelf with two or three others he still kept just in case. The card was in the drawer in his nightstand.

When it began to seem like a long time since Jennifer had left, and the thoughts of Grace and Rob and the Camaro started to crowd out the memories, he left the TV on, with that kid who played Spider-Man talking to Stephen Colbert, and went to go look at it.

It was a simple card. Off-white with nothing but *Thank You* on the front in a raised blue-gold calligraphic font. How many times had he read what she had written inside? Hundreds? Surely. He had a shoebox half-full of old cards and notes, most of them received in the aftermath of the incident. He hadn't saved many. A few from friends and colleagues, and several more from strangers who felt compelled to send him messages. He hadn't looked through those in a long time. But there were a few he kept next to the bed. So much of what had happened in his life before had been stolen from his memory that he kept these few things close. The last letter his mother wrote, the last birthday card before Peter's first surgery, a commendation from the chief, Jennifer's thank-you.

He looked at her card again, the handwriting so familiar he could almost feel the odd mix of pride and sadness he'd experienced the first time he'd read it.

> Ben,
> I wouldn't be going to Homicide if not for you. A lot of people could have taught me to be a better detective, but you taught me to be a better person. You're the best cop I've ever worked with and I'll always be grateful for what you've given me. I'll miss you.
> Jennifer

Sometimes when he read it now, silently mouthing the words as he worked his way slowly through each line, he could almost imagine what it was like to be the man to whom the note was written.

• • •

Even after he went back into the dining room and popped a couple of Peter's Advil PMs, he still couldn't go to sleep. He thought about the Ambien in his medicine cabinet but decided against it. When he leaned back on the couch and rested his head on the throw pillow, he realized that from that angle he could still see his old badge where he had attempted to hide it behind his mom's photo.

• • •

In the morning, as soon as he'd put the coffee on and started the water in the kettle for Peter's oatmeal, he sent Rob a text: I need to talk to you. He slipped the phone into his pocket and went to knock on the back-bedroom door. A few light taps, and he turned the knob and opened it. Peter was already up and in the bathroom. "You okay, Dad?" he said through the closed door.

The reply was even softer than usual. "Not much."

Ben cracked the door open and peeked inside. His father was sitting on the toilet, hunched over with his hand on his stomach and a grimace on his face. He grunted and Ben heard a squirt of diarrhea splash into the toilet bowl. He tried to smile. "I think it's a bad day," he said.

•　•　•

After Peter had breakfast and two more small bowel movements, his stomach was hurting, so he asked if he could lie down for a little while. Ben didn't mind, because he wanted to lie down, too.

He wasn't sure how long he'd been sleeping when he woke to the sound of a text message. When he tried to pick up his phone, it slipped out of his hand and thudded onto the hardwood floor.

"Shit!"

Leaning over the edge of the bed, he couldn't see the phone anywhere. It must have bounced underneath. He got down on his hands and knees and looked. There it was. About a foot back. In all the dust. He retrieved it and wiped the screen off with his T-shirt.

As he stood, he was startled by the shadow of a figure in the doorway and nearly dropped the phone again.

"I heard you shit," Peter said.

Ben didn't know what he meant. He hadn't gone to the bathroom.

"Are you all right?" Peter asked.

Then he realized what his father had meant. "Yeah. I just dropped my phone. It's okay. Sorry I yelled."

"You don't need to be sorry." Peter held a pile of dirty laundry in his arms. "Not for anything."

"Thanks, Dad." He felt bad. Ben tried not to get angry, because he knew it could upset Peter and knock things off track. Peter's earlier remark about it being a bad day still echoed in his head. "You need to do some laundry?"

Peter looked confused. He'd forgotten what was in his hands. Ben pointed and he looked down. "Oh. Yes, if it's okay."

"Of course it is. You want me to help you get it started?"

Peter nodded.

They stood in front of the washing machine and went through the pockets of Peter's clothes. For several months after Ben moved back home, his father would always double-check the laundry. It made Ben feel incompetent and infantilized, but he'd developed a habit of washing his notes and other things he'd folded into a pocket and forgotten, so he accepted it. Once, it had been the after-visit summary and instructions from the neurologist. Another time, the key fob for the Volvo. Peter didn't have anything of value in his pockets, though. They just went through the routine to spare themselves from having to go outside and shake bits of semidissolved tissues and paper towels off the clothes.

When the washer was full and Ben had helped his father add the laundry soap, he asked, "How's your stomach feeling?"

"Not too bad," Peter said.

He was relieved. Maybe it wouldn't be that bad a day after all.

• • •

Ben didn't remember the first text until the second came. They were both from Rob.

The first said can you meet me at the mariott by the airport at 9? The second had come at 10:30. How about 12?

Yes, Ben texted back. Where should I meet you?

lobby, Rob said. we'll grab lunch

>

• • •

Before Ben left the house, he made lunch for Peter. A small banana-berry smoothie and half a slice of the vanilla loaf cake he liked.

"You look good," his father said. Ben had put on khaki pants and a plaid shirt with a button-down collar, an outfit that these days qualified as dressed up.

"Thanks, Dad. So do you."

Peter chuckled.

"I'll be back in about an hour and a half, okay?" He'd made some fresh dishwater and emptied the drying rack on the counter so Peter would have something to do while he was gone.

"You don't have to hurry." Peter took a sip of the smoothie and frowned.

"I'll fix you some more coffee when I get home."

Ben kissed his father on the top of his head and locked the door behind himself on the way out. Halfway to the Volvo, he stopped, saw the neighbor's drone buzzing through the trees, and felt a flare of irritation cut through his nervousness. Then he thought for a moment, and went back inside.

"Sorry, Dad," he said. "I forgot something."

He went in the bathroom, opened the medicine cabinet, found the bottle of lorazepam, dropped two of the tiny tablets into his shirt pocket, and headed back outside.

• • •

He couldn't remember the last time he'd been in the Marriott. It was before. That much was certain. It looked like any other slightly-better-than-average airport hotel, except for the wall of windows that curved around the lush palm-lined pool area, making it all feel more tropical than anyplace in Long Beach had a right to.

Ben looked for Rob and didn't see him anywhere. He was a few minutes early, so he took a seat in a pale-yellow upholstered chair against the wall, which allowed a view of both the elevators and the main entrance. While he sat and waited, he took out his notebook.

1/11 11:52
Meeting Rob at Marriott
Something's up, but worried/anxious
Why isn't Rob talking to Becerra?
Should I be doing this—doesn't feel like I should be doing this

• • •

At five past noon, Ben was still waiting in the lobby. His phone rang. He knew it had to be Rob, cancelling or rescheduling. But it wasn't. Emma's name was on the screen. The awkward, panicked call he'd made to her yesterday had slipped his mind. He couldn't deal with it now, though, so he sent her to voicemail and put his phone back in his pocket. In his notebook he scribbled, *Call Emma.*

Absentmindedly, he rubbed his index finger on his chest, feeling the two small pills in his pocket. He should have brought the pillbox. If he needed the medicine, though, he didn't want to have to make a big production out of taking it. The way they were now, it would be easy to just pop one in his mouth and swallow. They were small enough he could even manage without anything to drink. He was about to go ahead and take one when Rob came in through the main entrance.

Ben stood up and raised a hand in an awkward, noncommittal semi-wave. It was just enough to cause a ripple of embarrassment to wash over him. Before he had a chance to worry about it, though, Rob strode over and extended his hand for a firm shake. Ben was vaguely aware of having shaken people's hands like that himself a long time ago. Rob wasn't wearing a suit, just a sport coat and jeans. No tie. Looked like a TV detective, mustache and all. Ben wondered if he was on the clock and what exactly he was doing in Long Beach.

"Let's eat," Rob said. "The restaurant's not actually too bad."

The Terrace Grille was tucked in the far corner of the ground floor. It supplemented the glass wall with numerous skylights that flooded the room with bright and beachy sunshine.

When the hostess left them at a table along the back wall with menus in their hands, Ben said, "Have you, have you heard anything from Grace?"

Rob shook his head. "Not yet."

"Why didn't you want m-me to call the LBPD?"

"I'll tell you everything I know. But let's just take a quick look at these menus before the waiter comes over. They've got a lunch buffet, but it's not as good."

Ben wasn't hungry. He found a club sandwich and decided he'd get that, folded the menu, and dropped it on the table. Rob was still examining his choices, as if his decision on what to eat was the most important thing he'd do all day. He looked different from the last time Ben had seen him. A little thinner, maybe? Older? Maybe it was just a haircut. It didn't matter. What mattered was Grace. Something weird was going on. And Rob needed to tell him what it was.

"I think I'll just get the burger. What are you going to have?"

"A sandwich?"

Rob eyeballed him. There was something in his expression Ben couldn't quite read. It hung there between them for what felt like a long time. The awkwardness came so quickly now. A few seconds of silence and Ben's gut started to churn. Had he said something wrong? Misunderstood something? What embarrassing thing had he done? Years ago, he wouldn't have been able to imagine himself like this. His greatest strength as a detective had been interviews and interrogations, always on the other end of the awkwardness, throwing a question or statement out into the empty space between himself and suspect or witness and letting it hang there, suspended for as long as it took for the silence to worm its way into the person's head and take hold. Then, the silence had been on his side, and he knew how to use it, how to manipulate it, how to make it into a tool, or a weapon. Now it seemed that in every conversation with anyone but his father, he was on the other side, looking right into the muzzle.

"What kind of sandwich?" Rob asked.

"The club looks good."

Rob nodded and smiled amiably.

Ben said, "Or maybe the Cajun chicken?"

"I had that yesterday. Not bad."

A server who looked like he should have been in high school instead of working a lunch shift approached the table and said, "Good afternoon. Can I get you gentlemen started on some drinks?"

They told him what they wanted and ordered their food, too. Ben went with the club, even though he felt it was probably a mistake.

"How's your dad doing?"

"He's okay." Ben checked his watch. How long had he been gone? It was close to an hour already and he still didn't know anything about Grace. Did Rob know that he had to get back home soon? "What's going on? Why didn't you want me to call the police?"

Rob glanced over his shoulder. The restaurant was still fairly empty. People were trickling in, but there wasn't much of a crowd. The nearest diners were three tables away. Still, though, he lowered his voice before he spoke. "I'm sure it's not a problem, there's nothing to worry about."

That made Ben worry. "Why no police?"

"Grace was involved in a case I was working on."

Shit. Of course the thought had occurred to him, that she had been connected to Rob that way. If she hadn't been, Rob would have talked more about how he knew her, what their relationship was, but he hadn't. No *She's my niece* or *My neighbor's kid wants to move to Long Beach.* There was nothing like that, so of course Ben had wondered. "Involved how?"

"She was a witness. Helped us make a big case, but the thing fell apart before trial."

Ben thought about it. It was a hell of thing, asking someone to give evidence in a big case. In some circumstances, it could put a person at risk. It wasn't at all unusual for the witness to want to get away, to put some distance between themselves and whoever they helped put in jail. But that didn't explain why he shouldn't have called the cops.

"What kind of case, though? Why wouldn't you want me to report it?"

The server came back with two iced teas and put them on the table. When the guy was gone, Rob looked down at the glass in front of him. "Think about it," he said.

Ben did. He had been thinking about it ever since Rob sent the text message telling him not to call the police. Knowing she had been a witness added a key piece to the puzzle. Grace was trying to get away from something, maybe even hide from it. If the case had fallen apart, that meant that whoever she was supposed to testify against would remain a threat. Still, though, why no cops?

Shit.

Shit. Shit. Shit.

"I didn't think to ask before," Ben said, not really wanting to know the answer. "Out in San Bernardino, what division are you with now?"

Rob looked at him. "Internal Affairs."

• • •

When their lunch was finished, Rob's plate clean and half a club sandwich on his, Ben still didn't know much more. It was a narcotics case. Rob wasn't worried about dirty cops in Long Beach, only that if anyone in an official capacity started asking questions about Grace in San Bernardino, word might get back to the suspect and give him some idea of where she might be. Or where she might have been. Ben thought about the red Camaro and wondered if it was too late on that account.

"Come upstairs with me for a minute," Rob said.

His room was on the fourth floor. Rob went straight to the closet, while Ben glanced at several bulging file folders spread across the small desk by the window. How much of Grace's past was laid out there?

Rob ripped the packaging off of a new prepaid cell phone and powered it up. He dialed a number, and a few seconds later an identical phone on top of one of the manila folders on the desk beeped. "Here," he said. "Take this."

"What for?" Ben asked.

"So we can get a hold of each other."

"You really think we need burners?"

"Can't be too careful."

Ben's stomach churned. There was more in those folders than Rob wanted him to know.

• • •

When Ben parked on the street in front of the house, he saw that the front door was open and his father was talking to a stranger on the porch. White guy, maybe thirty or thirty-five, old work boots and denim shirt fraying around the collar, lean and muscular, with blond hair cut short and a little too greasy.

Peter saw him coming up the walkway and said, "Here's my son. He can help."

Ben smiled, friendly and kind. "Sure. What can I do?"

"His car is broken," Peter said, concern and worry in his voice.

"Is it?" Ben said. "That's awful."

The stranger was wary, unsure what to make of Ben. "Yeah. I was telling your dad here I need a new fuel pump. Have a job interview tomorrow up in Santa Clarita. But I'm just a little short." The stranger looked as if asking for help was the most difficult thing he'd ever had to do.

"Santa Clarita's a long way away."

"Yes, sir. It is. I came to Long Beach for a job. Just a couple of days is all. To do some drywall on a remodel job just around the corner."

If any of the neighbors were having any work done, Ben hadn't heard about it.

Peter looked at Ben. "I said we could help him."

"How much do you need?" Ben asked.

The stranger looked like he was embarrassed to say. He was thin, not tweaker skinny but maybe on the way there. "Forty would do it, I think."

Ben took a step closer on the porch. There was nowhere for the man to go now except over the railing onto the lawn or into the house. "No problem," he said. Without looking at his father, he said, "Dad, would you go grab my wallet? I think I left it in the office."

"Sure." Peter turned and walked back into the house.

Ben reached over and pulled the front door closed without taking his eyes off the stranger. When the door latched, his smile was gone. Ben's left hand found the stranger's throat and he shoved him back up against the wall and held him there.

"How many people you rip off today?" He pushed the heel of his hand into the man's clavicle, thumb on one side of his neck, fingers on the other, ready to squeeze. His right hand found the place on his hip where his gun used to be.

The man started to say something, but Ben cut him off. "Don't lie to me."

"Five or six." His eyes were darting back and forth, searching for help or escape or something else Ben couldn't guess.

He grabbed the man's shirt in both hands, pulled him away from the wall, and shoved him hard, toppling him over the railing.

Ben didn't watch as the stranger hit the lawn headfirst and rolled down onto his side. He darted down the two stairs and caught the stranger, dazed, as he was pushing himself up onto his knees.

He was still on all fours when Ben's New Balance stomped down on his hand, pinning it to the ground.

Ben put his hands on the stranger's shoulders and leaned in close. "You ever try to take advantage of my father again and I'll fucking kill you. You understand?" He couldn't tell for sure, but Ben thought he nodded. He yanked him to his feet and pushed him toward the sidewalk. After a few shaky steps, the stranger found his balance and sprinted down the street.

Ben took several deep breaths on the porch, then went in and found his father in the office.

"I can't find your phone," Peter said.

"That's okay, Dad." Ben took his phone out of his pocket and held it up. "I had it the whole time."

Peter laughed and Ben tried to laugh with him.

EIGHT

1/11 2:30
lunch w/ rob Marriott
Grace witness—bad cop—hiding? Would rob know if he had her???
Asshole trying to scam dad, told him off
extra lorazepam (me not dad)

Jennifer answered the call right away and he told her everything. Ben thought he could trust Rob. He knew he could trust Jennifer.

"What if the guy he's looking at, the bad cop, what if he took Grace?"

"Did you ask Rob that?"

"No, I was too stupid to even think of it."

"Rob doesn't seem worried about that, does he?"

"No." Ben thought about that. Maybe Rob knew something about the guy. Maybe Rob had someone watching him. Maybe. But maybe it was even worse than that. "What if the guy just killed her?"

"Ben," she said, her voice soft and thoughtful. "Let's not get ahead of ourselves, okay? I think if Rob was worried she was in that much danger, he'd be acting a lot differently than he is. Don't you think so?"

She was right. Of course. "Probably." He felt bad that he'd called her. Interrupted her with his paranoia. "I'm sorry I'm bothering you."

"You're not bothering me. I talked to Becerra. He ran the Camaro. The partial plate number you gave him was enough to nail it down."

"Did he find anything?"

"No wants or warrants. Only a couple of parking tickets. Owner doesn't have a criminal record."

"Nothing suspicious at all?"

"Not really, no." She paused. "Just that he lives in Corona."

"Corona?" That was halfway to San Bernardino. More than halfway, actually. Ben tried to remember the county boundaries. Was Corona in Rob's jurisdiction? That wouldn't matter, though, if the guy worked for the sheriff's department. "What county is Corona in?"

"Could be Riverside," Jennifer said. "Let me check." The line was quiet for a moment. "Yeah," she said. "It's Riverside."

"Did Becerra dig any deeper yet?" Ben asked. "Find out what the Camaro guy does for a living?"

"I don't think so. You want to talk to him, or should I?"

Ben was glad she offered. He knew he'd get nervous if he had to make the call. "Would you mind?"

"Not at all," she said. "I'll ask him to get in touch with you if he needs anything else or comes up with anything."

"Thanks, Jennifer."

"I'm here if you need me," she said. "And not just about the case."

• • •

Peter hadn't been asking about Grace as much in the last two days. Sitting on the back patio in the Adirondack chair by her door, thinking about it, Ben was overcome with a wave of sadness. He knew the memories of her were fading for his father, and he didn't know whether or not to remind him. How much did Peter need to know? Too much information would just confuse him and make it even harder for him to understand. Not enough and he'd start to worry about Ben. His father could always sense his anxiety, and even if Peter didn't have the words to express or explain it, Ben knew it troubled him and made his symptoms worse. All of them—memory, language, even his stomach—they were all more troublesome when Ben was anxious.

He looked at the door and thought about what Jennifer had said about patience. What he'd said about it himself, a long time ago.

But Grace was gone now. Had she gone on her own? Was she running from the red Camaro? Or had something else, something worse, happened to her?

It had been easy for him to preach patience when he'd been a detective. Because then he had some control, some agency. Patience was easy when it was a choice. Of course you're happy with your speed when you're the one with your foot on the gas pedal.

Now, though, he wasn't even sure who was driving or where they were going.

Grace was gone now and getting further away, slipping out of his father's memories. Would she slip from his own, too? How long would it be until all he could remember of her was what he'd scribbled in his notebooks?

He thought about who she'd been before she'd gotten involved in Rob's case. Was she the same woman he and his father knew?

The more he thought about it, sitting there in the encroaching twilight, the more sure he was that the longer he waited, the further away she got. He was trying not to get caught up in his own projections, the way Emma had taught him, to ask himself how the situation would look to someone else, someone more objective. Like Rob, like Jennifer, like Becerra. Was that the right thing now? None of them knew the Grace who lived here, the Grace who drank coffee with his father on the patio and made him smile. None of them knew what was missing.

That was the moment he decided. If no one had any news for him by tomorrow, he'd start digging and he'd find it for himself. Becerra seemed like the good cop Jennifer said he was. He'd keep working the case. Before long he'd be here with a search warrant for the studio. If Ben was really serious about not sitting around on his ass anymore and actually doing something, he'd have to go back inside before that happened.

• • •

At first, Ben thought he was dreaming. He'd been sleeping fitfully, drifting off and waking again soon after. His dream had been one that had been visiting him recently, the one in which he relived his waking from the coma in the hospital and the slow realization that something was very wrong. He thought the moans were his own. Slowly, after two or three repetitions of the cycle, he sat up in bed, determined to leave the dream behind. Then he heard the moan again.

It was Peter.

In his haste standing up, Ben lost his balance and fell, fortunately hitting the edge of the bed on the way to the floor. The mattress absorbed most of the impact, so he was able to get back on his feet quickly and hurry to the back bathroom.

The door was almost closed, letting only a sliver of light out into the hallway. He tapped his knuckle near the knob as he pushed it open. "Dad?"

Peter was sitting on the toilet, hunched forward, hands on his abdomen, his face nearly touching his knees. He moaned again and Ben rushed to his side and kneeled next to him.

"What's wrong, Dad?"

"Hurts." Peter's voice was thin and weak. More breath than sound.

"Your stomach?"

He nodded.

"Is anything coming out?"

He shook his head.

"Can I look?"

Peter leaned to the side and lifted one cheek off the seat. There was nothing inside. The water was clear.

Shit. Did he have another bowel obstruction? *No, please. Please, please, please, no.*

Ben focused on his breathing, tried to slow it down, deepen it.

This wasn't how it had been before. No, then it was vomiting. Peter almost never threw up. The only times he'd ever thrown up were before the trips to the ER.

"Dad?"

Peter didn't seem to hear him.

He said it louder, firmer. "Dad."

Peter looked at him.

"Have you thrown up at all?"

The question didn't register. He wasn't getting it.

"Out of your mouth, Dad. Has anything come out of your mouth?"

He shook his head. Ben put his nose in front of his father's mouth and tried to figure out if he could smell anything unusual. It didn't smell good, but he couldn't detect any odor of vomit. "Are you sure nothing came up out of your mouth?"

Peter nodded. He was rocking forward and back on the toilet seat, still holding his stomach.

What was it? What *could* it be? Ben thought about it. He couldn't remember giving him his medicine. That wasn't unheard of—sometimes memories of their daily routines got lost in the shuffle. He must have, though. He wouldn't forget that. He couldn't forget that.

"Stay right here, okay? I'll be right back."

Peter nodded again and Ben rushed into his bedroom and turned on the overhead light. His notebook was on the nightstand. There was nothing there about his father's medicine. He flipped the pages back and forth. The entries went from dinner—*mashed potatoes, decaf/boost*—straight to Ben's note about his own evening meds.

It was his fault.

He'd forgotten his father's medicine. It was after four and he'd needed it nine hours ago. That was why his stomach was cramping and nothing was coming out.

It's your fault.

You worthless fucking piece of shit, you worthless fucking pieceofshit, youworthlessfuck—

"No," Ben said out loud.

"No."

He balled his hands into fists so tight he felt his fingernails digging into his palms. "No," he said again, this time almost a grunt.

Stop. Breathe. Breathe. Breathe.

The downward spiral he'd felt himself falling into seemed to be slowing. If he could just hold himself together for a few more minutes, long enough to help his father, he'd have the rest of the night to hate himself and spiral away into the nearest abyss.

Peter was still moaning when he got back to him on the toilet.

"Dad? It's going to be okay. I forgot to give you your medicine. I'm going to get it right now, okay?"

Ben mixed a big dose of Miralax into a cup of water. He had the bottle of Advil PM in his hand and decided it wouldn't be enough. In his medicine cabinet were a dozen hydrocodone tablets left over from his father's last surgery. He got one out of the bottle and hurried back to Peter's side. The painkiller might worsen the constipation, but Ben was hoping the laxative would be enough to counter that potential side effect.

"Here, Dad, take this." Ben held out the large pill and Peter pinched it in his shaking fingers and slipped it into his mouth. He needed help with the cup and it took two tries to get it down, but he did it.

For the next half hour, Ben sat on the edge of the bathtub and gave his father one small sip of laxative after another. By the time they finished, the pill had started to ease the abdominal pain and Peter was ready to go back to bed.

"Thank you for helping me," he said as Ben pulled the covers over him. "You always help me."

"And you help me, Dad. We help each other."

Peter smiled up at him in the dim glow of the night-light.

• • •

1/12 4:30a

Dad's meds very late b/c FORGOT THEM! Very bad stomach/constip.

-took hydrocodone b/c I FUCKED UP

Distracted thinking about Grace

Focus

Focus

Focus!!!!

Peter slept late the next morning. It was after ten when he finally woke up. That wasn't good. A solid start to the morning, keeping on track and following the routine, always made for a better day.

"I'm sorry about last night," Ben said.

Peter swallowed a small bit of oatmeal. "Don't sorry." He reached out and put his hand on his son's arm. "I was hurting and you helped me."

Ben wanted to apologize again, to explain what happened, to make sure Peter knew it had been his fault. The guilt was burning in his gut. He'd only had half a cup of coffee before he felt like he needed to vomit. If Peter understood—if he would only blame Ben, hold him responsible, get angry—then the shame would be validated. The dynamic was familiar. He'd talked about it with Emma over and over again. If no one else would blame Ben for all the shit that swirled around him, he would just have to do it himself.

"How's your stomach doing?" Ben asked.

"Not too bad."

"Can I feel it?"

Peter nodded, and Ben put his palm against his father's belly. It wasn't as tight and bloated as it had been early that morning. He'd filled the toilet before he came out for breakfast, so that was good. Maybe things were getting back on track.

• • •

At a quarter past noon, Ben hadn't heard anything from anyone except Emma, who had left another message about scheduling an appointment, so he went out into the garage and pulled down his old patrol bag from the shelf in the corner. It was wrapped in a big black trash-can liner to keep the dust off and the bugs out. As he slid it out of the plastic, he was hit with a flash of memory—hefting the bag into the trunk of an unmarked cruiser on the way to a callout. He couldn't place the case or even the time frame, but it seemed specific rather than generic.

The flashes hadn't been coming like they used to. For about a year after he came home, he'd have them all the time. Twenty, sometimes thirty a day. They were confusing, a disjointed jumble of seemingly random moments of his life before the incident. He'd never been able to make sense out of them, and on the worst days they left him unsure of where and even when he was. Just another of the many symptoms that had faded as the doctors fine-tuned his medication and his recovery progressed.

He unzipped the bag. The black ballistic nylon had stiffened and the zipper wasn't as smooth as it used to be. What he was looking for was right on top. All he had to do was nudge the Kevlar vest aside and he saw it. The box of latex gloves. When he opened them, though, he realized they'd been sitting there in the heat of the garage for years. The gloves were dried out and stiff and tore when he tried to pull them out of the box.

After a moment of disappointment, he cursed himself for his stupidity, went into his father's bathroom, and took a fresh pair out of the box on the counter that he'd brought home from CVS less than a week ago.

Honestly, he wasn't sure Becerra would even search the studio, or, if he did, that he'd bother checking for fingerprints. But if there was even a chance of that, Ben wanted to be careful. If they did dust the place, it would be normal to find a fair amount of the landlord's prints in a tenant's apartment, but if Ben did a thorough search, his prints would be everywhere, even on things Grace had clearly brought with her when she moved in. That would be enough to earn him a spot on the suspect list.

Peter was sweeping inside. He was way off of his normal schedule. Usually by this time of day he'd have the floors swept and the dishes done and be ready for lunch. Ben left half a cup of coffee and a quarter of a Hershey's bar for him on the counter.

"How you doing, Dad?"

Peter put a hand on his stomach and said, "Hurts, but not too bad. I'm almost finished."

"Okay," Ben said. "I left some coffee and chocolate for you. I'm going to be out in back for a while."

His father nodded and started in again with the broom.

• • •

Unlocking the door, Ben noticed a slight tremor in his hand and felt his chest and abdomen tighten. He ignored it and stepped inside. The plan was to start next to the door and methodically work his way around the perimeter of the room, looking for anything that might be out of place or that might give any information about Grace or anyone she was involved with. A new Moleskine was in his shirt pocket. He'd written *GRACE* on the blank beige cover with a Sharpie.

Next to the door was the small dining table. Her MacBook was still there, closed, in the same position it had been in the previous time he'd come inside. That would be last, though. He'd decided that before he started. After he was done with everything else, he'd remove it so he could take his time going through whatever he found. There was nothing else on the tabletop except a stack of mail. Ben went through it piece by piece. Nothing but junk. A couple of catalogs with women's clothes, a credit-card offer, and a stack of bulk-mail discount-ad flyers.

He flipped open the notebook.

1/12 12:42p
STUDIO
~~*Table*~~
~~*Mail*~~
Computer (save, search later in house)

The sofa bed was next. He looked underneath, took the cushions off, unzipped the cover of each one, and worked his hand all the way around the foam inside each one. Then he unfolded the bed and worked his fingers across every inch of the surface, top and bottom, feeling for the unusual or unexpected.

It wasn't until he'd folded the bed back into the frame of the sofa and tucked the cushions back into place that he realized the tension and uncertainty he'd felt on the threshold had disappeared.

~~*Sofa*~~

He didn't dwell on it, though, he just moved on to the end table, the chair, and the bookcase. She didn't have a lot of books. Some novels Ben figured were popular because he'd been vaguely aware of the titles that began with *The Girl Who* or *The Girl With* or *The Girl On*. His focus drifted for a moment as he wondered what a novel about Grace might be called.

Concentrate, he reminded himself. *Focus.*

There were some nonfiction books, too. Several memoirs. A few that looked more political. *Bad Feminist. Between the World and Me.* A couple of low-carb cookbooks. Ben thumbed through the pages of each one, looking for anything that might be tucked inside. There were a few stray receipts and slips of paper that looked like they were being used as bookmarks. Only one thing seemed like it might be useful. In an oversized paperback called *Atlas Obscura*—a kind of encyclopedia of weird and unusual places—he found a pale-blue Post-it note that read *Call Amy about job.* He left it where it was, but took out his phone and snapped a photo of it. *Maybe something,* he thought.

~~Bookcase~~

POST IT—WHO IS AMY? WHAT JOB? (see photo)

He was almost halfway around the room now, and any doubts about the rightness of what he was doing had faded with the note in the book. Maybe he would actually find something useful. Maybe he would be able to help.

•   •   •

Next was the chair. He knew there had to be a name for the style—small, squarish, with brown tweedy upholstery. There was nothing under the seat cushion or inside its cover. Nothing in the crevices and crannies other than the few crumbs of random detritus found in any piece of furniture that had been used for any length of time. He flipped it over and examined the bottom. A few of the staples that held the gauzy backing in place were missing, but there was nothing else to see. Ben wondered if they might have been removed intentionally in order to slip something inside. One of the staples, though, even though it was detached from the wood frame, still clung to the fabric. If you were going to go to the trouble of removing it, why would you leave it like that? It might scratch your finger or snag on whatever you were trying to stash inside. And there was nothing inside, anyway.

• • •

~~Chair~~

There was an end table next to the chair. He picked up the lamp on it and examined the felt cover on the bottom. Securely attached. There was nothing else, other than a single, unremarkable coaster. Ben reached underneath and ran his fingers along the underside. Nothing.

~~Table~~

There was nothing in the entertainment cabinet except the Blu-ray player Ben had installed when the TV was mounted on the wall above it, and the half dozen or so movies he'd left there himself. Still, he opened each case, one by one, and found nothing but the discs. *Elf* looked like it had a scratch, but whatever it actually was came off when he rubbed it on his flannel shirt.

~~Blu-ray Cabinet~~

Grace's dresser was next. He'd felt somewhat uncomfortable when he began searching, but that feeling had gradually slipped away as he became more engrossed in the process. Finally, he felt like he was doing something, taking action. But now his fingers hesitated on the knob of the top drawer. Was this a line he was ready to cross? The woman in the framed photo on top seemed to be staring at him. It had been taken on a bright day, outside, in what looked like someone's backyard. Lawn furniture and a row of flowering bushes along a wood-plank fence in the background. Who was she? He'd never asked Grace, but they looked like they could be related. There was something in the brown eyes. Not just the color, but in the shape as well, in the way the brows arched over them. The woman looked like she was in her late thirties or early forties. Was she old enough to be Grace's mother? Maybe, especially if the picture was a few years old.

Ben looked at her as he opened the drawer. He knew it was only his imagination, but her expression seemed to change as he did it.

"Sorry," he whispered.

Inside were several pairs of underwear. Mostly white or pastel cotton, but a few with lace trim, made out of something silky. Not quite as many bras. He couldn't tell if there were any matching sets. Along the back of the drawer was an assortment of socks rolled into ten or twelve identical little balls.

He only moved them enough to make sure there was nothing concealed underneath.

Something was off. He wasn't sure, but it seemed to him that there should have been more in there. Maybe she hadn't done laundry in a while. There wasn't a laundry basket anywhere. He'd be sure to look for one when he got into the bathroom.

The next drawer down held tops—T-shirts, tanks, a couple of lightweight sweaters, all folded and stacked by type.

That was how his drawers used to look. Before. Everything folded and neat. Now most of his clothes resided in two piles, clean and dirty. Once in a while, a shirt with buttons would find its way onto a hanger in the closet, but—he caught himself.

Focus.

Again, he ran his fingers under the clothes to make sure nothing was concealed below them, then moved on to the bottom drawer. Jeans, shorts, sweats. Something light and stretchy. Yoga pants? He wasn't sure, but this drawer wasn't as full as he expected, either.

~~Dresser~~
enough clothes?? check for laundry

Ben couldn't decide if he should search the bathroom next or go past the door to the closet and then go back. In the old days, he would have gone room by room. But the old days were different. He didn't expect a crime-scene unit or an assist from a partner, and he'd never be turning his notes into a report. There was no need for a systematic record that would make sense to someone else. No brass, no prosecutor, no jury. It made sense to him to work his way along the wall around the perimeter, so he went into the bathroom and flipped on the light switch.

The reflection in the mirror caught him by surprise.

"Someone's going to live here?" Peter asks.

"Maybe, Dad," you say. He's asked you the questions half a dozen times a day since you started cleaning the place out and painting.

"Who?" he asks again.

"Don't know yet."

He looks worried.

"We'll get somebody good," you say. "I promise." With the hammer, you tap the nail into the newly pale-blue wall over the toilet and rehang the framed sunflower print your mother chose for the spot. "How does that look, Dad?"

When he doesn't answer, you turn and look at him. He's crying.

Before long, you are, too.

Ben looked worse than he had in a long time. The dark circles under his eyes were back and the stubble on his fattening cheeks looked grayer than ever. He'd have to—

Focus.

There was nothing in the laundry basket except a blue sports bra and the old green oversized T-shirt with the owl on the front Grace used to wear when she hung around the house.

There was less makeup than he expected to find and nothing in the medicine cabinet except some Tylenol, a few other over-the-counter remedies, and one old prescription bottle. He picked it up and squinted at the label. Sertraline, the generic version of Zoloft. Grace had never mentioned taking antidepressants, and he knew he'd talked about them with her, how he and his father took some of the same meds. Still, would she be comfortable discussing something like that with him? His problems, and Peter's, too, were a lot more overt, and it felt natural to be open about them with her. Especially as they got to know her better.

Looking closer, though, what surprised him even more was that the name on the bottle wasn't hers. *Lisa Briard.* Was that Grace's real name? It would make sense to change it if she was trying to hide from whoever she'd been set to testify against. Ben had never done a background check because he trusted Rob's recommendation.

This was something important.

~~Bathroom~~
ANTIDEPRESSANTS—LISA BRIARD—GRACE REAL NAME???

After that discovery, the closet felt anticlimactic. Ben went through everything, checking pockets, looking for anything unexpected. He found nothing other than a few receipts, a movie-ticket stub for *La La Land*, and a barely used cylinder of Burt's Bees lip balm. There were a few nice dresses but mostly casual clothes, a couple jackets, and an assortment of shoes. There was nothing personal. He'd been hoping for something—a photo album, a box of mementos, or maybe even a journal. But there was nothing like that. Everything felt oddly impersonal.

~~Closet~~

There was even less in the kitchenette. A little bit of food in the small fridge. An assortment of dishes and utensils appropriate for a single person with no plans of entertaining company.

~~Kitchen~~

The only thing left was the area rug in the center of the room. He lifted it up, one corner at a time, until he was sure there was nothing underneath.

With that, he was back where he started, standing by the open door surveying the studio.

There was almost nothing of Grace here.

As he thought about it, though, he began to understand that it made a certain kind of sense. Maybe Rob had even advised her to keep her personal connection to the place as light as possible. To leave nothing there that linked definitively to her identity.

Was this all just temporary? Was she hoping to return to her old life when the case was made and she no longer had to worry about whoever Rob was trying to put away?

He could see that.

But where was she now? If she fled, why wouldn't she tell Rob? Had something happened between them? Had she discovered something about him that caused her trust to falter?

Or was it something worse? Had she been abducted? Or even killed?

The one thing that gave him some hope that she'd left on her own was the red Camaro. Ben was convinced that the car hadn't just been some rando passing through the alley, but rather someone specifically looking for Grace. If someone was looking for her, that meant they didn't have her, and they definitely hadn't killed her.

Judging by the studio, Ben knew she had at least some idea of how to cover her tracks. Would it be enough now that she had two cops—one good and one bad—looking for her?

NINE

Ben went back into the house with Grace's computer under his arm. He was headed into the office when he saw Peter in the living room, looking out the front window and pacing back and forth.

"Dad?"

Peter stopped and rushed over to him, a look of relief washing over him.

"What's the matter?" Ben said.

"I didn't know where you were." He was anxious and shaking.

Ben put the MacBook on the table and hugged his father. "I was just out in back."

Peter shook his head. "I looked in back."

"I was in the studio."

"I looked outside where the car is. I thought you should be here because the car is there."

"I was here, Dad."

He still looked confused, so Ben continued. "I was inside the studio, so you wouldn't have seen me unless you went all the way back and looked in."

"In the back where she is?"

Ben nodded.

Peter looked down at the floor.

"What's the matter?"

"I think she's mad at me."

"What? No, she's not mad. Why would you think that?"

"She doesn't come anymore."

"She's not mad, Dad. I promise she's not."

"Then why doesn't she come anymore?"

Ben thought about trying to answer, to explain everything to him again. Instead, he said, "She just had to go away for a little while. She'll be back soon. She misses you, too."

"She does?"

"Yeah. She really does. How about some lunch?"

While you're making the grocery list, you see Grace has joined your father on the patio. You were a little late getting breakfast ready, so you figured you'd missed her for the day. With a fresh cup in each hand, the yellow pad with the list tucked under your arm, and a pencil clenched between your teeth, you go out and join them.

"I'm going to Ralphs in a little while," you say to her. "Can I pick you up anything?"

She thinks about it and says, "No, I don't think so."

You wonder if she's just being polite or if she really might want something. "You sure?"

"Yeah. Thanks, though."

"Is there more . . . stuff?" Peter says.

"What kind of stuff?" you ask.

"For, uh, you know."

"I don't, Dad. What do you mean?"

He looks over at Grace, then back at you. There's something he doesn't want to say in front of her and you don't have the slightest idea what it might be. He motions you closer and when you get up and lean in close, he whispers, "For wiping."

"You mean Kleenex?" you say. "For your face?"

He shakes his head and whispers even more quietly, "For behind."

You feel the edges of your mouth pulling up and look at Grace, who has heard every word. She's trying not to laugh. "I'll go check, okay?"

He nods and turns to Grace with an awkward and embarrassed smile.

After excusing yourself, you go back into your father's bathroom and look in the cupboard under the sink. He's down to one roll. You make a mental note to add toilet paper to the list when you get back outside.

You also notice the toilet needs a little attention. You pour in some Mr. Clean and run the brush around inside a few times, then grab several baby wipes and use them to clean the seat, the tank, and around the rim of the bowl. The wastebasket is full, too, so you tie the corners of the plastic bag together, remove it, and replace it with a fresh one. Out in the kitchen, you think about leaving the bag by the door, but on the off chance Grace decides to come inside, you take it out to the trash can in the alley.

When you come back into the kitchen, you see Grace and your father outside at the table. It looks like she's adding something to the grocery list. But she keeps looking at Peter, then scribbling on the pad, then repeating the process. You watch for a few moments before you realize it looks like she's sketching him.

Outside, you see she's flipped the page on the pad. "I didn't know you were an artist," you say.

"It's just a doodle." She holds it up for you and your father to see. "What do you think?"

The portrait is remarkable. It's a good likeness, but that's not what you find so striking. Somehow, with only a few minutes and a crappy pencil and notepad, she's managed to capture a portrait of Peter that makes him look simultaneously joyful and sad. There's a light in his eyes that looks familiar, the sparkle of intelligence that you see slowly dimming day by day, fully restored.

"Oh my god," you say, choking up.

Grace locks eyes with you and you know she sees your gratitude.

"We should do a real one, one of these days," she says.

"Would you?"

"Of course." She puts the pad on the table and spins it around for your father to see. "What do you think, Pete?"

"Am I that skinny?"

The nearly empty page of the yellow writing pad stared back up at him. He'd needed something bigger than his notebook so he could try to lay out the information he had so far. But there were only two things written on it. Two names.

Lisa Briard.
Amy.

He wasn't sure what he expected to find in the studio. Had he really expected a clear answer, something simple that would point him directly to wherever Grace was now? He didn't think so, but the disappointment he felt, looking at what he had in front of him, led him to believe that, on some level at least, he'd been wishing for exactly that.

"Don't expect too much," he whispered as he opened the laptop. It was one of the new MacBook Pros that had only come out a few months ago, the base model without the fancy Touch Bar that could read your fingerprint. He'd looked at one the last time he'd gone to the Cerritos mall. His computer was getting old, but he didn't use it for much besides email and bills and the internet, so he'd decided against spending so much money. He made a note on the yellow pad.

Check release date of new Macs—before or after Grace moved in??

The screen lit up and he saw a browser window with a dozen or more still-open tabs. He scanned them, hoping to find Facebook or some other social-media site, but from what he could see of the tabs scrunched together and overlapping, it didn't look like there was anything like that there.

The open window was an Amazon page for a pair of Merrell women's Moab Mid hiking boots. They had four and a half stars with 692 reviews. It looked to Ben like they were beige and pink, but the color was listed as *Boulder/Blush*.

Grace had never mentioned an interest in hiking. Did this mean she was thinking about a new hobby, or that she was concerned about her safety and preparing to flee and disappear into the forest somewhere? He hit the "Back" button a few times and just saw five pages for similar boots. At least she hadn't been looking for survival gear. Ben wasn't sure why, but he found that a small relief.

He started clicking on the other tabs. There was one for REI, open on the same boots in a different color combination. They looked gray and green to Ben, but he didn't investigate any further. The next was the main page of the *Long Beach Press-Telegram*, then Vulture, Slate, and a few other news sites. There didn't seem to be any pattern to them besides the boots, and nothing that connected to her personally. It wasn't until he tried to check the browser history and found nothing there that he realized it was set to the private mode that didn't record the sites she'd visited.

Ben minimized the window and opened a new one. He typed *gmail* into the search window, hoping she might have saved the password to the email account she'd put on her rental application. But no luck—just the generic sign-in page.

He looked for files saved on the desktop or in folders, and there was nothing. Even the Downloads folder was empty. He clicked on the trash icon. Nothing. It looked like everything she did on the computer was online in private mode. Maybe if he still had help from the LBPD computer techs he could find something, but as far as Ben could tell, the laptop looked like it had barely been used at all.

Grace was being cautious not only with her physical space but with her digital space as well. Had she been covering her tracks all along, or had she cleaned everything up in order to disappear?

He couldn't find anything there. Would anyone else be able to? If Becerra came back and searched, he might be able to get something from the computer. But what about the red Camaro? If the driver really was a dirty cop, he might be able to get something from it, too.

He decided he'd keep the laptop in the house for now. If Becerra got a warrant, Ben figured he'd likely get a heads-up and have time to put it back in the studio. He scribbled a reminder on the yellow pad.

How much useful information he'd discovered, he really didn't know. Lisa Briard—was that Grace's real name? It made sense. Why else would she have the prescription? But she'd been so careful with everything else. Could that be another alias? Was it someone else's medicine? Maybe she needed the Zoloft but couldn't get it legally, and found another source. If it really was hers, why not just peel the label off or scratch out the name?

And who was Amy? Was she the woman he'd seen visiting Grace? He didn't know. He figured at some point he'd head to the Attic, the restaurant down in Belmont Heights where Grace worked. She'd said the woman was a friend from work, hadn't she? Ben thought he remembered that. Maybe he'd have to go a few times, see if he could spot her.

Ben realized he had stopped writing and was tapping the end of the pen against his bottom lip, and was seized by a memory of sitting at his desk, years ago in the Violent Crimes Detail, a yellow pad in front of him, doing the same thing with his pen.

It didn't startle him like the flashes usually did. It didn't make him uncomfortable or anxious.

No.

Quite the opposite, in fact.

It felt familiar. It felt right.

A jet rumbled in the distance. Ben got up and went into the dining room just in time to watch through the patio door as Peter, his hand raised and waving, followed the long arc of the plane across the sky.

• • •

Ben was in the kitchen making some fresh dishwater so Peter could help clean up when he heard the text-message sound from his phone in the office. He grabbed for a paper towel from the holder on the counter, but it didn't tear off like he expected it to and when he gave it a second yank, the whole thing tipped over and toppled to the floor.

"Shit!"

The towel in his hand was still connected to the wobbling roll on the floor by a rope of eight or ten more. He grabbed the strand, pulling off the two on the end and letting the long tail float down to the tile.

He dried his hands and went into the office, hoping to see something from Rob or Becerra or even Jennifer. But when he depressed the button on his phone, he saw that it was just CVS notifying him that one of Peter's refills was ready for pickup.

While he was there, he checked his email again. There was nothing from anyone who mattered. He knew Rob was trying, and he believed Jennifer when she told him Becerra was, too. But he couldn't help feeling like he was all alone.

In the kitchen, Peter had put the spindle holder back on the counter and was holding the roll in both hands, slowly and carefully winding the long strand of excess towels back into place.

• • •

Sometimes Peter liked to go with Ben on errands to get out of the house, so he rode with him to CVS. He didn't want to go inside, though, so he waited in the Volvo with the windows rolled a quarter of the way down and the satellite radio playing Willie's Roadhouse.

Ben came out with a small bag in his hand, got in the driver's seat, and said, "Would you mind if we made one more stop?"

"No. Where do we need to go?"

"I heard about a place that has some good biscuits and gravy. Want to try them?"

"Sure."

While he'd been waiting in line at the pharmacy window, Ben had looked up the Attic on his phone. When he saw that they served breakfast until four, he thought it might be a good excuse to stop by for a visit and phoned in a takeout order. The timing, he hoped, would be helpful. They were right between the lunch and dinner crowds, so he could get a decent look around without having to wait too long for the food. At that time of day, he might even be able to score a spot in the tiny lot behind the restaurant instead of having to park in the surrounding neighborhood a block or two away.

Ben couldn't figure out why his father liked country music so much now. Neither of his parents had ever listened to it while he was growing up. It was all Beatles and Van Morrison and early British rock and folk stuff. After his mom died and the avalanche started, though, things began to change. With each of Peter's surgeries, he became less interested in the music he'd listened to before, and more and more he'd be drawn to the classic country stuff. Ben had never met his paternal grandfather, he'd died before Ben was even born, but he'd often been told the story of how Peter was born in Oklahoma and moved with his family to California when he was still a toddler.

Sitting in the left-turn lane at the light on the corner of Seventh and Redondo, Ben remembered something he hadn't thought of in years. In the ninth or tenth grade, he had to do a project for class about a career he was interested in, so he asked his father why he'd become a history teacher. "When I was about your age," his father had said, "I read *The Grapes of Wrath* and I knew I'd be either a novelist or a historian." Ben could remember his father's grin as if it were yesterday. "Turned out I was a lousy writer."

Ben started to look at his father, hoping to see a trace of that smile, but the driver in the car behind him leaned on the horn. The light had turned green.

• • •

They did get lucky with a parking spot in the lot. Ben had been worried about leaving Peter in the car on the street far away from the Attic, so he was glad he didn't have to try to convince him to come inside. Ben left things just the way he had at the drugstore, and walked around to the front of the building.

The restaurant was in what had been, decades ago, a fairly good-sized Craftsman house. For years it had been another place, called Lasher's, but Ben had never eaten there, and he'd only been here once since it changed owners. With the change, they'd added a large outside patio area that ran the full width of the building along Broadway and back around one side. It was much more popular now that they'd made the changes and updated the menu, and that was one of the main reasons he'd never come back after that first visit. He'd really liked the food, but not the crowd. He'd had to wait forty minutes, and then, once he got inside, all the people in the small dining area had made it loud and hot and his anxiety kicked into high gear.

But now, at three thirty, with only two people inside and a few small parties scattered around the patio, he could imagine himself enjoying a meal here.

The hostess came up and greeted him. She was wearing jeans and a black shirt that looked identical to the ones in Grace's laundry basket. "Hi," she said. "How many?"

"Oh, it's just me."

"Would you like to sit inside or outside?"

Ben wondered how old she was. Eighteen or nineteen? Quite a bit younger than Grace. "Oh, no," he said. "I'm sorry. I called in a takeout order?"

"Oh, okay. Can I have your name?"

"Ben."

"Give me just a sec, I'll go check on it."

While she was gone, Ben sat on a bench on what had once been the front porch and looked across the street and down the block at the Reno

Room. For decades it had been an authentic dive bar, and then in the nineties, as gentrification began to take hold in the surrounding neighborhoods, it became a hipster hangout. When he'd been in uniform patrolling the East Division, he'd responded to more calls there than he could count. He'd only been there once off duty, and the fourth time someone pointed out the pool table Charles Bukowski had vomited on, he decided he probably never needed to come back.

She returned with a white plastic bag in her hands. "Biscuits and gravy and an OG Mac?"

"Yes," he said. "That's me."

He paid cash for the order.

"Anything else for you?"

He decided to take a chance. "Is Amy working today?"

"Oh," the hostess said, "you just missed her. She did breakfast and lunch."

"Okay," Ben said, his stomach tingling. "Thanks."

Peter waved at him as he approached the car. Ben opened the back door on the passenger's side and put the bag on the seat. The he covered it with his fleece jacket, hoping it would stay warm long enough to get it home.

"What did you get, something good?" Peter asked, twisting around and trying to get a look under the jacket.

Ben slid in behind the wheel. "Yeah," he said, "I think it is something good."

• • •

1/12 3:40
Amy works at the attic!!!
Morning shift—check back—tomorrow???

• • •

108

He tried not to get too excited about this new information. But since he'd searched the studio, things had felt different. They'd felt right. He knew Jennifer would tell him to stop what he was doing. And he thought about it. All those years as a cop, how many people had he told to stay out of things, to let the police do their job? More than he could count.

This was different. He wasn't just some amateur going off half-cocked and interfering with an investigation. Hell, as far as he knew, he was the only one actively investigating anything. There was no doubt Becerra was doing his best. But how many cases did he have on his plate? How much time did he have for a case he couldn't even be sure was really a case? Even with Ben's history, and Jennifer putting in a word with him, there was no way it was a high priority for him. And Rob— was he more interested in helping Grace or in putting his dirty cop away? Suspects and witnesses were very different priorities. Tightening the screws on somebody dangerous always put witnesses at risk. If Rob had to choose between Grace's safety and his case, which would it be?

No. Ben had to keep going. There was nobody else he could trust.

• • •

They bumped into Bernie and Sriracha on their evening walk again.

"Hey, guys," he said. The little dog had been pulling at her leash for the last fifty feet so she could get closer to Peter. When she jumped on his legs, he bent over and scratched her behind the ears.

"How's it going?" Ben asked. Like always, he stopped to chat mostly just to give his father time with the dog.

"Not bad. What's up with you two?" Bernie asked.

Before Ben could answer, Peter looked up and said, "She's still gone."

Bernie looked puzzled, and when Peter turned his attention back to Sriracha, he whispered to Ben, "Your mom?"

Ben shook his head. "No. Grace is missing."

"Really? She skip on the rent or something?"

"No, nothing like that. She's all paid up and things are good, but she hasn't been home for several days."

"Wow. You going to do anything about it?"

"I called a friend from the LBPD. They took a missing-persons report. Someone's looking into it."

"I hope everything turns out okay."

"Me too."

Peter stood up straight and smiled at them.

"You guys think any more about a dog? I've got a friend with some puppies. Little terrier mixes like that one." He stuck a finger out at Sriracha, then looked Ben in the eye and added, "A lot mellower, though."

"Dad," Ben said. "Should we get a dog?"

Peter thought about it and said very seriously, "They poop a lot."

Ben and Bernie laughed, and, after a few moments, Peter joined in, too.

• • •

Ben gave Peter his evening meds and noted it in his book. He also made a big check mark with a Sharpie on the note on the refrigerator door. He needed to find a balance with the obsessive-compulsive behaviors, but for now, he decided that if he would err, it would be on the overly cautious side.

He waited while Peter brushed his teeth and changed into the long-sleeved T-shirt and gym shorts he liked to wear to bed.

"Thank you for taking me out," Peter said when Ben came in to say good night.

"You're welcome."

"The food was good." He'd only eaten one of the biscuits and a bit of the gravy. Ben wasn't sure, but he thought it was too peppery for Peter, who didn't have much tolerance for spiciness anymore.

"I know, I thought so, too." He'd eaten the leftovers, in addition to his mac and cheese. It had been too much and his stomach was just beginning to let him off the hook.

Ben leaned in and kissed his father on the forehead. "Good night."

"Good night." Peter looked like he wanted to say something.

"What is it, Dad?"

He just shook his head and squeezed his son's hand.

•   •   •

The yellow pad was staring up at him again. He made a to-do list.

1. *Check for Amy at Attic*
2. *Call Rob*
3. *Call Becerra*

It wasn't much. Not yet, anyway. He was hoping Amy would be able to help, to give him something else to go on, or at least a nudge in a particular direction. It didn't even have to be the right one at this point.

He wasn't good at being spontaneous anymore, and even the need to make an unplanned phone call could sometimes send him into an anxious spiral.

But he looked at number two and checked the time again. It was five minutes after nine.

Fuck it. He was just going to do it.

Three taps of his thumb on the screen of his phone and he was waiting for Rob to answer. He decided not to say anything about Amy to him yet. If Rob hadn't already talked to her himself, he wasn't the cop

Ben thought he was. No, he would just press Rob for information. He'd felt hints of his old confidence already, and the memory was enough to embolden him. If he pushed, Rob would give him more. Ben was confident of that. And he was ready to push. On the third ring his confidence crescendoed and began to fall as he became more certain that he'd be talking not to Rob but to his voicemail.

Ben left a message telling Rob he needed to talk to him, and disconnected.

Crossing that item off the list didn't give him the sense of accomplishment he'd been hoping for. Staring at the phone in his hand, he saw the little red bubble over the green icon at the bottom of the screen reminding him of Emma's voicemails. He knew he should see her. But what could he really tell her? How much would he have to hold back? The idea of withholding or even lying to her seemed overwhelming, but he knew he would have to if he saw her. She'd never approve of what he was doing. He called her back, knowing it was safe, that there was no chance of her answering the phone at this time of day. When her recorded greeting finished, he said, "Hi, Emma, it's Ben. I'm doing okay. Had a few rough days with my father, but I'm doing better now. I won't need the extra appointment after all." Apparently, lying to her voicemail was an altogether different story.

Unable to think of anything else productive to do, he went out into the living room to try to find something interesting to watch on TV.

He struck out there, too, so he added a few thousand more steps to the readout on his Fitbit.

• • •

Ben had dozed off on the couch and was surprised by Peter standing over him. He looked like he'd been crying.

"Dad?" he said, one hand pulling on the backrest and the other on the cushion under his shoulder, pushing him upright. "What's wrong?"

"The dog," he said.

Ben was puzzled. "What dog?"

"The dog," he repeated, his voice thin and reedy. He wiped at a tear on his cheek.

"Sit down," he said, patting the cushion softly. "I don't know what you mean. What dog?"

"We can't take the dog."

"Okay." Ben couldn't understand why he was so upset or why the idea of getting a dog was so troubling.

"It would be bad." He seemed wracked with grief—over what, though, Ben had no idea.

"Why, Dad? Why would it be bad?" Ben squeezed his thigh, worrying again about its thinness.

"Because Benny."

"Benny? You mean me? Ben?"

"No." Peter shook his head. "Benny."

"Bernie?"

He nodded.

"Why do you think Bernie wouldn't like it?" He didn't understand. Bernie was the one encouraging them.

"He's our friend."

"I know. He's been our friend for a long time."

Peter looked more confused than ever and tried to pull away from Ben on the couch. "How could we do that to him?"

With far more firmness than he intended, Ben said, "Do what, Dad?"

"Take his dog away from him!"

As his father's misunderstanding became clear to him, Ben felt something break open inside his chest and clenched his teeth hard to hold back his own tears. He knew nothing worried Peter more than watching his son cry.

Peter resisted as Ben tried to pull him into a hug, but ultimately didn't put up too much of a fight.

"No," Ben said. "No. We'd never take his dog from him. We wouldn't do that. We're the good guys, right?"

Peter nodded his head against Ben's shoulder.

"We'd get another dog, a different dog. One for us. Not Sriracha. She'd stay with Bernie."

Peter pulled back so he could look Ben in the face. "Another dog?"

"Yeah. A completely different one. We'd never take anybody's dog away from them."

"A different dog?" He finally seemed to understand.

"That's right."

The clouds drifted out of his expression and were replaced with a childlike brightness. "A different dog?" he said again.

Ben nodded.

Peter nodded back, grinning. "Okay."

• • •

They had breakfast early, and once Peter had his laundry in the washer, Ben said, "I need to run a couple of errands. Will you be okay?"

"Yes."

"I'll probably be about an hour and a half."

"I'll be fine," Peter said. "I'll do my clothes and get started." He made a sweeping motion with his hands.

Ben poured one more cup of coffee and Boost, covered it with a folded paper towel, and put it next to a quarter of a Hershey's bar on the counter. "You can have this in a little while."

"Got it," Peter said.

• • •

The Reno Room wasn't the only establishment across the street from the Attic. Next to the old bar was a coffeehouse called the Library. He sat there at a table by the window and watched the outdoor patio on the other side of Broadway while he pretended to read a *Washington Post* article on his phone.

He hadn't forgotten everything—he was confident none of the other morning patrons had any idea that he was doing anything other than keeping himself up to date. Ben had always gotten a charge out of surveillance. He'd always been good at it. The idea of disappearing, of making himself invisible, had always given him a sense of mildly transgressive power. Now, though, he wasn't feeling the same excitement he used to.

A server he hadn't seen yet came outside to take an order from one of the tables along the sidewalk, and for just a moment, Ben thought it might be her. But no. Her hair was too long and too dark. And she was taller than the woman who'd visited Grace, who he hoped was Amy.

She went back inside and he realized something. What had been so appealing to him in the old days about surveillance wasn't just the power or invisibility.

No.

It was the transformation that gave him the sense of power. The old Ben Shepard was visible. He had presence and people noticed him. They paid attention to him. They saw him.

Hardly anyone saw the new Ben Shepard. Partly because he rarely wanted to be seen, but mostly because nobody wanted to see him. PTSD and traumatic brain injury and all the other associated conditions he carried with him were not things at which many people wanted to look too closely, and Ben wasn't one to challenge that inclination.

Now he realized that becoming invisible wasn't that big a deal when you were barely visible to begin with.

He almost didn't notice her. She came from the covered side patio area with two plates for a table along the sidewalk. It was the same woman he'd seen with Grace at home, tall and thin, with her light-brown hair pulled back. Was that Amy?

It didn't look like anyone was waiting for a seat. It was late enough for the breakfast surge to have waned. He didn't think he'd feel too self-conscious asking for a solo table. Ben tossed his coffee cup in the trash and went to the corner to cross the street. While he was waiting for the traffic light to change, a nervous excitement swirled in his abdomen. This was it. He was crossing a line. So far he was the only one who knew he was looking for Grace. When he talked to Amy—if the woman he'd just seen really was Amy, he reminded himself—someone else would know. He wasn't sure why, but he believed that would make his search real in a way it wasn't yet. The moment he involved someone else, he would be crossing a threshold. He'd be working a case.

"Inside or outside?" the hostess asked. It wasn't the same person as yesterday. That was good. He didn't want to draw any more attention than he needed to.

"Outside would be good," he said. It was still gray and cold, but the weather report had said partly sunny. Maybe it would clear up.

She led him over and sat him down at a table next to the one that the server he believed to be Amy had been working. It wasn't very busy and he guessed that she was the only one working outside.

He pretended to look at the menu but tried to keep his peripheral vision focused on the side patio area where he'd seen her come and go. Earlier, at home, he'd looked at the menu online and decided what to order. The crème brûlée French toast and the Belgian waffle had both been appealing, but he didn't want the sticky mess that breakfast foods with syrup always seemed to result in these days. No, he'd just go with the simple steak and eggs.

"Can I start you off with something to drink?" she said. She'd come down the steps from the front porch and almost managed to surprise him.

"Hi, uh, coffee?"

"Sure. Cream?"

"Yes." If she recognized him, he couldn't tell. He hadn't expected her to, though. The plan had been to see if she seemed to know who he was, and if she didn't, to just come right out and ask if she was Grace's friend and hadn't she been to the house?

"Are you ready to order?" He was, but how did she know that? Oh. The menu was closed on the table. *Ask her,* he thought. *Just go ahead and ask her.* But she'd already asked him a question. He had to answer that first, right?

He told her what he wanted.

"And how would like your steak?"

"Medium." *Ask her.*

"Are the potatoes okay with that?"

"Yes." *Ask her.*

"Toast?"

"Yes." *Ask her.*

She smiled. "What kind?"

"Sourdough?" She didn't write anything down, Ben noticed. It wasn't crowded. She probably didn't need to. He felt a twinge of envy.

She told him she'd be right back with his coffee and he swore to himself that he'd mention Grace as soon as she got back to the table.

He didn't say anything when she brought his coffee.

Or when she brought his food.

Or when she checked to see if everything was okay.

Or when she cleared his plate and dropped off the check.

It was only when she returned his debit card and told him to have a great day that he finally felt the balance tip, and his fear of failing to help Grace outweighed his fear of risking an actual substantive conversation with someone he didn't know.

"Excuse me," he said, just as she was turning away from the table.

She stopped and looked back at him, eyebrows raised with a pleasant curiosity.

"Aren't you—I mean, don't you know Grace?"

The pleasantness vanished and something darker and more questioning took its place.

"Will you help me find her?"

117

When he explained who he was and what was going on, she apologized for not having recognized him, said he'd looked familiar but that she thought she must have just waited on him before. She agreed to meet him back at the Library when her shift ended at two. By the time he got home, it had been more than two hours since he'd left. He found his father by the dryer, holding his blue plaid flannel shirt in his hands. It was covered in tiny white shreds of Kleenex. Ben hadn't been there to remind him to double-check, and he'd left a tissue in one of his pockets again.

"I messed up," Peter said.

Ben helped him carry the load of laundry out to the patio table. The sky was a lighter shade of gray than it had been, but the sun still seemed a long way off. He took a pair of jeans over onto the lawn and started shaking them, first holding the waistband and snapping the legs out away from the house, then switching his grip and flapping the waistband into the breeze. As he did, the air filled with little bits of white fluff that drifted and swirled and finally settled onto the damp green grass.

Peter brought a T-shirt and joined him. Together they worked their way through the whole load.

When they were finished, Ben looked down at the mess on the lawn and thought about what he'd need to do to clean it up. Could it wait until the gardener came?

Peter bent over and ran his fingers across the shredded mess and said, "It looks like snow."

• • •

Ben had already left Peter alone for more than two hours that morning, and it would probably take at least another two to meet with Amy. He couldn't remember a day he'd left him alone for that long, not since the last surgery, at least. Asking for help wasn't something he was very comfortable with, but the more he thought about it, the more he considered asking Bernie if he could help. Bernie offered all the time and Ben had almost never accepted. For more than a minute, he just stared at the text message.

You around this afternoon by any chance?

Bernie answered right away. sure what do you need?

Got an appointment. Going to be kind of a long one. Could you check on my dad around 2 or so?

Sure

Thanks

no worrys

Ben used to say that himself.
No worries.
But that was a long time ago.

• • •

Amy had put on a zip-up hoodie over her black shirt. Ben wasn't sure if that was what made her seem younger than she had when she'd served him breakfast, or if it was just that sitting down to talk with him about Grace put her in a more uncertain and vulnerable position. Earlier he had estimated her age at late twenties, but now he guessed five or six years younger.

"Thanks for doing this," he said, pulling his notebook out of his shirt pocket. "Sorry. I might need to write something down."

She had both of her hands wrapped around the oversized cup on the table in front of her. "It's okay."

"When was the last time you saw Grace?"

"Last week. Thursday, I think. We both worked the early shift. We talked about doing something on the weekend." She looked down at the whipped cream on top of her mocha. "I didn't know anything was wrong until I heard she missed her shift on Tuesday."

"Did she call in or get anyone to cover for her?"

"No, that's what seemed so weird. Not like her at all."

"You try to get in touch with her?"

"Yeah. I even called when she didn't answer her texts."

"And no replies?"

"No." She lifted her cup halfway to her mouth but stopped before drinking. "Something bad happened, didn't it?"

"I hope not," Ben said. "But that's what I'm trying to figure out."

"She liked you and your dad a lot," she said.

Ben felt himself blink. He hadn't expected her to say anything like that but didn't quite understand why not. As soon as he'd put the notebook on the table, he now realized, he'd slipped into interview mode. Detached. Impersonal. For just a few minutes, he'd forgotten this wasn't a case and that he wasn't a detective on the job. Grace wasn't just a victim. She was a friend.

"She said that?" he asked.

Amy smiled, and he saw her teeth for the first time since he'd paid his bill after breakfast. "Yeah. She was always talking about how much she liked renting from you guys. Super nice, but no creepy vibes at all."

"Is that a thing? Super nice people usually have creepy vibes?"

"Well, when they're landlords they do."

He laughed at that, but for the first time, he wondered what it must have been like for a young single woman to rent an apartment from two old men. Did that mean she really trusted Rob? Or just that she was desperate enough to take a chance?

"How well do you know her?" Ben asked.

"Pretty well. She's only been working here for what, like four or five months? But we hit it off. Before she switched to mostly nights, both of us liked the early weekday shifts."

"Why is that? You can make a lot more money working evenings and weekends, right?"

"Yeah, it's only like half as much, but it's even less than half as much stress. It's actually fun sometimes in the mornings."

"What's fun about it?"

She shrugged. "I don't know. We've got regulars. It's nice to be able to talk to them, get to know them some when things aren't as busy."

Ben tried to remember if he'd enjoyed meeting and getting to know people before. He thought he used to be friendly, people used to tell him he was, but did he actually enjoy it? Honestly, he didn't know.

"Is that what Grace liked, too?"

"Not as much, but she seemed like maybe she used to?"

"What do you mean?"

"Well, she never really wanted to talk very much about San Bernardino, but I know she had a really hard time there with the bad relationship and everything. I think she was a lot more reserved and quiet, especially when she first started. But it seemed like she relaxed more lately. Like she was adjusting, finally putting it behind her. Having more fun, doing stuff, you know?"

He didn't, really.

"Just being more social, going out more and stuff."

"Do you know why she switched to nights?"

"The money, is what she said."

Something in Amy's expression gave Ben the sense that there might have been more to it than that, but he didn't press. "Did you guys hang out a lot?"

"Yeah. Not at first, though. But then more and more."

Ben wondered why he hadn't seen Amy at Grace's lately.

When he didn't say anything, she continued. "After we worked a few shifts together, I started asking her if she wanted to hang out. I'd just broken up with somebody too, but not bad like her. She said no a few times, so I stopped asking. But after a few days, she asked me if I wanted to grab a coffee after work. We came here." She looked at a table over by the window. "Sat right there and talked for a long time. I knew I liked her at work, but you know how sometimes work relationships don't translate?"

Ben didn't know what she meant.

"Like to real life? Sometimes you get away from the office or wherever and you realize you don't have anything else to talk about?"

He thought about all the cops he used to be friends with. All he could remember ever talking about with them was work. But was that just him? He didn't like sports, didn't go to the movies very often or have any hobbies. He could remember other cops talking about playoffs or politics or whatever, but did he ever join in?

"Yeah," he said. "I know what you mean."

"At first she just wanted to hang out and watch Netflix and stuff."

"That was when you started coming to her place?"

"Yeah. After a while, we started going out more and doing stuff."

"Like what?"

"Oh, different things. She liked the aquarium. She'd never been before, so we went there a few times. You know when they have live music at Fingerprints? The record store? We both really like that. We saw Tall Walls there. Do you know them?"

He shook his head.

"They're so good. You should check them out. They won Buskerfest."

"They did?" Ben didn't know what Buskerfest was.

She seemed to misread his confusion. "Not this year. Last year."

He tried to play into her mistake. "Oh, okay." That seemed to satisfy her.

They were quiet for a moment and Amy finally took a sip of her drink.

"When was the last time you talked to her?" he asked.

"Friday, maybe? We were supposed to go to the movies, but she cancelled. She wasn't feeling good. Then a couple of days later, when she didn't answer my texts, I started getting worried. Even went by her place to check one night, but she wasn't there."

Ben's stomach tightened. "What kind of car do you have?"

"A Prius." She smiled. "Same color as Grace's, even." Apparently, she could read the relief on his face. "Why?"

"I saw a car in the alley one night. I wasn't positive, but I thought they were checking out the studio. Wasn't a Prius, though."

"What was it?"

"A Camaro."

Amy narrowed her eyes. "That's weird."

"Why?"

"One day when Grace and I got off work, we walked out back through the parking lot and one of our managers was just parking there for the evening. Grace got this really intense look on her face as we watched him walk inside. I asked her what was wrong and she said, 'Is he an asshole?' and I asked why and she went, 'Camaros are for assholes.'"

• • •

On the way back to the Volvo, Ben passed the little parking lot. He hadn't asked Amy specifically, but he assumed, because she walked up the block in the opposite direction, to where she'd parked her car, that only managers got a spot behind the restaurant. He saw what he was looking for, backed into the corner spot nearest the back door—a gleaming yellow Camaro.

He didn't believe there was any connection. Camaros weren't that popular, but there were enough of them around that they didn't seem unusual. What had caught his attention, though, was Amy mentioning the strong reaction Grace had to the make of the manager's car. The kind of reaction that came from personal experience. Grace didn't hate Camaros. She hated one specific Camaro. And Ben was certain the one she hated was red.

• • •

He'd tried to get as much information as he possibly could from Amy before they left the Library, but Grace hadn't shared much about her past, and the only person she seemed to be spending any time with was Amy. He'd hardly written anything at all in his notebook.

Fri 1/13
Coffee w/Amy—Grace's friend
Grace doesn't like Camaros
Look up BUSKERFEST

As he reread the entry behind the wheel of the still-parked Volvo, he realized he'd forgotten to ask Amy about the Post-it he'd found when he searched Grace's room. *Call Amy about job*, it had said. What could that mean? Hadn't they met working at the Attic? Was it something about her job there, or was it another job altogether?

Shit. Ben had exchanged numbers with Amy. He thought about texting her right then. She'd probably be driving, though. He'd wait. He added another line to the notebook entry:

ASK AMY ABOUT JOB

He made good time getting home. It was still too early for the after-work traffic on Cherry to have really started to stack up, so it had been just over ninety minutes since he'd left. A car he didn't recognize had parked at the curb in front of the house and left him a smaller spot than usual. He'd always hated parallel parking, and he seemed to be getting worse at it since the injury. It took him three tries to get the tires close enough to the curb that he wouldn't worry about anyone judging his competence.

Inside, he expected to find Peter in the living room watching *Ellen* like he usually did at that time of day. But his father wasn't there. He wasn't in the dining room, the kitchen, or the bathroom, either. Just as the worry began to wash over him, a blur of motion out the back door caught his attention. Someone had thrown a tennis ball onto the patio. It thumped off of the door and rolled back toward the grass. Before it could get there, though, Sriracha came scrambling into view, jaws opened wide like a feeding shark, and scooped it up. She spun and bounded off back in the direction she had come.

Ben went into his father's bedroom and peeked out between the slats of the plantation shutters. Peter was standing near the back fence and Sriracha had just dropped the ball at his feet. He picked it up and hurled it across the lawn again.

Bernie wasn't anywhere to be seen. Did he just leave them out in the backyard like that? Where the hell was he? Ben wasn't sure what to do. Just go out and ask where Bernie was? He looked through the window again. They were still going at it—Peter tossing the ball and Sriracha fetching it. Neither one showed any signs of slowing down. His dad seemed so happy. It didn't look like anything hurt. So normal. It seemed wrong to interrupt them.

His phone pulsed in his pocket with a text message. Maybe it was Amy getting back to him. He checked the screen. It was Bernie.

you home?

Yes. How did you know?

your cars out front

Where are you?

over on the side by the kitchen

Instead of replying, Ben went back through the house and out the side door.

Bernie was standing there, a grin widening his face.

"What are you doing over here?" Ben asked, his voice lowered. He didn't think Peter would hear them, but he didn't want to take a chance.

"Jorge called. Welding thing at the shop. So I came around here and talked to him for a minute, and when I started to go back, I saw the two of them going like that and thought, why not let them go a while?"

"How long ago was that?"

"Twenty minutes, maybe?"

Bernie fiddled with his phone, then turned it around so Ben could see the screen. It was Peter and Sriracha playing. "I recorded it in case you didn't get to see it."

"Would you send that to me?"

"Sure."

"And could I get the name of your friend with the puppies?"

• • •

Ben was surprised when he saw Becerra's name on the screen of his ringing phone. The detective had told him he would call, but he didn't expect to hear anything so soon. Or at all, really. Ben couldn't shake the feeling that he was just being humored, that pacifying him was some-how more important than just another missing waitress.

"Detective Becerra," Ben said. He'd thought about answering with just a generic "Hello," but he wanted to give the impression that he was more on top of things than he really was.

"Detective Shepard," Becerra replied.

Ben wondered how calculated the use of his former title was. He tried to remember the old days. Had he ever referred to a retired cop by their title? It certainly wasn't standard practice when he'd been work-ing. He couldn't think of a time when he'd done it himself. So what was going on? Was it an act of respect or was he just being patronized? Ben didn't have any idea and he wished he could quit caring about it. Confronting his insecurity only ever made it worse.

"Just calling with an update." Becerra sounded as if he was report-ing to his lieutenant rather than informing a concerned party about the progress of an investigation. "Detective Tanaka notified you about the lead we're pursuing with the Camaro, right?"

"Yes." They really were communicating, and even more signifi-cantly, they really were keeping him in the loop.

"Good," Becerra said. "I have some new information for you. Grace hasn't used her phone or accessed her bank account at all."

"Okay," Ben said. Most people would find that alarming, and they would probably be right to see it that way. It could be read as evidence of foul play. But Ben was still working on the hopeful assumption that Grace had left on her own to avoid someone who was trying to find her, and to him it made perfect sense that she'd be careful not to leave a digital trail that someone could follow.

"I don't think we should worry about that too much, though."

Ben wondered why Becerra would say that. Simply to placate him, or because he suspected the same thing Ben did—that Grace was on the run? He tried to coax some more out of Becerra. "Why not?"

"Well, for one thing, she's a waitress, so she gets a lot of her income in cash, right? She probably hasn't needed to make a withdrawal."

Ben knew Becerra would have checked her account activity, looking for patterns of transactions to get an idea of whether or not a few days of inactivity was normal for her. "How often did she make deposits?"

"Usually at the end of the week."

"When was her last deposit?"

"Ten days ago."

"Had she ever gone that long without putting something into her account before?"

"No."

"But it's a new account, right?"

Becerra paused. "How did you know that?"

A wave of anxiety rolled over Ben. Had he said something wrong? Revealed something he shouldn't have? How did he know that?

"Detective?"

He knew but he couldn't remember how. A drop of sweat fell from his eyebrow and rolled down his cheek like a tear.

Becerra said, "Did she ever—"

"Her rent checks." Ben let out the breath he didn't realize he'd been holding. "The numbers were all like single digits. I remember thinking how odd that seemed, that it must have been a brand-new account."

"Yeah," Becerra said, "that makes sense."

"And she hasn't used her phone at all." It wasn't a question.

"No."

Still, Ben thought, *that fits.* If she knew enough not to access her bank accounts, she'd know not to use her phone. "Did you try to locate the GPS?"

"We did. No sign of it."

"When was the last hit?"

"The night before you realized she was missing."

"Where?"

"Your house."

Grace had turned off her phone before she disappeared. She knew she was going and she didn't want anyone to be able to find her.

Becerra broke the silence. "You know what that means, right?"

"I know what it means for us," Ben said. "What does it mean for you?"

"If she chose to disappear, there's no crime to investigate."

"So you're done?" His voice was sharper than he intended.

"Not yet. She probably took off of her own free will. But I'm not comfortable with 'probably.'"

Maybe Jennifer was right about him.

• • •

As Ben got Peter ready for bed, he thought about Becerra's call. He was glad to have received it and still surprised they were sharing so much information with him. Maybe if he'd been a family member or something, it would make sense. But it seemed strange to him and he couldn't help wondering why Becerra was so forthcoming. He didn't believe it was the hero shtick that the detective had mentioned when he came to the house.

It had to be Jennifer. Nothing else made sense. One thing he remembered clearly from his days with the department was how fiercely he and everyone else had protected investigative details from anyone not directly involved in a case. Everything was strictly need-to-know. Did he need to know? It was hard to believe anyone would think he did, except maybe for his old partner.

Rob had certainly known much more than he shared with Ben.

That had to be it. Rob knew there was real danger out there for Grace. As far as Becerra and Jennifer knew, this wasn't a big deal at all. Someone decides to go off the grid for a while, why not help an old colleague who'd had some hard times feel a little better?

He needed to talk to Rob again.

Ben picked up his notebook, opened it, and realized he hadn't recorded his father's evening meds.

"Shit," he said out loud.

He wrote them down and added:

ALMOST FORGOT AGAIN—DON'T FORGET!!!

Then he went back to Peter's bedroom to see if he was finished in the bathroom yet. He found him already in bed with the lights off and his blankets pulled up to his chin.

"Why didn't you tell me you were ready for bed?" he asked.

"I didn't want to bother you," Peter said.

Ben leaned over and kissed him on the forehead. "It's never a bother, Dad."

Peter smiled but didn't look like he believed the words.

ELEVEN

Ben texted Rob asking for another meeting not long after he put his father to bed, but he didn't see the reply until he woke up at seven the next morning. According to the time stamp it had come at 3:37 a.m. The night had been all tossing and turning and worrying, so it was a surprise that the message hadn't woken him. He would have sworn that he hadn't slept deeply enough at any point to have missed the message, so at least he had slept a little better than he thought.

He read the message one more time and copied the details into his notebook.

Meet Rob. 10:00. Marriott—Room 406.

It was raining again. He couldn't remember the last time they'd had so wet a winter. When was the last big El Niño? There was supposed to be a very wet season last year, but the heavy rain had never come. This year was making up for it, though. Some people were saying it might even be enough to end the years-long California drought. That would make Peter happy. Ben had never had much success trying to explain the new county watering regulations to his father. Maybe now he'd be able to reset the sprinklers and keep the lawn as green and full as Peter liked it to be.

Ben didn't go out of his way to be quiet while he was making break-fast. He turned up the classic country music on the Echo and let the teakettle whistle for a minute so Peter would hear. The right balance was tricky. He had to be noisy enough for his father to hear if he was already awake, but not so loud that he'd startle him if he wasn't.

He knew he'd gotten it right a few minutes later, when Peter shuf-fled out in his thick gray socks and sat at the counter.

"How'd you sleep, Dad?"

"Good."

"Is your stomach okay? Did you poop yet?"

Peter nodded. "Big one."

"That's good."

Putting the half-full coffee cup and instant oatmeal on the place mat in front of him, Ben said, "Go slow, okay?"

Peter nodded and lifted a spoonful to his mouth. "It's good," he said.

Remember this, Ben thought. *Remember what it feels like to do some-thing right.*

• • •

Ben double-checked the room number and knocked again. Still no answer. He took the burner out of his pocket and called Rob. Just before it went to voicemail, he thought he heard something from inside the room. The second time he dialed, he held the phone down by his hip and put his ear close to the door.

A phone was ringing inside.

Rob wasn't there and didn't have his phone with him. Hadn't he told Ben he'd have it with him all the time? He was sure he had.

What should he do? Maybe Rob was in the shower or out on the balcony or something. Or maybe he'd gone downstairs for food or coffee.

Ben thought about what to do. Should he be worried that Rob didn't have the phone? Had something happened to him?

All he could do at the moment, it seemed, was go downstairs and look for Rob. Maybe he had just stepped out for a minute. That would make sense, wouldn't it?

On his way back to the elevator, he passed a cleaning woman who'd just come out of a room and returned to her cart.

"Good morning," she said to him, smiling.

Ben nodded and smiled back, hoping he didn't seem too anxious.

There was no sign of Rob downstairs. Not at the Starbucks stand in the lobby or in the restaurant or out by the pool.

Think, he told himself, *think.* It didn't seem likely that Rob would have forgotten their meeting or changed the plan without calling or texting him. What did that mean? Could something have happened to him? Maybe he was in the room. If he'd been asleep, surely the multiple calls would have woken him. What if someone else, someone he was looking for, found him here first?

Ben's hand was beginning to shake. Sometimes mild tremors came with his anxiety. But why was he so anxious? Was it worry that something had happened to Rob, or was it just that the plan for the meeting was thrown off? He tried to breathe deeply and think it through. The last time he remembered noticing a tremor in his hand was at Ralphs not long ago, when he realized he'd forgotten the grocery list he'd made. Another deep breath. The feeling had been almost exactly what he was feeling now. This was what Emma had taught him to do. To examine the anxiety, to place it in context, to ascertain whether it was proportional to the situation. He took another deep breath and he was confident that it was just the plan going off track that was upsetting him. There was no real reason to be concerned about Rob, and no evidence at all that anything serious was wrong with the situation. He rubbed the back of his head and thought.

Ben decided he'd have a cup of coffee and wait in the lobby for a while to see if Rob showed up or returned to the room.

As the barista was making his decaf vanilla latte, though, he remembered the cleaning woman upstairs and got an idea.

He added a muffin to the order, and in the elevator on the way back upstairs, he punched in the number to Rob's phone again, but didn't hit the "Send" button.

The cleaning cart was still in the hall, one room closer to Rob's door. Ben hoped that meant she'd spent the time he was downstairs cleaning that room and would soon be finished. He walked past the cart and waited in front of room 406.

It was only about two minutes before the maid came back out into the hallway and found Ben, coffee and muffin balanced precariously in his left hand while he frantically pretended to search his pockets with his right.

"Is everything okay?" she asked.

He gave her a befuddled look and said, "I'm expecting an important call and I think I left my key card inside with my phone."

She came closer and he found the "Send" button on the phone in his pocket and pushed. Just as she got to the door, the faint ring sounded from inside. Without hesitation, she slipped her master key into the lock and opened the door for him.

"Thank you so much! You saved my life." He slipped inside and let the door shut behind him before she could finish saying "You're welcome."

"Thank you," you say to her. "You saved our lives."

Grace laughs at the hyperbole and hands you a bag of ground Starbucks House Blend, decaf. You feel like an idiot.

Half an hour ago, you'd been on the verge of an anxiety attack because Peter was already up and asking for coffee and you hadn't realized you'd run out until you tried to brew the morning pot. You hadn't showered. You were still wearing the sweatpants and T-shirt you'd worn to bed. You were still trying to shake off the nightmare that woke you an hour later than usual.

Then you heard a tapping on the patio door and saw Grace outside. You opened the door and she said, "I'm going to Ralphs. You guys need anything?"

Now, with a cup of coffee in each hand, you go out and join her and your father at the patio table. If either of them can tell you've been crying, they don't let on.

He stood there in the middle of the room, staring at the pale-yellow wall behind the king bed's headboard. It had really worked. Even more surprising was that when he opened his hand and held it in front of his chest, it was no longer shaking.

What had happened? Just a few minutes earlier, he'd been in the lobby trying to derail an impending anxiety attack, and now here he was in Rob's hotel room. The idea had come to him and he'd acted on it. He hadn't thought about it. He hadn't considered his options. He hadn't doubted.

Ben had taken action and now, at least for a moment, he felt a kind of satisfaction that seemed unfamiliar to him. The more he thought about it, though, the more he felt the calmness beginning to slip away.

Focus, he reminded himself. *Breathe.*

No one else was inside.

In front of him, the bed looked like Rob had made it himself after he'd gotten up. It wasn't as neat and tightly tucked as it would have been if the housekeeping staff had done it, but it was more than a rudimentary effort. Did people do that in hotels? Make the beds themselves? He didn't think so. At least, he'd never done it himself.

On the desk was a thick manila folder. Before he examined it, though, he took a quick look around the room. In the closet hung an unwrinkled navy-blue suit and what he believed was the shirt Rob had been wearing when they'd had lunch downstairs. A carry-on-sized suitcase was perched on the folding luggage stand. There were no extra shoes or dirty clothes. In the bathroom on the counter was a small waxed-canvas toiletry bag, and one apparently used towel was balled up on the floor next to the shower. A blue toothbrush had been placed in a water glass so the bristles wouldn't touch the counter.

Rob kept things neat.

Ben made his way over to the desk by the window that looked out toward the airport. A jet was taking off. He watched as it sped up the runway and into the sky. As it grew smaller in the distance, he couldn't help but wonder if his father had been watching.

What he'd been hoping to find when he made the snap decision to lie his way into the room, he wasn't sure. He'd been concerned for Rob, sure, but a part of him knew even before he came upstairs that wasn't really what was driving his impulsivity. No, it was information he was after.

Rob knew things about Grace.

Ben wanted to know them, too. He wondered how much time he had before Rob came back. It was worth the risk, he decided, so he sat down at the desk and opened the folder.

The first page was a printout of cell-phone records. It had been years since he'd looked at something like that, and the formatting was different than it had been back when documents like that had been a regular part of his job. There was more information now, more columns, more numbers that he didn't know the meaning of. He started turning the pages—there were maybe forty or fifty here—and saw similar documents. Not all phone records—some were bank and credit-card statements, others were spreadsheets and forms he didn't immediately recognize. Some were stapled, some paper-clipped, others single sheets. Disappointment washed over him.

There was nothing here that would be helpful without analysis, and maybe not even then, without the context he was sorely lacking. He had hoped for straightforward reports and case notes. Names. Addresses. Photos.

A more thorough search of the room revealed nothing. The dresser drawers were empty. Rob's suitcase only held a few spare items of clothing, socks and underwear, a T-shirt. The kinds of things you don't hang up.

Maybe there was something in the small safe on the closet shelf, but it was locked and he'd never know.

He still had no idea how much time he had, but he decided to try to make the most of the opportunity and went back to the desk. He opened the file folder again, took out his phone, and opened the camera app. Slowly and methodically, he worked his way through the pages and took a photo of each one, careful to replace the paper clips and stapled packets just as they had been.

Forty-eight pages into the process, he heard the unmistakable key-card click of someone unlocking the hotel-room door.

TWELVE

Ben quickly closed the folder, stood up from the desk, and faced the door, his mind grasping for possible explanations that Rob might buy for his presence in the room.

But the man who opened the door wasn't Rob.

The stranger took two steps into the room before he realized he wasn't alone. He was clearly as surprised as Ben. Immediately he shifted his stance, taking a small step forward with his left foot and turning his right hip back toward the door. He lifted his right shoulder as his hand opened and slid around behind him. "Who are you?" he said. "What are you doing here?"

The door closed itself behind him with a click.

Two things were obvious to Ben. One, the guy was armed, and two, he was trained well enough to instinctually prepare himself to draw his weapon, but not so well that he was at all subtle about it. The man was about the same height as Ben but leaner and more muscular, with blond hair cut short.

"What am I doing here?" Ben said. "Rob gave me his key and told me to meet him here. Who the fuck are you?"

There was confusion in the man's eyes.

Ben watched and waited for what seemed like a very long time.

Something seemed to click in the man's head and the confusion gave way to an angry gleam.

Before the stranger's hand could clear his shirt and get a solid grip on his gun, Ben's shoulder was already buried in his chest, driving him backward and ramming him into the door.

Ben pulled him back into the room and body slammed him to the floor, bringing his own weight down on top of the stranger. The man was gasping for air, but Ben didn't give him a chance to catch his breath as he punched him wildly again and again, only stopping when he felt a sharp pain shoot up his hand and into his wrist.

Looking down at the bloody and swollen face lolling to the side on the gray carpet, Ben tried to understand what had happened. He rolled the stranger onto his side, pulled the Glock out of the holster behind his hip—it was the same model Ben had carried himself when he'd been on the job—and tossed it onto the bed. It was clear the man wasn't going to be getting up on his own anytime soon.

Ben hoisted himself to his feet while the last ninety seconds replayed in his head. He had to steady himself on the wall with his hand.

His left hand. The right was throbbing and bloody. Was it the stranger's blood or his own? It took a few seconds for him to realize it was both.

The man he'd beaten was nearly motionless on the floor, and Ben realized that from the sink in the bathroom he'd still be able to see the man's feet if he started moving. He went in and ran cold water on his swollen right hand. As the blood rinsed away, the throbbing became more intense. Outside the door, one of the feet moved. Ben shut off the water, grabbed a hand towel from the rod next to the counter, and went to check. The stranger had rolled onto his side and thrown up on the carpet.

The sour acidic odor reached Ben and stimulated his gag reflex. The sensation of having to hold back his own vomit triggered something, and the adrenaline-fueled confidence and certainty flowing through him were flushed away and it felt like a hand had taken hold of his intestines and started twisting. He looked across the room and saw the folder on the desk. Cautiously, he stepped around the softly moaning body on the floor. As he reached out for the documents, he tried to steady his shaking hand.

Wait.

Could the folder be what the stranger had come for?

And if it was, would they come after him to get it?

Almost everything in it was now in Ben's phone. Could there be anything in the last few pages worth taking the risk?

No, Ben decided. It wasn't worth it.

He squatted down. "Can you hear me?"

The man mumbled something Ben couldn't understand. He wasn't unresponsive, but he wasn't alert, either. Ben patted him down. No wallet. No ID. Just a Samsung smartphone, a spare magazine for the Glock, and a few hundred dollars folded into a money clip.

He couldn't open the phone without a code. There didn't seem to be a fingerprint sensor he could use to access it, so he went back into the bathroom and dropped it into the toilet. Then he picked up the Glock on the bed and tucked it into his waistband at the small of his back.

As he stood surveying the room, a flash of memory struck him.

Another hotel room, a long time ago, somewhere far away, quadruple checking to make sure he hadn't forgotten anything, Kate grinning and teasing him about his obsessiveness.

Should he try to wipe everything clean of his fingerprints? Not enough time. And he doubted he could even remember everything he'd touched.

Should he try to help the stranger? Maybe. He probably had a concussion. A broken nose. Maybe the jaw, too. If he fully lost consciousness, he could choke on his own blood and phlegm. *No. Fuck him.* He'd been going for his gun. He wouldn't have done that unless he was willing to use it.

Should he do something else? The answer to that question had to be yes, but Ben knew he'd never be able to figure out what else it should be.

He glanced one more time in the bathroom, grabbed the towel spotted with the blood from his knuckles, took one more deep breath, and went to the door. Just as he was about to grasp the handle, he stopped and turned around to look at the stranger on the floor.

Ben cautiously walked back to him. He was still only semiconscious, but there was a hint of fear in him as he saw Ben stand over him and reach into his pocket.

Ben took out his phone and snapped half a dozen pictures of the man's swollen and battered face. An ID might be difficult, but it would still be better to have the photos.

He was out in the hall and halfway to the elevator when he heard the door close itself behind him.

Downstairs, he exited the hotel through a side door to the parking lot so he wouldn't have to pass the front desk.

It had started to rain again, just a drizzle, really, but the forecast had said it would come down harder that night.

• • •

When he pulled the car up to the curb, Ben realized he had no memory of the drive home. He'd been so focused on what had happened, what he'd done and what the repercussions might be, that he had zoned out and made the trip on autopilot. The realization frightened him. During the early months of his recovery, he'd often lose time. Sometimes he'd have complete blackouts, but later, as his health improved, they became less frequent and were supplanted by incidents where his mind would get fixated on something—an idea, a fear, a memory—and he'd find himself somewhere with no recollection of how he'd gotten there. He'd be on the couch watching TV one minute, get lost in his head, and find himself in the backyard. Once he'd even gone from sitting down at lunch with a turkey sandwich to washing the dishes from a dinner he couldn't remember eating. Had it ever happened while he was driving? He didn't think so, but he couldn't be sure.

The blood on his knuckles was starting to dry and scab, and his whole hand was swollen and throbbing. He needed ice and something for the pain, but he was afraid to go into the house. What would he tell Peter?

On his way to the door, he realized the sole of his left shoe was brushing the concrete with each step. What was happening? His gait was off. The same way it had been after his shooting. It had taken him two years of physical therapy to overcome it. High steppage, the neurologist had called it. He'd worked as hard on that as he had on anything, because he knew if he could get past it, he'd finally be able to walk through a crowd again without anyone noticing him.

Why was it back now? Was it just the stress and exertion, or had he injured something other than his hand? Could it be neurological? Jesus. If it was, he might—

The door opened and Peter said, "Are you okay?" Ben could hear the worry in the high timbre of his voice.

"I will be." Ben carefully stepped up onto the porch, right foot first so his father wouldn't notice what was going on with the left. "I tripped and fell down in the parking lot at the drugstore."

"Oh, no."

"It's not too bad." He lifted his arm and displayed his scraped and swollen knuckles. "Fell on top of my hand, though. Need to put some ice on it."

Peter helped him dig an old pot they hadn't used for years out of the cupboard. They dumped half the ice from the freezer into it and filled it the rest of the way with water. Peter lugged it over to the dining-room table, careful not to let any slosh over the sides.

The ice water stung at first, but soon his hand started to numb. Ben looked at the empty coffee cup on the counter. His father had fashioned a makeshift lid out of a paper towel folded into quarters. "You need something to eat, don't you?"

"No, I'm okay," Peter said. "I had a . . ." He couldn't find the word he was looking for. "A little one?" He held his thumb and forefinger up, half an inch apart.

"A Hershey's bar?" That was pretty much the only thing he still got for himself. Sometimes he'd get a bottle of water out of the fridge, but usually if he opened up the door, he'd spot the chocolate in the butter compartment and break off a piece.

"I'm sorry," he said.

Ben bought them by the package, six each, specifically for his father, but somehow Peter always thought he was doing something wrong when he ate them, taking candy away from his child.

"That's all right, Dad. You can always have as much chocolate as you want. We're still trying to gain some weight, okay?"

Peter nodded. "Does it hurt bad?"

Even the sting of the icy water had faded. When he moved his fingers in the pot, he still felt a sharp pain in the back of his hand and there was stiffness in his wrist, but it wasn't nearly as bad as it had been. "No, I think it's going to be okay."

He hadn't noticed that the Echo on the counter was still playing music until Peter smiled and started tapping the table in rhythm to Buck Owens singing "Act Naturally."

• • •

After three cycles of twenty minutes in and twenty minutes out of the ice water, Ben's hand felt pretty good. The knuckles weren't as bad as he had feared—only the first two had lost any skin, and they didn't look like much more than scrapes. Most of the swelling had disappeared, too. He'd been worried about a metacarpal fracture, but that was seeming less likely.

Ben knew he had to talk to Rob as soon as he could. He didn't know how to get a hold of him, though. The burner phone Rob wanted him to call had been in the hotel room. Would it still be there? Would Rob have it by now? Ben thought about how long it had taken Rob to reply to some of the text messages. Maybe he always left the phone in the room. That would make sense. He'd go out and do something, then only check it and answer when he came back.

Could he have come back already? Ben tried to figure out how long he'd been in the room. He really had no idea. The initial search and then the later altercation hadn't taken that much time at all, maybe two or three minutes each at the most. The variable he couldn't account for was how long he had spent taking photos of the documents in the folder. It could have been five minutes or it could have been twenty-five. He really had no idea. Was there a way to figure it out?

He opened the camera on his phone and looked at the picture of the first page. The time stamp told him it was taken at 10:14 a.m. The last at 10:23. He must have been out of the room by 10:30 at the very latest.

It wasn't a stretch at all that Rob could have been half an hour late. And without the only phone he used to talk to Ben, how could he have let him know he'd be late?

The stiffness in his hand made typing difficult and clumsy, but he sent Rob a text message. Thinking vagueness would be to his advantage if the stranger had somehow managed to recover enough to leave with the phone, he wrote I was there. Contact me ASAP and hit "Send."

Ten minutes later, when Ben had just about given up on a quick reply, he got one.

we need to meet

Where? When?

An hour later, when he got up to ice his hand again, there was still no answer.

• • •

The real rain hadn't come yet, so Ben spent half an hour walking back and forth on the damp grass in the backyard. One thousand four hundred thirty-eight steps. His gait seemed to have returned to normal. What had been going on when he'd come back from the hotel, he couldn't figure out. It could have just been the stress. He'd taken a lorazepam to calm himself down while he was waiting for the text from Rob that never came, so stress would make sense. Maybe it was just coming down from the adrenaline rush from the fight. He hadn't experienced anything like that since before his injury, so he had no frame of reference by which to judge it.

Or did he?

During Peter's recovery from the last surgery, about two-thirds of the way through the two-week hospital stay, one of his father's doctors saw Ben walking back from the cafeteria and asked if he was all right. He'd said he was just exhausted, and the doctor asked if he was still seeing a neurologist. Most of the staff knew about his history—one of the night-shift nurses had recognized Ben from his own hospitalization years earlier, and soon everyone else seemed to know the story. He told the doctor he was two months away from his next neuro consult and asked why she was curious. She said he'd been shuffling in a way she hadn't seen before and wanted to make sure he was okay.

He hadn't thought much more about it at the time, but over the next few days of Peter's recuperation, he became more conscious of how he was walking.

That was how he felt now, in the backyard. His gait felt normal. It was just the stress. He repeated that quietly to himself, over and over. *Just the stress. Just the stress.*

He kept walking and muttering until Peter came outside and said, "Is it time for TV?"

Ben checked his watch. It was Saturday, but it was time. He left his damp shoes, stray blades of grass sticking to the toes, by the patio door and went into the living room with his father to watch one of the episodes of *Ellen* saved on the DVR.

• • •

All evening Ben waited. For Rob to get back to him. For the police to knock on his door. For something.

Had Rob found the stranger in his hotel room? Had the cleaning staff? Had he somehow managed to get away on his own?

At least until Peter went to bed, he'd had something to distract him. Now, though, all he had were the TV and the sound of the rain falling on the roof. He knew he should have called Becerra or Jennifer, but he didn't. That might escalate things even more than he already had. He suspected the stranger was a cop or had been at one point. The way he'd twisted his body and prepared to draw his weapon had been conditioned into him through training or experience or both. Where would that have come from if not the police? He could have been one of the dirty cops Rob was trying to take down, and reporting could trigger alarm bells and maybe make things more dangerous for Grace. Even worse, he might have been a cop who wasn't dirty, and then the felony Ben had committed would definitely come back to haunt him.

But if he wasn't dirty, where was his badge? If he was a cop, whatever he was doing in Rob's room was off the books, or he would have had his badge and ID with him. Your shield was more important than your gun. You weren't really police without it.

Shit.

Where was the Glock? What had he done with it? He'd had it when he got into the Volvo at the Marriott, he remembered dropping it onto the floor in front of the passenger's seat, but he hadn't thought about it since.

He hurried into the kitchen and grabbed the car keys from the small bowl where he'd trained himself to put them every time he came home, and he ran out the front door into the rain. Already soaked through when got to the car at the curb, he fumbled to get the key into the lock of the passenger's door. The light wasn't too bright anymore, but there it was, right where he had left it. The sense of relief was more palpable than the rain pelting his back and splashing onto the seat below him. Hugging it to his chest as if it might melt if it got too wet, he hurried up the walkway, locked the front door behind him, and took the pistol straight into his bedroom.

He opened the drawer next to the bed, removed the magazine from the Glock and cleared the chamber, then inserted the extra cartridge back into the magazine. His mother had taught him how to shoot and the fundamentals of gun safety when he was thirteen, just as she'd taught his father when they first moved in together. He could almost hear her voice saying, "If you're going to live in a house with a weapon, you're going to learn how to use it properly."

There was a gun in the nightstand again.

It didn't make him feel any safer, though.

Walking back into the living room, he looked at the wet footprints on the floor. He was still making them, and even when he stopped moving, he was still dripping. In the bathroom, he took off his wet shirt and dropped it on the floor, then grabbed a bath towel off the rack to soak up the mess. He pulled a hoodie out of the closet and put it on, cleaned up the water from the storm, then did almost three thousand more steps on the living-room-kitchen circuit.

• • •

When he'd replaced his old iPhone a year and a half ago, Ben had set up photo sharing on the new one, so when he sat down at the desk and brought the computer to life, all the pictures he'd taken of documents in Rob's hotel room had been uploaded into the cloud and were waiting for him.

He went through them one by one. They still didn't make much sense to him without the necessary context. Seventeen pages of phone records with no names attached. They seemed to track three different phone numbers. He wondered if he should start cross-referencing them to see if each of the numbers showed up in each other set of records. Ben assumed they would or that there was some common pattern of outgoing or incoming calls to be found. Why else would Rob have them together in the file? He wondered if Rob had done this already. It didn't appear that he had, because the printouts had no notes or marks on them. Ben remembered how he used to go at phone records with a dozen different-colored pens and highlighters. There would have been no mistaking whether or not he'd gone over documents like these. Even before he went out on disability, though, things were changing. Maybe these records had already been sorted and cross-referenced digitally. Why spend hours hunched over piles of paper when you could do the same thing more reliably by typing in a set of search parameters?

Context, he thought again. Unless he knew what he was looking for, it didn't seem worth the time and energy.

The ten pages of bank records and credit-card statements presented similar issues. They were identified only by account numbers. Whose account numbers were they? They might be Grace's. But even a casual examination showed quite a few more transactions than he expected based on what Becerra had told him of her activity. She could have accounts under another name, but if she was trying to keep a low profile, that didn't seem likely.

Next were six pages of spreadsheets. Ben had no idea what any of them meant.

What came after that, though, was interesting. Fourteen single-spaced pages, in a tiny font, of what he thought were time-stamped GPS coordinates. Again, there was no name or identification other than a six-digit number on the top of each page. It could have been from a phone, but he suspected they came from a tracking device, because of the level of detail and the formatting. Just dates along the left margin and dozens of entries for each day. They covered a span of nine days. The most recent was the day before Grace disappeared.

This was something. Ben knew he could look up the coordinates online. All he'd need would be Google Maps and a lot of time. He made a note on the legal pad. *Look up coordinates?*

The last document was different. He hadn't taken a close-enough look at it in the room. It was a page of typed case notes.

There had been several more pages when he was interrupted. He clicked to move to the next photo and saw the stranger's battered face gazing slack jawed into the camera.

"You fucking idiot," he whispered to himself.

Why hadn't he finished the job before he left?

Ben clicked back to the case notes and used the "Z" key to zoom in until the photo displayed at close to its actual size. Rob had used abbreviations for names, some of which he could guess, but the others were as meaningless as the other documents. He copied the notes he believed he understood onto the yellow notepad.

G—first barista job in Long Beach
Talk to manager, coworkers
4245 Atlantic

G had to be Grace, Ben thought. If he was right, then the Attic wasn't the first place she'd worked in Long Beach. That address wasn't too far from where he sat. He tried to think of the coffeehouses on Atlantic. It had to be either the Coffee Bean or that other place just up the street. The one that used to be It's a Grind. It was something else now, had been for a few years, but he couldn't remember what. Still a coffee place, though.

Apartment—Bluff Heights
Contact Roommate
307 Orizaba

Had Grace had another apartment in Long Beach, too? Another job and another home. That seemed odd to Ben. Why switch? And how long had she been in those places? She'd been in Long Beach longer than he had realized. He tried to think it through. If he didn't know what he knew about Grace's past, it would make sense. The job at the Attic likely paid more than the one at the coffeehouse, and the rent for the studio here would be less than something comparable in Bluff Heights, so maybe the decision was strictly financial. If she or Rob suspected her cover was shaky, she'd put a lot more distance between herself and the new life she'd been trying to make in Long Beach, wouldn't she?

Find K. BF?

That one was more cryptic. Ben assumed *BF* stood for *boyfriend*. It didn't seem to be too big a leap. If she had been involved with someone and it hadn't worked out, that would give more credence to the theory that moving and switching jobs had more to do with her new life than her old one.

Ben didn't need to spend too much time or energy with the last note he copied. It was perfectly self-explanatory.

Talk to B, don't let him get too close

Too late for that one.

• • •

Back in the living room, just as he was about to sit down on the couch, he caught a glimpse of the Lucite brick encasing his shield. He walked over to it, moved his mother's picture to the side, and took it down off the shelf.

He held it in his hands and looked at it more closely than he remembered ever doing before. It had been polished before they put it inside, the brass bright, almost glowing. "POLICE," it said on the top edge of the ring in the center. On each outer edge was the distinctive logo with a capital *L* centered on top of and bisecting a capital *B*. On the bottom, "CITY OF LONG BEACH." In the center of the circle, a star with the city seal. But it was the banner above the ring that he focused on. It read "DETECTIVE."

It had meant something once.

Maybe it still did.

Ben carried it back into the office and put it on the desk next to the computer. It took him half an hour of Googling, but he finally found what he was looking for by following a link in the forum section of the American Numismatic Association.

Before falling asleep on the couch watching Carpool Karaoke, he texted Bernie to ask for another favor.

THIRTEEN

"I'm not sure about this," Bernie said the next morning. "You positive it's not against the law or something?"

They were in his garage, where Bernie maintained a small welding shop to work on personal stuff—he'd become an amateur sculptor after he retired—and do small projects, mostly as favors for friends and family.

"Nothing I'm asking you to do is illegal," Ben said, hoping he wasn't lying.

"How about what you're going to do with it when I'm done?"

When Ben didn't answer, Bernie sighed and said, "Let me see it again."

Ben held up the iPad and showed him the page on the numismatics message board where he'd found the instructions.

"Put these on and stand over there." Bernie handed him a pair of safety glasses and waved his hand toward the closed garage door.

Ben watched him heft a dark-green metal cylinder—it looked kind of like a scuba tank with handles on top—out from under the workbench and put it in the middle of the floor.

"That's the liquid nitrogen?"

Bernie nodded and put on a pair of welding gloves, grabbed one of the handles with his left hand, and used his right to twist the top. It was a removable lid, Ben realized.

Bernie looked at the rim of the cylinder, then at the block of Lucite, then back at the cylinder again. He shook his head. "I don't think it's gonna fit, but I'll give it a try." Next to the badge was a pair of large tongs. Bernie used them to pick up the block and attempt to dip it into the top of the tank. It almost fit.

"Crap." He put the block back on the bench, then went to one of the shelves that lined the back wall and came back with some kind of heavy-duty metal bucket, which he placed on the floor next to the cylinder.

He carefully tipped the tank to the side and poured its contents into the bucket. White wisps of mist rose from the liquid. Bernie picked up the badge with the tongs again and lowered it into the bucket. As he held it there, he turned his head toward Ben. "It's a felony?"

"Is what a felony?" Ben asked.

"What you're planning to do with this." There was a tone in Bernie's voice that Ben hadn't heard since he was a teenager.

His own voice was hardly louder than a whisper when he answered. "Misdemeanor."

Bernie didn't say anything but kept looking at him with something like judgment in his eyes. There was something else there, too. Sympathy, maybe, or concern.

He lifted the block out of the bucket and put it down on the workbench, laid the tongs next to it, and reached for a ball-peen hammer on the pegboard wall. Bernie took a quick glance over his shoulder to make sure Ben hadn't moved, then lifted the hammer high and smashed it down onto the block.

The Lucite shattered with a loud crack, sending tiny fragments everywhere. Ben felt one bounce off his forearm. Bernie's body blocked his view of the badge, so he took a few steps to the side.

"Did it work?"

Bernie held up the badge under the light and used a gloved finger to brush and pick away stray bits of plastic. "Son of a bitch," he said, trying to conceal his grin from Ben. "It looks pretty good."

Ben couldn't look away from the glints of light reflecting gold from his shield.

"There's still some bits of plastic stuck on here." Bernie grabbed a clean shop towel from a box under the bench and put the badge down on top of it. Then he put on a pair of reading glasses and went to work with a small hooked tool that looked like something a dentist might use.

Ben watched him silently while he worked. After about ten minutes, he held the badge up again and examined it in the light. "Looks pretty good," he said. Then something else caught his attention. He tried to work the clasp on the back. "Uh-oh."

"What's the matter?"

"This isn't working. Must be some plastic in the little hinge there." He pointed to the tiny jewelry-like mechanism that allowed the pin to swing out and slip through the grommets on a uniform or badge holder. He gave it a few more gentle tugs. "Nah. It's stuck."

"Anything you can do?"

Bernie put the badge back down on the towel and used a propane torch with a tiny flame to heat the hinge. He kept pulling gently on the pin until the last bit of Lucite let go and it swung free.

"It worked," Ben said.

Bernie put the torch down, but kept rotating the pin. When he saw the question in Ben's eyes, he said, "Gotta keep moving it until it cools off so it doesn't get stuck again."

When he was satisfied that it was okay, he put a tiny dab of some kind of polish on the shop towel, rubbed it over the badge, and buffed it off. Then he gave it to Ben and said, "Be careful."

Ben examined the shield, felt its familiar weight in his hand. "Thank you. Really, I—"

"No problem. But I mean it. Promise me you're going to be careful."

"I will," Ben said. "I promise."

• • •

He found the old badge holders in his patrol bag in the garage. Even though he knew he would only be using the one with the belt clip, he took both of them. The wallet would be preferable, but he wouldn't have anything to put in the empty window slot where the valid ID should be. This time he didn't bother putting the patrol bag back into the trash-can liner and hoisting it back up onto the shelf. After he zipped it up he left it on the floor in the corner. Who knew what he might need next.

Inside, Peter had just finished a yogurt for lunch and was rinsing out the container in the kitchen sink. He didn't say anything to Ben when he came in.

"You okay, Dad?"

"Fine."

Among the many things his father had lost was the ability to conceal his emotions. He was utterly and completely without guile. Sometimes Ben thought the best way to handle things when Peter was upset was to let it go, to pretend like nothing was wrong at all. He didn't want his father to know he could see right through the attempts to hide his feelings, because it would be just one more thing Peter would know he couldn't do anymore. It was kind of like the way he'd wait until Peter was in the other room, where he couldn't see, to make sure the spoon he had washed was actually clean enough to put back in the drawer. There was about a fifty-fifty shot, Ben knew. But it was worth the subterfuge to let his father believe he was still capable of something as simple as washing the dishes.

Now, though, he couldn't walk away. He needed to try to fix this so it wouldn't be hanging over him for the next two hours.

"What's wrong, Dad?" His voice sounded much harsher than he had meant it to.

Peter doubled down. "Nothing." His eyes were narrowed and he stared at the drain in the sink.

"Something's wrong," Ben said, trying to soften his voice. "Tell me what it is." He put a hand on his father's shoulder.

Peter pulled away. "My stomach hurts. I'm going to lie down." He walked around Ben into the hallway and closed the door hard. Not quite a slam, but enough to make his point.

"Shit," Ben said, slapping the counter in frustration. A sharp pain shot through his hand and wrist. He knew he should ice it again, but the idea seemed like too much trouble, so he popped a couple of Advil and sat down at the counter with a cup of coffee and one of Peter's Hershey's bars. If he waited a few minutes, maybe he'd be able to calm down enough to go talk to his father and figure out what was wrong.

He ate a piece of chocolate and checked the burner phone. Still no message. Rob had left him hanging. Again. It felt different this time, though. They were in the middle of arranging a meeting with the last text. Ben wondered if Rob had found the stranger in his room. Even if he hadn't, if the man had somehow gotten up on his own or even with the help of an accomplice and made it out, Rob must have known something was wrong. There had been blood and spit and vomit on the carpeting. Surely in the struggle they had disturbed other things as well. But what if the stranger had gotten out and the cleaning staff had attended to the room? Was it possible that Rob wouldn't have noticed?

It was, Ben decided. It was.

Then why the silence? Maybe the stranger or whoever he was working with was looking for Rob, and maybe they had found him. Maybe Rob had caught a break and he needed to see it through. Maybe Ben was just another problem for Rob to deal with and he'd finally tired of humoring him. Too many maybes.

Ben took the shield out of his pocket, opened the clasp, slid the pin through the holes in the top layer of the black leather holder, and fastened it securely. Then he clipped it onto his belt and tucked his flannel shirttail in behind it.

You feel awkward because Peter has invited Grace inside to watch Ellen. *He's in his chair in the corner and she's on the end of the couch closest to him. You wonder if you should sit down with them. Is that the polite thing to do?*

"Can I get you a cup of coffee or Diet Coke or anything?" you ask.

She smiles and says, "No, thanks. I'm okay."

You wonder if she can tell how surprised you are, how awkward you feel. She's been in at the kitchen counter in the morning half a dozen times now because of the rain or the cold, so it shouldn't seem like a big deal, but for some reason it does.

You realize you're still just standing there looking like an idiot, so you go over and sit on the other end of the couch.

Tom Hanks is talking to Ellen about his new movie, some Da Vinci Code sequel or something, but you're not really paying attention. Grace laughs and Peter laughs with her.

This is good for him, *you think.* This is good.

So why are you so nervous?

After the commercial, Ellen does the thing where she surprises someone with a lot of money. This time it's a special-ed teacher who has been buying art supplies for her students herself because the school has no budget for that kind of stuff. There's a whole big thing about how much she does for them and how they love her and how it's such a struggle to get them what they need. When the guy in the cap comes out with the giant check, the teacher is so shocked and overwhelmed that she starts weeping right there onstage.

You feel yourself starting to get choked up, and you get even more nervous than you already were because what if Grace sees you crying? Especially about something so stupid. You turn your head away toward the bookshelves. You look at the picture of your mother, the other things on the shelf.

When you've finally composed yourself, you cautiously sneak a glance back, hoping she hasn't seen you. Hoping you haven't embarrassed yourself too badly.

But when you look, you see she's pulled a tissue from the box on the coffee table and is drying her own eyes.

"God," she says. "That gets me every time."

Me too, *you think,* me too.

The door to Peter's bedroom was shut. It was almost never closed all the way. Even at night when Ben would watch TV out in the living room, he still left it cracked open in case his father called out or groaned in his sleep. Only when Peter was upset about something did the doorknob ever get a chance to really do its job.

Ben tapped lightly on the door with one knuckle. "Dad?"

There was no answer.

He knocked and said it again, just a little louder. "Dad?"

Still nothing. He delicately turned the knob and cracked the door open.

"It's just me," he said, his voice as soft and gentle as he could make it.

"What?" Peter said.

Ben peeked in and saw his father sitting on the side of his bed, looking out the window into the backyard. "You okay?"

"I'm fine."

"Can I come in?"

"It's your house."

Ben pushed the door open wider and took a tentative step into the room. "No, it's not," he said. "It's your house. I live here so you can take care of me." He knew from experience that line was likely to soften Peter's resolve. And he also knew that it was a petty and manipulative tactic on his part. Reminding his father of the aftermath of the incident, of the days before anyone knew that Peter's forgetfulness was due to something more than his advancing age, was one of the dirtiest tricks in Ben's playbook. Every time he used it, he swore it would be the last. But it never really was.

Peter's stiff posture relaxed slightly, but the shift would have been invisible to anyone other than Ben.

"I'm sorry about before, after I came home. I didn't mean it." Ben had no idea what he was apologizing for, but he had neither the time nor the energy to try to figure it out.

His father looked at him, saw the contrition in his face, and forgave him. Ben could tell. He could see it in his eyes, the same way he'd seen it so many times before.

"I'm sorry, too," Peter said.

"You don't have anything to be sorry for, Dad." This time the sincerity was genuine.

• • •

His good suit was in the back of his closet, hanging in the same dry-cleaning bag it had been in for the past two or three years. The last time he'd worn it was at the funeral of one of his first training officers. A guy named O'Malley. Retired at sixty-five, old for a cop, after spending his last eight or ten years driving a desk. Got a stage-four diagnosis two months after his last day on the job and died six months after that. Had a good turnout for the funeral, though. The chapel at All Souls was standing-room only.

Ben thought about his own funeral often enough. Back in the early days of his recovery, he'd even planned it, wrote down a few songs he thought would be good. It made him feel—not better, exactly, but relieved in a way that none of the other things he tried to focus his attention on did. The prospect of just being done with all of it had been appealing to him then. And he liked the idea of an O'Malley-sized turnout. Hell, he wouldn't have had any trouble topping that, not back then. Hero cop and all. They'd need to get a bigger place. And besides, he wasn't Catholic, so All Souls wouldn't work anyway.

But he didn't think that way anymore. He couldn't say he was happy, really, but he knew his father needed him. That was something. On the rare occasions that he imagined his funeral these days, he didn't hope for the same things he used to. Now, he liked to imagine the place empty, with no one there to remember who he used to be.

When he tried the suit on, the pants were uncomfortably tight and he could barely button the coat. It didn't fit anymore.

He did have an old brown sport coat that still fit, though. It had been tailored more loosely and was still in good shape. With a dress shirt, a nice tie, and the right pair of khakis, it would work. It was the kind of outfit that, back in his detective days, might have raised a lieutenant's eyebrow but would still pass muster.

After his first shave in a month, he put it on and clipped his shield a few inches to the right of his belt buckle. Looking at himself in the mirrored closet door, he knew it would work. Sure, he could use a haircut, but with a little product he could pull it off. It would really work.

FOURTEEN

The last several years had seen a real resurgence for Bixby Knolls. Decades ago, people in Long Beach referred to it as "Uptown," and it was among the first bastions of significant wealth in the city. The Virginia Country Club, on the neighborhood's western edge, was still surrounded by multimillion-dollar homes, just as it always had been. And while the area had never been hit with the downturns that many parts of the city had seen, it had never really generated the kind of trendy heat and coolness of places like Belmont Shore and the East Village. But more recently, as new restaurants and brewpubs and wine shops moved in, that was changing.

DRNK Coffee + Tea was in a small shopping center with a Subway and a dry cleaner and a few other shops. Ben couldn't remember the last time he'd been there. He was pretty sure it was before It's a Grind had failed in its ambitious attempt to become the dominant regional coffee chain. It still looked pretty much the same to him.

He pulled the flap of the jacket back and held it there with a hand in his pants pocket to make sure his shield was clearly visible as he approached the counter. There was only one other customer. An old man with a newspaper, a small coffee, and a muffin, sitting at one of the tables by the window.

The young woman at the counter said, "Hi. Can I help you?"

Ben smiled. "I hope so. I'm investigating a missing person. Is there a manager on duty who I could speak with?" He was careful about what he said. Just the badge was enough to constitute a crime. But if he actually claimed to be a cop, that would make matters significantly worse if it ever caught up to him.

She looked surprised but not troubled. "Let me see, I think Marcus can talk to you." She went in back and came out in less than a minute with a tall and gangly young man who looked to Ben like he couldn't be long out of high school.

"Hi," Marcus said. "I'm the assistant manager."

Ben extended his hand, and Marcus gave it a weak and noncommittal shake. "Is this about Grace?"

"Yes," Ben said. "Has Detective Kessler already been here to talk to you?"

"Yeah." Marcus gestured to an empty table close to the restroom at the back of the shop.

Ben sat down. "I'm afraid I'll have to ask you some of the same questions again. He's running the investigation for the San Bernardino Sheriff's Department, but because Grace lived here in Long Beach, we need to look into it, too." He hoped the kid wasn't a criminal-justice major or an Explorer or anything else that might lead him to suspect that something wasn't quite right with the interview or how carefully Ben was framing his words.

"That's okay," Marcus said. "I just want to do whatever helps."

"Thank you," Ben said. "I appreciate that. And I'm sure Grace will as well."

"I hope so. Can I get you a coffee or a tea?"

"No, that's okay. This should only take a few minutes." He took a fresh notebook out of his inside jacket pocket, opened it, and put it down on the table. "How long did Grace work here?"

"Not very long, actually. A little over two months."

Ben thought back to when she moved into the studio. "That would have been around August and September?"

"Yeah," Marcus said. "I checked the exact dates for the other detective. It was the second week of June to the first week of September."

She'd still been working here when she moved. Her employment here overlapped with her server position at The Attic. That was a good sign. It supported his theory that both the job change and the new housing arrangements were financial choices and not safety related. He made a note in his book, as much to convince Marcus that he was being useful as to record the information. "Did she say why she was switching jobs?"

"It was because she could make a lot more. We hated to see her go, though—she was really nice and everybody liked her. It's hard to keep good people, you know?" He sighed like a fifty-year-old middle manager.

Ben looked at the young barista behind the counter and wondered how long she had worked there. Did Marcus think she was good people? "So would you say you got to know her pretty well?"

"Just workwise. We never hung out or anything."

"Do you know if she hung out with any of the other employees?"

"I don't think so." He turned around in his chair and looked at the barista. "Ashley?"

She looked surprised to hear him call her name. "Yeah?"

"You remember Grace, who used to work here last fall?"

Ashley nodded. "She got that server job at the Attic, right?"

"That's her," Marcus said. "You guys ever hang out or anything?"

"Not really. She wasn't here very long."

"You know if anybody else did?"

"I don't think so. Like I said, she didn't work here very long."

Ben just sat back and listened. It was okay with him if Marcus wanted to do the job for him.

"Yeah, that's what I thought. Thanks." He turned back around and folded his hands on the table, ready for the next question.

"Was she a good employee?"

"Oh, yeah. Always on time, learned everything really quick, cleaned up without having to be reminded. I was sorry to see her go."

It was becoming clear that Marcus relished his small slice of managerial authority. Ben played into it. "Did the rest of the management team feel the same way?"

"Oh, yeah. Hannah, our manager, gave her a really good reference. In our leadership meeting that last week, she even said we needed more staff like her. Hannah doesn't usually gush like that."

Ben had what he'd come for. Grace had been a solid and reliable employee, but apparently hadn't gotten too close to anyone here. He decided to throw out one more question on the off chance Marcus might know more than he realized. "Did you ever meet Grace's boyfriend?"

"No, he never came here that I know of."

"But you knew about him?"

"Only that she was involved with someone."

"She told you about him?"

"Not really. Sometimes guys would hit on her and she always said she had a boyfriend."

It didn't seem to occur to him that not every woman who used that line in that situation was actually involved with someone. "That happen a lot?"

"It happens to most of the girls. A lot of the guys who come in are assholes." When he realized what he'd just said, he nervously turned toward the old man with the muffin, as if worried that he might have been overheard. When he saw that the customer was oblivious, he relaxed again.

"I believe that." Ben shot him a knowing smile. "Thanks for your time, Marcus. You've really been a big help."

"You're welcome, Detective."

They stood up and Ben headed for the door.

"Don't you have a card?" Marcus said behind him.

Ben turned back.

"In case I think of anything else?"

"I'm sorry, I don't. I just ran out. I'm supposed be getting the new ones any day now. I'll drop one off. In the meantime, you can just call the station if you need me, okay?"

"Okay," Marcus said. "I will."

Ben hurried out to the car so he could get away before Marcus realized he hadn't told anyone his name.

. . .

By the time Ben got home, his father seemed to have forgotten about whatever had upset him earlier in the day.

"You look nice," Peter said.

"Thanks, Dad."

"Did something happen? To dress up for?"

"No. I just had to go talk to some people."

"Talk about what?"

"It was about Grace."

Ben could see both the concentration behind his father's eyes and the frustration at not being able to make the connection. "We haven't seen her in a while, remember?"

Peter nodded, but Ben still wasn't sure he got it.

After a few seconds, his face lit up as he made the connection. "Our friend? Who we have coffee with in the morning?"

"Yes, Dad. Grace."

"Oh! We haven't seen her in a long time. Where is she?"

. . .

He didn't want to leave Peter there by himself again, but he didn't think there was any alternative. Bernie probably would have helped, and Ben considered calling him, but he'd already imposed too much. And besides, Bernie would know exactly why he was wearing a coat and tie.

No, Ben thought. *It won't take long.* A quick trip down to Bluff Heights to check out the address of the apartment from Rob's notes and a knock on the door. It was only three o'clock. There probably wouldn't be anybody home to talk to anyway.

When he parked across the street from 307 Orizaba, he was surprised. He expected an apartment building or maybe one of the big old houses that had been subdivided into multiple units after World War II. But it was just a small Craftsman bungalow that couldn't have had more than two or three bedrooms. The lack of an apartment number should have been a clue, but Ben had gone out on lots of calls with addresses that lacked specific unit numbers.

The house was painted two shades of green and seemed well maintained, even though it apparently hadn't been updated in decades. Ben walked under the shadow of a large shade tree in the front yard and up onto the porch. The front door looked like it had been painted more recently than the rest of the house, in a pleasantly contrasting orange. He unclipped the shield from his belt and knocked on the door. No one answered. Thirty or forty seconds later, he tried again. He waited a bit longer and had just turned to leave when he heard the door open behind him.

A woman of about forty, in yoga pants and a sweatshirt, opened the door.

Ben held up his badge and said, "My name's Shepard and I'm—"

"Another detective?" the woman said with raised eyebrows.

"Yes, I'm sorry to bother you. I'm working with Detective Kessler on a missing-persons case."

"Which one was Detective Kessler again?"

It was Ben's turn to raise his eyebrows, but he caught himself, hoping she hadn't registered his surprise. Someone other than Rob had been here. Becerra? It must have been. Who else would have been able to figure out Grace might have lived here?

"Tall guy, white, brown hair?"

"That's both of them."

It wasn't Becerra.

Shit.

"Mustache?"

"Okay," she said. "The first one." Rob had been there first.

"The second one was from San Bernardino, too, right?"

She nodded. "Seemed weird that they'd send two from so far away." Who was the second? The most likely possibility was also the most frightening—the dirty cop Rob was investigating. Ben thought about asking if she remembered his name but didn't want to risk sounding like he didn't already know what was going on.

He gave her the same line he'd given Marcus at the coffeehouse about separate investigations in separate jurisdictions, and it went over just as well here.

"Could we talk inside?" he asked.

She led him into the living room and they sat on opposite ends of the sofa. Her name was Amanda, and she was renting the house with her wife. They had sublet the spare bedroom to Grace for a few months, from the beginning of June until just before she moved into the studio behind his house.

"Did she tell you why she was leaving?" Ben asked.

"She said she wanted to be closer to work. But I think she wanted more privacy, too. I mean, who wouldn't rather have their own place, right?"

"Right." Ben thought about Rob's note about a possible boyfriend, the one he'd abbreviated with only *K.* "Did Kevin spend any time here?"

Amanda looked puzzled. "Kevin?"

169

Ben said, "Her boyfriend? I thought it was Kevin." He thumbed back the pages in his notebook and pretended to search for the name.

"Oh, you mean Kyle?"

"Yes, that's it. I got the *K* right, at least."

She gave him what he thought was a courtesy laugh. "A few times, but they both seemed really self-conscious about it. I think that ended before she moved, though."

"Did she tell you that?"

"I asked her about it once, after he hadn't been here for a while. She said she'd rather not talk about it, so I let it go."

"Did you tell the other detectives about Kyle?"

"Just the first one, with the mustache."

"Was Grace a good roommate?"

"Oh, yeah. Clean. Quiet. Always on time with the rent."

That sounded like her. If someone had asked Ben if she was a good tenant, he probably would have said the same thing.

"Thanks, Amanda," he said. "You've been a big help."

She looked at him as if trying to decide if she wanted to say something that was on her mind. "I hope you find her."

"We will." Ben smiled reassuringly. Something felt familiar. It took him a few seconds to realize he was using what he used to think of as his detective smile, the one he'd practiced to perfection. Smiling with the mouth, but with concern and a touch of sadness in the eyes. Hadn't used it in years, and he nailed it on the first try.

"No. I mean you specifically. You really care about her. I can tell. Those other two guys were assholes."

• • •

Driving home, he felt a fresh pang of loss and something shifting in his head. Somehow, when Rob had told him the bits and pieces of Grace's story, he'd thought of a clear-cut before and after, a bright dividing line between who she used to be and who she was now. Like he had, before and after he'd been shot. Like his father had, before and after his first surgery.

He had assumed that line for her was when she moved into the studio. But that was wrong. After talking to people who'd known her in that window of time between when she left the Inland Empire and when Ben met her, she had been the same woman he'd met a few months later. Was she the same woman she'd been before she ever got involved with Rob and the cop he was investigating?

Ben knew he wasn't the same man he used to be. He'd never chosen to be someone else. That had been completely out of his hands. What was it like for her? Did she feel the same way? Like her life had been broken in two?

She had a new name, a new job, a new home, but maybe she was still the same person she always had been. If so, then this wasn't just about finding her. If she still had that, Ben realized, he'd do anything to help her keep it.

• • •

Ben's hands tingled on the steering wheel as he drove the Volvo up Redondo toward home. An electric buzz coursed through his body. It was the same sensation he used to feel when he caught a big break on a case, the rush of new information, new leads, new possibilities. How many years had it been since he'd felt like this?

Admittedly, he wasn't sure he was any closer to finding Grace, but he'd learned more about her, about who she was, and that felt significant. And he did have one solid new lead—Grace had been involved with someone named Kyle. If Ben could find him, he would likely be of help, not necessarily in finding Grace, but certainly in filling in more of her story.

He knew he should turn everything over to Becerra and let him run with it. It was important, and with the resources of Long Beach PD behind him, he could do much more with the information than Ben could himself. Rob knew what Ben knew, but where was he? And who was the other cop who'd talked to Amanda? Of all the new information, that was the most troubling. Could it be the dirty cop Rob was investigating? It had to be. There was no way someone else from San Bernardino would come all the way to Long Beach.

Rob was the key. Ben needed to talk to him and get him to open up about everything he knew. But he still hadn't replied to that last text. He had to be on to something big. That was the only thing that made any sense. Or was it? Ben thought of that last note he'd copied from the photos. *Talk to B, don't let him get too close.* Rob might have just been ignoring him.

At the north end of Redondo, where it dead-ended at the airport, waiting in the left-turn lane, Ben checked the rearview mirror and caught his reflection. For a moment, he thought he was looking at someone else. Then the car behind him honked and he made the left turn.

FIFTEEN

"I know she's gone," Peter said. He'd been sitting in the Adirondack chair in the backyard, staring at the door to the studio, when Ben got home.

"Of course you do." Ben could tell his father was upset. He didn't know why. Maybe it was connected to what had happened earlier in the day, or maybe it was something new. With the two interviews today, Peter had been home by himself for more than four hours. Ben had come home in between them, but the amount of time he'd been gone was surely the longest since Peter's last surgery.

"It's because of me."

"What do you mean, Dad?"

"I did something bad."

"No, you didn't," Ben said. "You never do bad things."

"Because I'm not a real person anymore."

"I don't understand," Ben said. "Of course you're a real person."

Peter shook his head. "You should put me someplace else so I don't ruin it all."

"Where else could you go?"

"There's places for people like me."

"No, there aren't," Ben lied. He knew all about the places for people like his father, because he'd visited half a dozen of them. Even the nice ones, the ones where selling the house would only pay for two or three years, left him feeling hollowed out, empty of everything except his own guilt for even considering them. "At least not any good ones."

"It doesn't have to be good. Just get rid of me."

Ben put a hand on his father's shoulder. "What's wrong, Dad? Why are you so upset?"

"She left because of me and now you are, too."

"You think I'm leaving?" Ben felt like he'd been punched in the stomach. He squatted down in front of Peter and took both of his father's hands in his own. "I'm not leaving you. I promise. Not ever."

"You got dressed up and didn't come back." The anger in his voice was slipping away.

"I'm sorry, Dad. I wasn't leaving. I'm trying to find Grace."

"Because I made her leave?"

"You didn't make her leave, I promise. She had to go, but it wasn't because of you."

"It wasn't?"

"No way. I think she wants to come back now and I'm trying to help her. We want her to come back, right?"

As Peter nodded, he leaned forward and his expression shifted from darkness to light. "I want to help, too. Can I help?"

"Absolutely."

• • •

There was no rain in the forecast for that evening, so Ben asked his father if he'd like to go for a walk. They'd missed the last few days. Ben blamed the weather, but he knew that wasn't the only reason. Peter was reluctant. His mood had improved, but he still wasn't quite himself.

"You sure you don't want to go?"

"Can we go tomorrow?"

"It's supposed to rain, so we might not be able to."

"I don't think so."

"Okay," Ben said. "Think about it for a little while. We still have some time before it gets dark if you change your mind."

Ben went back into the office and had no sooner sat down and tapped the spacebar to wake up the computer when he saw Peter at the door holding his floppy beige hat.

"Is it too late to walk?" he asked.

They were halfway around the block when Peter stopped and looked toward the sound of the first plane to take off since they'd started out.

Ben knew from the sound it wasn't one of the big jets, but rather a small prop plane. He didn't think his father could tell the difference anymore. They saw it as it emerged from behind a big tree. It began to bank around to the north, and as Peter watched it curve through the sky and wobble, its wings leveling out in front of him, he kept his hand up and waving the whole time. Ben realized it was one of the training flights that would take off, do a big loop around the airport, and approach from the opposite direction, landing in the same spot from which it had just taken off. They'd repeat the pattern five or six times over about an hour and a half. Sometimes he'd sit with his father on the patio long enough to see the whole cycle.

When they were almost home, Peter spotted a man with a dog up the block, maybe twenty yards ahead of them. His face lit up and he pointed.

"That's not Bernie, Dad." He was surprised at his father's mistake and worried about his eyes. Dusk was coming, but it still seemed too light out for that kind of error. For the last couple of years, Peter had been getting injections in his eyes to treat his macular degeneration. Sometimes, at the end of the six-week window between treatments, his vision would start to decline. But it wasn't—

Had they missed the appointment with Dr. Boswell? Ben suddenly remembered the day last week when Peter got up early and got ready for the appointment and it turned out to be the wrong day. One day too early. But they didn't go the next day. They had missed the appointment. Ben had fucked up.

"Shit."

Peter had still been watching the dog, but as soon as he heard the muttered profanity, he turned and asked, "What's wrong?"

"I forgot about your eye appointment. We missed it."

"That's not your fault."

"Yeah, actually it is."

• • •

There was no point in calling the doctor's office on Sunday to reschedule, so Ben wrote a big note with a Sharpie on a yellow pad and taped it to the refrigerator. It wasn't more than ten inches away from the other note for the appointment he'd missed, but he was counting on its size and color to catch his attention in the morning.

Peter had gotten over what was bothering him. Either he'd forgotten, or Ben's self-flagellation over missing the appointment had softened his mood and reengaged his usual sympathies.

He made it through his first two pills with his customary *"Quod"* and *"Erat,"* but when the Double Jeopardy round came on, he held the plastic cup and his Donepezil tablet up in front of himself with a nervous confusion in his eyes.

Ben saw his hesitation and said, "What's wrong?"

"I'm supposed to say something."

"Demonstrandum, Dad. *Demonstrandum."*

"Demon— demon—" He cut himself off in frustration.

As he tried to say the word, Ben remembered. Peter hadn't used the Latin for months. Maybe even a year. "It's okay, Dad. It's okay. Try one more time. Repeat it after me."

Peter nodded.

He spoke clearly and slowly. "Demonstration."

"Demonstration," he said.

Ben saw a wave of relief wash over him as he sat up straight, put the pill in his mouth, and washed it down.

"Little sips, now?"

"That's right. Little sips."

After his father was in bed, Ben sat down in the living room and took out his notebook.

1/15 9:15 pm
~~Quetiapine~~
~~Escitalopram~~
~~Donepezil~~
Dad forgot last part of QED—Slipping?

He couldn't remember the last note he'd made other than the meds for Peter and himself, so he flipped back through the pages to go over them. To his surprise, he discovered he hadn't written anything at all other than the dates and times of his father's medications for the last three days. He hadn't even been keeping track of his own. Had he even been taking them? He must have taken them. But he couldn't remember actually dumping the pills out of their bottles into his hand and swallowing them.

Ben went into the bathroom, took his own meds, and made a point of recording it in the notebook. The more he thought about it, the more convinced he was that he hadn't missed any of his medications.

It had been a good day. For a few hours, he felt better than he could remember feeling for a long time. He'd made some real progress and genuinely believed he might actually be able to find Grace. This was the first time since she'd disappeared that he'd felt optimistic at all.

It was nine thirty when he went to bed, and only five minutes later he was asleep.

• • •

Ben woke early and had a plan for the morning in place before the coffee had even finished brewing. If he got Peter up a little early, he could be at the Marriott by eight. He didn't think it likely that Rob would be out earlier than that. Of course, Ben had no idea what had happened there after he left or what he'd find when he got there. But Rob was still his best shot at putting the pieces together. Ben didn't care anymore about what Rob wanted or who he was worried about getting "too close." If Rob didn't like it, Ben would tell him he was going to the LBPD.

He wasn't quite ready to do that yet, though he wouldn't tell Rob. There were a few more things he wanted to check on himself before he went to Becerra. He needed to talk to Amy again and ask about Kyle. She hadn't said anything about Grace being involved with anyone, but even if she didn't have any direct knowledge of him, she might know something she didn't realize could be useful.

In all likelihood, Kyle was just someone Grace had been briefly involved with before moving on. But he was a loose thread. "You pull on a loose thread," he remembered saying to Jennifer years ago, "and it either comes off in your fingers, or everything starts to unravel."

Ben would go to Becerra, but not until he'd pulled every thread he could find.

As soon as he had Peter set up with breakfast, he showered, shaved, and put on his khakis and his only other dress shirt. He'd need to do a load of laundry if he was going to dress for work the next day. He folded the tie and put it in the pocket of the sport coat. It would be too much if Rob answered the door when he knocked. Without the tie, though, he could just say he had an appointment or something, if Rob asked why he was dressed up. But he wanted to be able to put the tie on in case he needed to use the shield with the front-desk or cleaning staff.

"You look nice," Peter said. He was just finishing his coffee. "You have to go somewhere?"

"I do, Dad. I'll be gone for an hour or two. Will you be okay?"

Peter nodded.

"How's your stomach?"

"Not too bad." He rubbed his belly as if he weren't quite sure that was true.

Ben took Peter's cup and refilled it with coffee, sugar, and Boost. Then he covered the cup with a folded paper towel and put it down on the corner of Peter's place mat on the counter. "This is for later, okay?"

On the way to the Marriott, Ben felt like he was finally on the right track. The pieces of the puzzle weren't exactly all fitting together yet, but he was beginning to see them. It was almost as if Grace was a corner and he had just found the first matching piece.

As he drove east on Spring and emerged from the tunnel under the airport, Ben got the first inkling that something was off as an LBPD black-and-white sped past him. Stopped at the signal at Lakewood Boulevard, he couldn't get a good look at the Marriott parking lot across the street, but there was already a twisting tightness in his stomach. The light changed and he crossed the intersection to see at least a dozen LBPD cruisers crowding the front of the hotel.

The entrance to the parking lot wasn't on Spring, but rather on a connecting road. As Ben turned right onto Airport Plaza Drive, he saw there was also a mobile-command trailer and a coroner's-department van in the crowd of vehicles.

Someone was dead.

Ben turned the Volvo around in the Auto Club parking lot and headed back home.

●　●　●

"Is something wrong?" Peter said through the closed bathroom door.

"No, everything's okay," Ben said, hoping his father wouldn't be able to hear the lie in his voice. "I just need a few more minutes."

He took another lorazepam and washed his face.

"Breathe," he whispered to his reflection in the mirror. "Breathe."

"Can I ask you something?" she says.

You fight the overwhelming urge to cringe, because you know what's coming. "Of course," you say. "Anything."

It's late. You're pretty sure the two of you have never had a conversation this late at night before. Peter had already been in bed for a couple of hours when you heard the soft tapping on the patio door. You were surprised to see her, but happy to help when she told you that she'd locked herself out of the studio. She'd been planning to meet some friends for a late dinner, but realized she'd left her keys inside when she tried to get into her car. You opened the door for her and they were right there on the counter in the kitchenette. Instead of picking them up, she put her bag down and kicked off her shoes. She'd been outside for half an hour trying to figure out another way to get inside so she wouldn't have to bother you, and now she was too late to meet her friends. She'd already texted them to say she wouldn't be able to make it after all.

You felt bad, told her not to worry about knocking no matter what time it was. The two of you chatted for a few minutes, then the question.

"What happened when you got hurt?"

"Rob didn't tell you?"

"Only that you got shot and retired early." She can see the weight of it on you and it looks like she's sorry she's asked. "It's okay. I didn't mean to pry."

"No, it's all right." You smile at her, but it feels awkward. Still, though, you want to answer. "I figured you would have Googled it."

"I thought about it, but that seemed kind of intrusive."

You nod, a little surprised. "I got shot in the head."

"Oh my god."

You raise your finger to the little scar on your cheek. "It went in the back, came out here."

"That's from a bullet?"

You nod.

"It's so small."

You turn your head and tap your finger on the indentation in the back of your skull. "Feel this."

She gently rubs her fingertips over it. Her eyes widen but she doesn't say anything. You try to remember the last time anybody who wasn't a doctor touched you like that and draw a blank.

"Does it still hurt?"

"Not the scars so much, but lots of other stuff hurts."

"I thought bullets made a small hole where they go in and a big one where they come out."

"Sometimes they do. Sometimes not."

"How long did it take you to get better?"

"I spent two years learning to walk and talk again."

"But you're okay now?"

"Not really, but I can fake it well enough that most people can't tell."
You laugh softly. She doesn't.

"Is that enough?" The question is full of both sadness and curiosity.

You shake your head. "No, but I'm still working on it."

You try to read her face. She's been focused on you, but just for a moment you can see that she's thinking about something else, too. You want to ask what it is, but you don't want to pry. If she wants to tell you, she will.

"Do you ever just want to give up?" she asks. There's more than curiosity in her voice now, and you can see the weight she's carrying, how much she needs to let go of it.

"Every day."

"Why don't you?"

"My dad needs me." It's not the answer she's hoping for. She tries to hide her disappointment but you can still see it. You want to tell her something else, something that will help her, but you've got nothing.

"Thanks, Ben," she says.

"For what?"

"Letting me in."

Peter was still waiting outside the bathroom when Ben finally felt composed enough to come out.

"What's wrong?"

"I'm having kind of a bad day, Dad."

"Hurting?"

Ben nodded. He was hurting, but not really in the way his father thought. There was a headache, but most of the pain wasn't physical. Seeing the callout at the Marriott had rattled him badly. It was as if the walls of every carefully constructed and managed compartment in his psyche had been shredded, and everything he'd been so carefully containing had spilled out and was roiling in an uncontrollable turbulence. He didn't feel like he could even get a hold on anything, let alone begin the arduous task of getting everything he'd been so carefully containing—life before, the trauma, the recovery, his dad, Grace, the mess of his life—back under control and compartmentalized again. But he needed to keep his father from seeing any of it. There was no way he'd be able to maintain even a semblance of control if his father started spiraling, too.

"Yeah," Ben said. "My head is really bad."

"Oh, no. Did you get some medicine?"

"I did, yes." Three lorazepam and two Advil. The PTSD/TBI full house. Hopefully, he'd feel them start to kick in soon. He would have taken four of the antianxiety pills instead of three, but even though they'd surely provide relief, he probably wouldn't be able to stay awake.

"You should lie down."

Peter was right. He should. "I will. I just need to get you something to eat first."

"No, that's okay. I'm not hungry. You rest."

"I'm going to fix you something just in case."

Peter followed Ben into the kitchen. Ben poured him a cup of coffee and Boost and turned to put it on the counter. He stopped when he saw the cup he'd left before going to the Marriott. The paper towel was still on top of it. That was when he realized it had been less than an hour since he left.

Peter opened the refrigerator and found a Hershey's bar. He held it up so Ben could see. "I'm okay. I have food."

"You sure you don't want some yogurt or some more oatmeal?"

"No, this is good."

Ben acquiesced and went into his bedroom. He took off his shoes, lay down on top of his bedspread, and stared at the ceiling. The anti-anxiety meds were starting to kick in.

Before he had a chance to think about anything, though, Peter knocked lightly on the door and pushed it open. In his hands he held his favorite blanket, the one his wife had crocheted twenty years ago. He spread it over Ben, leaned over, kissed him on the forehead, and said, "Rest."

Not long after Peter closed the door softly behind him, Ben rolled over on his side, clutched his mother's blanket to his chest, and began to weep.

SIXTEEN

It turned out that even three lorazepam were enough to put him to sleep. He woke an hour and a half later, angry that he hadn't been able to keep himself awake. The mild headache he'd had earlier had developed into the full-blown ice-pick-through-the-forehead pain he used to feel when the cluster headaches were at their worst, during the early days of his rehabilitation. He went into the bathroom and swallowed two more Advil.

The first thing he did when he came out was to check his burner for word from Rob. Then his regular phone for a text or voicemail from Jennifer or Becerra. There wasn't anything from anyone.

Was it possible that the death at the Marriott had nothing to do with Rob? Yes, but Ben didn't think it was remotely likely. That would be way too much of a coincidence. Especially considering that when he was there, someone had entered Rob's room prepared for violence. He wondered if it might have been the stranger who'd been killed. Maybe he died on the floor and they had only just discovered the body. That didn't seem to fit, though. If the guy wasn't able to get away, Rob would have found him. And even if Rob hadn't come back to the room, housekeeping would have gone in to clean. The only way Ben could figure that it could have been the stranger was if someone had found him, left him there, and then hung the "Do Not Disturb" sign on the door. That was a possibility, but it didn't seem likely.

Ben was afraid to think about what he believed was the most probable situation. That when he'd been in Rob's room, the stranger had in fact come to kill Rob, and that either he or someone else had come back and completed the job.

It was the mobile-command unit that concerned Ben more than anything else. A hotel room makes for a very contained and controllable crime scene. The trailers were usually only brought in for large or complex scenes that would require a significant amount of time and manpower to fully process. Or for multiple murders. Or if the victim was of great importance or someone whose death would be particularly interesting to the press.

Like an out-of-town detective working a case in Long Beach.

What if Rob really was dead?

Ben thought about calling Jennifer and telling her everything he'd found out since the last time they talked. She'd be angry with him. But if there was a murder in Room 406, they would be certain to place him at the scene. If by some miracle he had managed to get out of the room without leaving any physical evidence of his presence, they were sure to see him on the hotel's security recordings. They would definitely have him in the lobby and the elevators, and probably even going into and out of the room.

He should call her and try to get out in front of it. That was surely the wisest course of action.

There was just one thing he needed to do first.

Amy was probably at work, so he thought about a text message, but decided the urgency of the situation warranted an actual call. He tapped his thumb on her name in the contacts on his phone and waited to connect. After the third ring, he got her outgoing voicemail message. He paused long enough for a single deep breath, then said, "Hello, Amy. This—this is Ben Shepard. Quick question: Did Grace ever mention anyone named Ky . . . Kyle? His name came up in the investigation and I need to get a hold of him as soon as I can. Thanks." On top of the stutter, he caught himself slurring the last few *s* sounds, but hoped she wouldn't notice.

Headache. Slurred speech. Ben knew he should be keeping track of the symptoms. But he didn't want to deal with the notebook now. There was too much going on, too much to figure out before he went to Jennifer. Or before someone knocked on the front door.

• • •

Ben spent twenty minutes in the shower with his head under the hot water. By the time he got out, the heat and the extra Advil had cut the pain in his head by about half. While he was in there, he figured out how he might be able to find out what happened at the hotel. It would be a bad idea to contact anyone at the department. Just one more thing that could possibly connect him to the crime scene. But he was certain that the media would already be paying attention. There was a columnist at the *Press-Telegram* he used to know pretty well when he was still working. Ben had bumped into him at CVS a few weeks earlier and they'd agreed they should get together for lunch sometime soon. Of course, Ben had never followed through, but it was a good excuse to reach out.

He went back into the office and sat down in front of the computer. A phone call would have been more expedient, but he didn't think he could maintain a tone that sounded casual enough. And he was pretty sure he'd never sent a text message to him before and that might seem odd. It would have to be an email.

Hey Tim,

Sorry it's taken so long to get back to you. I'd love to get that lunch we talked about a few weeks ago if you're still up for it. What's your schedule like?

I'm pretty wide open so let me know what works for you.

BTW, I just drove past the airport Marriott. A big crime scene there. From the looks of it, somebody got killed. Any idea what happened?

Best,

Ben Shepard

He hit "Send," hoping it wouldn't take too long for an answer. Newspaper guys had to be punctual with email replies, right?

• • •

The response to the phone call came first. Ben saw the name on the screen and answered right away. "Amy," he said. "Thanks for getting back to me so quickly."

"I'm on my break at work."

"I won't keep you, then. Did Grace ever mention someone named Kyle?"

"Yeah, one time. It didn't seem like anything, though. I'd completely forgotten about it until your message."

"Tell me about it."

"We were at her place. Watching Netflix. I think it was *Master of None*? She paused it because she had to go to the bathroom. While she was in there, her phone rang. I looked at it and took it over to the door in case she wanted to answer, you know? So I knock on the door and tell her someone named Kyle is calling and do you want to take it? She says to let it go to voicemail. When she comes out I ask her who Kyle is. 'Just a guy I know,' she says. 'From where,' I ask. She laughs and says,

'San Pedro.' She knew it wasn't what I meant. Before I could push her for more, she unpaused the show and that was pretty much it."

"Did you ever tell anyone else about that?"

She thought for a moment. "No one."

"Are you sure about that?"

"I'd forgotten all about it until you asked."

"Did she ever mention him again?"

"No. I thought about asking her after we were done with the show, but I forgot and that was pretty much it."

"And no last name?"

"It just said *Kyle* on the phone, and she never said it."

"Thanks, Amy," Ben said. "That's a big help."

"It is? Good. Have you found anything else out?"

"A few things." He filled his voice with as much feigned optimism as he could. "I'm getting closer."

"You'll tell me, right? When you find her?"

"Absolutely."

Ben wished he could get a look at her phone records. He wondered if Becerra had tracked Kyle down. Probably not. In all likelihood, he'd already moved on to his next case. Ben wouldn't blame him if he had. He knew the job. You worked a case as long as you had leads to pursue, and when they dried up, you put it aside and worked something else until you got another break. And if another break never came along, well, there was no shortage of new cases.

He'd need more to find Kyle than knowing he was from San Pedro, if he even really was. Who could know what Grace might have meant when she said that? Maybe she met him there, or maybe he worked there, or grew up there. Maybe. He needed more to go on, and he didn't know where to find it. What really mattered, though, was that Ben was confident that he was the only one who knew about Kyle and the San Pedro connection.

Ben wasn't sure what else to do at that point, so he sat with Peter in the living room and watched a movie he'd never heard of, with Morgan Freeman and Diane Keaton playing an old married couple who had to move out of the New York apartment they'd shared for decades. It wasn't a great movie, but the actors were appealing, and the fear it instilled in him of ever having to move out of the house was enough distraction to push everything he'd been thinking to the side for a little while.

• • •

By dinnertime, the LBPD still hadn't knocked on the front door, so Ben was allowing himself a sliver of hope that he'd been wrong about what he had seen at the hotel that morning. His headache was gone and his anxiety had normalized. He couldn't deny the fact that he was experiencing some disconcerting symptoms. All the stress of the last several days was taking a toll. It was possible, he thought, that he was making too much of what he had witnessed. The Marriott was a big hotel. They had hundreds of rooms, conferences, meetings, all kinds of events. Thousands of people must go in and out every day. To think that the police response he had seen there this morning was connected to him might very well be grandiose thinking, even paranoia.

Ben was feeling better, carefully recompartmentalizing everything, just as Emma had taught him to do in their sessions. The thing she always came back to with him was the idea of managing his thoughts and feelings the same way he used to manage a case. Don't jump to conclusions. Don't personalize. Don't rush to action. Be careful with your instincts—trust them, but only act on them after significant analysis. Step back. Strive for objectivity. Consider other perspectives. And breathe. Always breathe.

He felt a kind of calmness he wouldn't have believed possible only a few hours ago. Then he sat down at the desk in the office and checked his email.

Ben,

Happy to get lunch. Maybe Monday or Tuesday
next week? Just tell me where.

As for the hotel, you were right. There was a
homicide. A cop from San Bernardino. Don't have
much more, but there are rumors he used to work
for LBPD. No ID yet. Hope he wasn't someone
you knew.

Tim

When Ben read the email, the piercing pain behind his eyes
exploded and the room began to spin. He rolled the chair back away
from the desk and leaned forward, putting his head between his knees.
For a few seconds it worked and the spinning slowed. It seemed safe to
sit up again. But as soon as he began to move, something in his stomach
let go and he vomited on his feet.

SEVENTEEN

The rain came again in the middle of the night. Ben was awake in bed. He had nodded off two or three times, but the sleep never took hold, and after half an hour or so, he found himself each time staring at the ceiling again. He got up before dawn and sat at the table in the dining room, watching through the patio door as the darkness gradually lifted and the rain continued to fall.

The coffee maker had just started dripping and he was filling the kettle to boil water for Peter's oatmeal when he heard them.

Nobody knocks on a door like a cop.

Whoever it was, though, either wasn't very sharp or hadn't done their homework. You knock on a door at seven thirty in the morning when you want to catch someone to question them before they go to work. It's a courtesy so you don't have to interrupt them at their job. But if you know you're going to arrest them, you go earlier, before the sun comes up, so you get them while they're still sleeping. Anybody who knew him or who had been watching should have known he'd be at home most of the day with his father, and rousting him early for an interview wouldn't be a courtesy at all, just an annoyance that would complicate the situation and make him less forthcoming and willing to talk. It didn't make any sense. Was somebody trying to rattle him?

It wasn't Long Beach at the door—they would have known better— so he was glad he'd already put on his shoes.

Ben grabbed his phone, activated the voice-recorder app, and slipped it in the pocket of his T-shirt. With his left foot planted firmly behind the door, he put his hand on the knob and opened it six inches, bracing it with his shoulder. Whoever was on the other side might still be able to get in, but they'd have to be willing to knock him over to do it.

"Yeah?" Ben said.

"Mr. Shepard?" The cop on the other side was tall, with dark hair and a good suit to go along with a deputy-sheriff's badge. There was a younger, blonder cop in a cheaper suit behind him. "I'm Matthew Lopez, from the San Bernardino Sheriff's Department. We need to ask you a few questions." He didn't introduce the other man. You always introduce your partner if you want a comfortable witness. You don't if you want to play alpha-dog intimidation games.

"About what?"

"We're following up on a case Rob Kessler was working on." Lopez smiled amiably, but Ben could see something darker behind his eyes. "Could we come inside? It's coming down pretty hard out here."

They were on the porch. It was covered.

"No," Ben said.

"That's okay. Would you mind stepping out onto the porch?"

"Yes, I would mind."

Lopez stopped smiling.

"Are you going to arrest me?"

The younger cop made a soft grunting noise, and Lopez shot him a sharp glance over his shoulder. "No, Mr. Shepard, not at this time."

Ben took the phone out of his shirt pocket, swiped left on the lock screen, and snapped a few photos of their faces. "Then we're done here."

He closed the door and threw the bolt. His knees buckled, but he managed to catch himself on the knob and remain on his feet.

"What's wrong?"

The sound of Peter's voice startled him. "Nothing, Dad. Just some guys knocking on the wrong door. How about some breakfast?"

• • •

After they had eaten—Ben had a bowl of oatmeal, too, something he hadn't done in ages—Peter said his stomach was hurting and he'd like to rest a little more before he got started on his cleaning.

At the desk, Ben swallowed a lorazepam and wrote *MATTHEW LOPEZ* on the yellow pad he'd been using for his notes on the investigation. Then he underlined it. Then he underlined it again.

Something was wrong about them showing up at the door this morning. When he heard the knock, even though he questioned the timing, he'd expected it to be the Long Beach Homicide detail. Not Jennifer, of course. If she was next up in the rotation, the investigation of Rob's murder would go to someone with no personal connection to the case. Then again, maybe no one knew how connected Ben was to Rob. He'd told Jennifer about talking to him, but that was when things were a lot less complicated than they were now. Maybe it would be a good thing if Jennifer caught the case.

He figured that depended on why Lopez came to see him. The San Bernardino cop would have no jurisdiction in Rob's murder case, and unless he was a complete idiot, he'd stay away from Ben if he were a suspect or even a person of interest in the killing. It could be that Lopez was just a loose cannon who wanted a piece of someone he thought was involved in the murder of a fellow deputy.

But Rob was Internal Affairs now. IA guys didn't inspire much loyalty, except maybe within their own squad. It wasn't like in the movies, where they were just about always portrayed as the evil mortal enemies of the rank and file, but they didn't make a lot of friends, either. Lopez didn't seem like IA. Ben was wary of profiling, but he seemed like a narc. He had the swagger and tough-guy posturing in his physicality. It was obvious he was trying to underplay it, but when Ben didn't go along with the script, it ruffled Lopez's feathers. He tried not to let it show, but Ben pissed him off.

Had he made himself an enemy, Ben wondered? No. Either Lopez was already an enemy or he wasn't. The encounter on the porch wouldn't have been enough to tip that scale one way or the other.

The big question was what to do now. He didn't have anything else to go on in his search for Grace. He wanted to find Kyle, but there was nothing he could think of that would get him any closer, not with his limited resources.

He was hesitant to contact the police before he had a solid plan, but what about Becerra? How involved would he be in the investigation of Rob's murder? The detective already knew Rob was connected to Grace. And Jennifer said she'd reach out, too. Whoever was working Rob's case would know about it by now.

Maybe the best thing to do would be to contact Becerra and tell him what he'd found out about Kyle and about Grace's previous job and home. The only problem with that would be explaining how he found the information to begin with. He couldn't tell him that he'd broken into the hotel room, photographed Rob's files, and left a man bleeding on the floor.

But he could say he learned about Kyle from Amy. That wouldn't even be a lie. There was a slight risk that Becerra would follow up with her, but was it likely that he'd press her hard enough to discover who mentioned the name Kyle first?

Shit. It was all such a huge clusterfuck.

He closed his eyes and listened to the rain pattering on the roof. The sound calmed him, so he just sat and focused on his breath for a few minutes.

In and out.

He rolled the chair a foot or two back from the desk and rested his hands in his lap.

In and out.

He noticed the tension he was holding in his shoulders, the tightness in his neck.

In and out.

He noticed the hollow feeling in his stomach.

In and out.

He noticed the dull ache in his right hand, and his mind started to drift to the stranger in the hotel room. He acknowledged that memory and gently brought his focus back to his breath.

In and out.

In and out.

In and out.

Ben brought his attention back to the room, to the sound of the rain, and slowly opened his eyes.

There were really only two things that mattered right now. Keeping his father and himself safe and finding Grace.

When Ben checked on Peter, he found him still napping on his bed. Ben eased the bedroom door closed and walked softly to his own bedroom, where he eased that door closed, too. He went to the side of his bed and sat down. Then he reached out and slid the drawer open. The Glock and its magazine were right where he had left them. He picked up the pistol and slid the magazine into the well in its grip until it clicked into place.

But he didn't chamber a round.

Not yet.

Your father gets up to go to the bathroom and leaves you and Grace sitting at the patio table.

"What was he like before?" she asks.

"He was nice," you say.

She smiles. "He still is."

"Smart, too." He really was, you think. You didn't think so when you were younger. You always got annoyed at the way he seemed to have an answer for every question, and even more annoyed when they inevitably turned out to be right. There's a pang of guilt in your chest when you think of how little time you spent with him in those last few years before your mom got sick. Once a month, maybe, you'd come over for dinner. And that was only because Kate . . . You saw your mom a little more often, even after she left the department. She had been a cop for a long time. She knew what it was like. And even though she said you didn't have to hold back with your father, that he understood the weight you carried, you were never comfortable really letting him in. You remember the time you told him about a little boy who'd been repeatedly abused by his stepfather with his mother's consent, and the pain you saw in your father's eyes. You never wanted to see that pain again, so you held back. Eventually, you understood how hard that was, and how it got easier if you kept your distance. So you kept it.

You realize you're drifting away and worry that Grace has noticed. If she has, she doesn't give you any indication, and even though you know the awkwardness you're suddenly sensing is self-inflicted, you feel the need to fill it with the first thing that comes into your head. "He wrote a book once," you say.

"Really?"

"Yeah. It was about World War I."

"Like a textbook?"

"No, it was nonfiction, but it was the story of this one group of soldiers that he followed all the way through the war and then for a while after it ended."

"Wow. Did you read it?"

"Yeah, but I was too young. I was in high school. Thought it was boring."

"You should read it again."

"I wish I could. It's out of print. He used to give them to anybody who asked. We thought he had more in his office at school, but after he retired, we could never find them. Ten boxes of books and I went through every one again and again and couldn't find a single one of his."

"He gave away all the copies of his own book?"

"That's my dad."

Ben didn't really know what to do next. There wasn't anything he could come up with that might help him get closer to locating Grace. He had a lead, sure, but no real way to pursue it. At the very least, a conversation with the LBPD was surely going to take place soon, but he decided to let that come to him because he had no idea where it would lead. Bernie had been willing to stay with Peter, when Ben told him he'd have to go in to the station for a few hours sometime in the next few days, but he feared he was being wildly optimistic. There was a real chance he'd be gone longer than a few hours. What if he'd hurt that stranger more seriously than he thought? What if they tried to hang Rob's murder on him? He couldn't discount that possibility. It was all too much for him to process.

Just as the anxiety found a foothold and began to pull at the edges of his focus, his phone rang. *Boswell*, the screen read. Ben picked it up. "Hello?"

"Hi, Mr. Shepard?"

"Yeah."

"I'm calling to confirm your appointment with Dr. Boswell at one today."

For a moment, he was offended that they thought it necessary to remind him, as if they were implying that he wasn't capable of getting his father there on his own. Which, of course, he wasn't, as he had so clearly demonstrated a few days earlier. "Yes, we'll be there." He didn't bother pointing out that it wasn't his appointment at all, but his father's. What would be the point?

Peter was in the living room, sweeping the hardwood floor in front of the couch.

"Hey, Dad?"

His father looked at him, surprised like he'd been caught doing something he shouldn't.

"Thanks for cleaning up."

"You're welcome."

"I'm sorry," Ben said. "But I forgot we need to take you to the eye doctor today."

"For this?" He raised a finger and touched his eyelid.

"Yeah."

Peter's shoulders slumped. "Is it time now?"

"We have to go in about an hour."

He looked at his son, trying to smile back at him, then gently lowered the broom to the floor and went into his bedroom to change his clothes.

• • •

Ben was relieved when his father did slightly better on the vision test than he had the last appointment. Though the trajectory of Peter's macular degeneration was a long downward slope, there were plateaus and even a few occasional upticks. The treatments, as awful as they were, still seemed to be working. With everything that had been going on, it was a relief to have a bit of good news.

The office was busy, so even after they did the retinal imaging and the medical assistant had put in the drops and they'd waited twenty minutes for Peter's eyes to dilate, they still had to wait another half hour in the small windowless exam room for the doctor. Usually Ben tried to read something while they waited, but today he couldn't focus. He always felt like the wait was harder for him than for his father, then felt guilty since he knew it was probably because Peter didn't remember what was coming.

Up until his father's second-to-last surgery, Ben would always excuse himself and go out into the waiting room. But with the most recent cognitive decline, his father had become more fearful and more easily agitated, so Ben sucked it up and sat there for the whole procedure.

When Dr. Boswell came in, Ben stood and shook his hand. He tended to get along much better with his father's doctors than he did with his own, partly because they genuinely seemed to be friendlier people and partly because he took better care of his father than he did of himself.

After he greeted Ben, Dr. Boswell turned to Peter and shook his hand, too. "How are you doing, Peter?"

"Hanging in there," Peter said pleasantly, as he always did.

The doctor turned to the computer, examined the retinal images on the monitor, and said, "This looks very good." Then he turned down the lights and looked into Peter's eyes, both through a device mounted to the wall on a swing arm and through a handheld lens. "It looks like the Eylea is still working." He turned to the medical assistant and said, "We'll do both eyes."

He left the room while the young woman prepped Peter with different eye drops. Ben watched his father with a kind of admiration. He wasn't sure how he did it. Maybe he wasn't fully aware of what was coming, but even going back a few years, to when they started with Dr. Boswell and he hadn't experienced much memory loss at all, he'd never complained or showed any hesitation. They even used to laugh when Ben got squeamish and went out to the waiting room until they were done.

A few minutes later, Dr. Boswell came back into the room, rolled his stool over, and inserted the retractor into Peter's left eye. Ben still couldn't help but think of the end of that old movie, *A Clockwork Orange*.

But it got even worse.

Dr. Boswell said, "Look down and to the right," and then inserted a needle into the sclera of Peter's eye and injected the medication.

Ben had seen his father go through this almost a dozen times now and still winced and shuddered with the same intensity as the very first time he'd watched it happen.

Before he'd even fully recovered his composure, they were done. Dr. Boswell was shaking Peter's hand again and saying, "We'll see you in six or seven weeks, okay?"

How his father managed to smile warmly and say "Thank you" after having a needle jabbed into each of his eyes, Ben would never understand.

• • •

The voicemail message from Jennifer had been left shortly after they got home. Ben didn't hear the phone because he'd turned the ringer off while they were at the appointment and forgotten to turn it back on when they left. It was another hour and a half before he realized what he'd done and found the message.

When Peter's eyes were dilated, he was always worried about doing something that might hurt them. Ben explained, as he always did after the appointments, that he didn't have to worry about anything except being uncomfortable, but he still always went out of his way to make sure all of the blinds were closed and the lights turned off for a few hours after an eye appointment. It helped Peter relax.

It was only after his father was settled in the darkened living room watching *Walk the Line* on one of the cable channels that Ben thought to check his phone. As awful as it was to watch his father get the shots in his eyes, at least it was a distraction that allowed him to substitute a tamer anxiety for the one he felt rushing back when he saw the message waiting on his phone.

"Hi, Ben," she said. "You've probably already heard this by now, but if you haven't, I'm afraid I have some bad news. Rob Kessler was murdered." She paused. "Dave Zepeda is the primary on the case and he needs to talk to you. Can you get someone to take care of your dad for a few hours tomorrow? Give me a call as soon as you can and let me know."

He held the phone in his hand and stared at it for a long time.

If they wanted him to get someone to look after Peter, that meant they were expecting him to go to the station. That wasn't a good sign. But they also let Jennifer give him a heads-up, so he didn't know what to make of it. Maybe they were going to charge him and she was just trying to make things go as smoothly as possible.

No. He trusted Jennifer more than anyone in the department. If they were planning a takedown, she wouldn't help them with it.

Still, he thought, he could say no, that he didn't have anyone who could stay with Peter while he went to the station, that they'd have to come to the house if they wanted to talk. If they agreed to that, he would feel a lot less pressure, knowing it meant they were more interested in an interview than an interrogation.

What would Jennifer say if he just asked her what was going on? Would she tell him? He wanted to believe she was still his friend, but what evidence did he have? A pity lunch every month or two wasn't much to go on.

"Stop," he whispered. "Just stop."

He called Jennifer back.

"What's going on?" he asked.

"Zepeda needs to talk to you about Rob."

"What happened?"

"Someone killed him." She wasn't saying much.

"At the Marriott, right?"

"Yes."

"I met him there a couple of times." He wanted to be as honest as he could. But in the back of his mind, he knew it would be better to admit he'd been there so it wouldn't seem like he was holding anything back.

He half expected her to say she already knew that, but she didn't. "It was pretty ugly. Someone cut his throat while he was sleeping."

It surprised Ben that she told him that. He expected her to withhold any specifics. Maybe he was being paranoid and they weren't looking at him as a suspect at all. "Jesus," he said. If she told him that, maybe he could push a little further. "Any suspects?"

"That's why we need to talk to you. The only thing he seemed to have going on here was your missing-persons case. We're hoping you might know something that can help us get more of a handle on that."

Ben sighed loud enough that Jennifer heard it through the phone. "What was that?"

"Nothing. I was just worried."

"About what?" she said. "Do you think we were looking at you for it?"

"No," Ben said, embarrassed. "Not really, no."

She was silent a moment before she asked, "Are you all right? I know this has been a lot of stress for you. Is it triggering any of the old symptoms?"

"I'm doing okay. I mean, I'm worried about Grace, but . . ." He lost the thought briefly, but recovered. "But I'm okay." He knew she heard the stutter. Before she could ask anything else, he added, "What time do you want me to come in tomorrow?"

"Let me check with Zepeda. We can probably come to you. Would that be better?"

"Really, I'm okay," Ben said, certain she wouldn't believe him.

• • •

An hour after the end of the call, Ben had four and a half pages of notes that covered everything he'd learned from the time he realized Grace was missing until he found out that Rob had been murdered. Even the stranger in the hotel room. He felt comfortable taking his chances with that. The only thing he left out was his shield. He would tell them he'd talked to Marcus and Amanda, and even that he told them he was looking into Grace's disappearance. Just not that he had impersonated a police officer. Maybe it would come up in the subsequent investigation, and if it did, he'd admit to it then. But maybe it wouldn't and he'd be spared that indignity.

The notes were almost complete when he heard Peter shuffling through the dining room toward the office. Ben got up and saw that he'd put his sunglasses back on. With the blinds closed and lights off, it was so dim that he was using his hand on the chair backs to guide himself past the table.

"Hey, Dad, what's up?"

"Could I have another one?"

"Another one of what?"

"To drink?"

"Coffee?"

Peter nodded.

"Of course. I think maybe we should take these off, though." Ben reached out and delicately slipped the old Ray-Bans off of his father's face. His pupils were still three times their normal size and he squinted as his eyes found Ben's own.

"Is it okay?"

"Does it seem too bright in here?"

"No."

"Then it's okay."

Ben went into the kitchen and poured half a cup of coffee into his father's mug. Reaching for the Boost to top it off, he realized there was only one empty bottle on the counter. There should have been two by now. *Shit.* His father would be low on calories for the day, and there wasn't enough afternoon left to make up the deficit.

• • •

After dinner and their walk and their evening meds, Ben went over the notes again to prepare for the meeting with Zepeda and Jennifer in the morning. He was exhausted, but there was a sense of relief, too. Nothing was really resolved. Rob was dead. Grace was still missing. But talking to Jennifer had made him feel better. She still had his back. He would talk to her tomorrow and she'd take some of the weight off his shoulders. Maybe finding out about Kyle would be enough for Becerra to track down Grace. Or maybe she'd actually escaped and was far enough away from all this to find some real freedom. As much as he missed her and needed to know she was safe, he also understood that none of this was really about him. The old Ben Shepard was the hero in the heart of the action, but the new Ben was just a supporting player in someone else's story.

He took the shield out of his pocket and put it away in the top drawer of the desk.

● ● ●

That night, there was no moon and the clouds had cleared out to make way for the next storm. Ben sat in the Adirondack chair and looked up at the sky. Even with all the light pollution, he could still see more stars than he had in a long time.

"Like eight or nine months," you say.

"And it's all just gone?" You've never seen Grace look as sad as she does now.

"It's kind of like there's me before, and then there's just this giant empty hole, and then there's me after and I'm someone else, someone broken and—" You stop yourself before lapsing completely into self-pity.

When it's clear that you aren't going to continue, she says, "That must be awful."

"The worst part is what I lost before I got shot. There's like six months that I can't remember at all before it happened. People told me things, tried to fill in the lost time, but it's still . . . I don't know. I can't really describe it." You think of Kate, what she told you about those six months, but put it out of your head as quickly as you can. "It's just gone."

She looks away, across the yard, at your mother's jasmine planted along the fence. "Sometimes I wish I could forget a few months."

"What do you mean?" you say, thinking that maybe she'll open up and share something about before she came to Long Beach.

But she doesn't. She turns back to you, but she seems further away now. "Maybe forgetting isn't like I imagine."

EIGHTEEN

Ben called Jennifer early and told her he'd rather meet at the station. He left Peter with Bernie and Sriracha and drove the Volvo downtown. Something still didn't feel quite right about parking in one of the spaces reserved for visitors. It had been two or three years since he'd been inside the building, and he hadn't been upstairs to the Homicide Squad since he was still on the job.

Jennifer had told him to let her know when he arrived so she could come downstairs and meet him, but he wanted to spend a few minutes inside by himself before he did that. He wasn't prepared for the odd sense of dissonance he felt as he checked in and picked up his visitor's pass. At least the desk sergeant wasn't anyone he knew. It was a bit like when he'd moved from the rehab center back into his father's house and he realized it was possible to feel both comfort and discomfort at the same time. It was more intense here, though. He hadn't lived at home since he'd been a teenager, but this was the place he most associated with his previous life. This was the place that made the old Ben Shepard who he had been. The place that had given him his identity.

"Hey, Ben," she said.

He had been so lost in thought that he hadn't noticed Jennifer come around the corner from the hallway. "I was just going to call you," he said.

"The desk let me know you were here. You want to go upstairs?"

In the elevator, she said, "How's your dad doing?"

Ben considered his answer. He'd promised himself he was going to be as honest as he could. "He seems to be doing pretty good, but when I get stressed about something, he knows and it gets him, too. I can't hide as much from him as I think I can." He could see she wasn't expecting his frankness, but he continued. "And he can hide more from me than I think he can. It's pulling him down, too, even if I can't really see it."

The door opened and she led him down the hallway to the conference room that the various squads of the Violent Crimes Division shared. Ben remembered the layout, but everything else had changed. New paint. New furniture. New aesthetic. If he didn't know better, he could easily believe he was in a midlevel insurance company instead of a police station. Only a few years gone, and everything felt different.

Until Dave Zepeda came in and sat down. He was old school all the way. The burly old detective had already been crusty and grizzled when Ben graduated from the academy. He extended his leathery hand across the table. "How's it going, Ben?"

"Not bad."

"Been a long time. Five years?"

"A little longer." Ben felt like he had the first time he came to work in the new suit he bought as soon as he found out he made detective. Like he was in over his head and convinced he'd made a terrible mistake.

Becerra came in then, with a file folder and laptop sleeve under his arm, and joined them at the table with a nod and smile. That made Ben feel a little better. He knew the younger detective was thorough and competent, but his relative inexperience balanced out Zepeda's seemingly all-knowing gaze. He thought about the shield in the desk drawer at home, then looked at Jennifer and took a deep breath.

Becerra opened up the laptop and Zepeda said, "Why don't we get started?"

• • •

Zepeda eyed him warily. "So you just left him there on the floor?"

Ben swiped through the photos on his phone and when he found the one he was looking for, he held it up so Zepeda could see the stranger's face.

"Looks like you rang his bell pretty good."

"He didn't say anything, didn't identify himself, just went for his weapon. What would you have done?"

The old cop thought about it. "In your shoes, probably the same thing."

Becerra opened a pocket on the laptop sleeve, took out a USB cable, and said, "We need copies of all those. Do you mind if I download them?"

Ben hesitated, wondering if there was anything on his phone he wouldn't want them to see. He hadn't specifically mentioned his Lucite-encased badge to Bernie in any of his text messages, he was sure of that. He had only asked for a favor.

"I won't look at anything else," Becerra said, as if he knew exactly what Ben was thinking.

"No, it's okay." He stopped himself from adding that he didn't have anything to hide. He remembered being on the other side of the table. People who said they didn't have anything to hide almost always did. He slid the phone across the table to him.

Zepeda tapped his fingers on the notepad in front of him. "Let's keep going."

As Ben nodded, he realized there was one other thing he hadn't mentioned.

The Glock.

•   •   •

Two and a half hours after he rode up in the elevator with Jennifer, they were riding back down. "Think Becerra will be able to do anything with Kyle?" he asked.

"Did you see the way his eyes lit up? He certainly thinks he can."

"Is he usually right about stuff like that?"

"Yeah, he is." The elevator doors opened and she walked him out to the Volvo. There was supposed to be more rain later in the day, but just now the clouds were letting a little bit of sunlight through and it felt warm.

Ben was relieved and maybe just slightly hopeful. He should have gone to Jennifer earlier. That much was clear. "Thank you," he said as she gave him a hug and said goodbye.

Something smelled odd, almost like burning rubber. At first he thought it might be Jennifer, but the smell got stronger as he watched her walk back into the building. He took a look around, but didn't see anything unusual, so he got in behind the wheel and put the key in the ignition. The music surprised him. Was it the radio? He double-checked to make sure he hadn't already started the car. What was happening?

Then it felt like someone stabbed an ice pick into the back of his head and he was gone.

NINETEEN

There was a pattering noise coming from somewhere above him. Ben couldn't figure out what it was. His head hurt and he felt like he might vomit. He turned to look around and everything was spinning, so he closed his eyes and let his head fall back against the rest.

Rain, he thought. That's what the sound was. Rain. On the roof of the car.

The last thing he remembered was Jennifer saying goodbye, the odd smell, the glow of the sun.

He thought about the day he went into the studio after Grace had disappeared. How long it had been, he couldn't say. A week? A month? It couldn't have been longer than that, could it? He'd been afraid of what he felt that day. Just like he was afraid right now.

And this time he couldn't pretend it wasn't really a seizure.

Ben wished he had noticed what time it was when Jennifer walked him to the car, so he could figure out how long he'd been sitting here. Then, maybe, he'd be able to estimate how long the seizure had lasted. He knew he had arrived at a few minutes before ten this morning and it was almost two now. It felt like he had known how long the meeting lasted, but he couldn't seem to recall it anymore.

The ground had been dry. It hadn't started raining yet. Now it was coming down steadily. Not too hard. Any softer and he probably wouldn't be able to hear it on the roof. The windows were fogged, so he wiped a circle clear on the driver's side with the cuff of his shirt. There were puddles forming on the asphalt of the parking lot. He watched the rain hit the ground for a few more minutes. Between half an hour and an hour, he decided.

He took his phone out of his pocket and saw that Bernie had texted him forty minutes earlier. everything ok?

Yes. Sorry, he replied. Took longer than I thought, but wrapping up now. Be on the way soon.

no worries

Ben read that last message and started to giggle, then that grew into full-bellied laughter that went on and on and on. He couldn't help himself. He couldn't stop. When it finally began to wane, his chest aching and his throat sore, he caught a glimpse of himself in the rearview mirror and realized he hadn't been laughing at all. He had been crying. And he still was.

It's going to be a bad day. You know it as soon as you realize you're awake. The pulsing in your head is already at full tempo and the weight of the day to come is pressing down on you, pinning you prone.

But it's morning.

It's likely your father tapped on the door a few minutes ago and whispered your name, then snuck away when he realized you weren't yet conscious. You think you remember that. But it doesn't really matter whether you remember or not. It's time.

You're needed elsewhere.

The air feels so thick that it takes both arms just to sit yourself upright in bed. Your feet are concrete blocks hanging off the ends of broomsticks. The first attempt to stand fails and you collapse back down onto the tangled blankets. The second is barely an improvement. With the third, you find a fragile balance and, with some effort, lift your arm and plant your hand on the wall.

Eventually, you feel like you might be able to move. Slowly, you work your way into the bathroom, sit down on the toilet. You don't realize you're sleeping again until you start to fall off. Your hand finds the edge of the countertop just in time to prevent you from planting your face on the bath mat.

You clean yourself, struggle to your feet again, and work your way over to the sink, where you Listerine the sticky crud out of your mouth and splash some water in your face. There aren't any more of the little plastic bathroom cups, so you try to hold enough water in your cupped palm to wash down three Advil. It feels like dry-swallowing a peach pit.

At least you're up and semimobile. Ten minutes, *you tell yourself,* ten minutes to fix your father's breakfast, and you can be back in bed for a few more hours. You can do ten minutes. You've done it before and you'll do it again.

You shuffle toward the kitchen. Notice something odd. The music is already playing. Peter never starts the music himself anymore.

Then you turn into the dining room and see. It's confusing for a moment. Even disconcerting.

Grace is making your father's breakfast.

You stand and watch. Her back is to you, but you can see she's just adding the sugar to his coffee and Boost. He's already got his oatmeal.

"Ben," he says softly, with a worried smile on his face.

Grace turns when she hears him. You see her biting her lip, an apology in her eyes.

"He was out on the patio by himself," she says. "I hope it's okay."

You nod, say, "Thank you," but your voice is so soft, you barely hear it yourself.

"You're welcome," she says.

You manage to make it back into bed without needing a hand on the wall to steady yourself.

After the slow and careful drive home, Ben went inside and found his father standing by the door, wringing his hands.

"I'm sorry," he said, eyebrows raised and lower lip trembling. "I did something bad."

Bernie called out from the kitchen. "No, you didn't, Pete!"

Following the sound of his voice, Ben found him in the kitchen on his hands and knees, wiping muddy paw prints up from the floor. Sriracha was next to him, soaking wet and wagging her tail.

"Your dad found her scratching at the door and he let her outside. No biggie. I'll have it cleaned up in just a minute."

Ben stood there in the kitchen, watching Bernie with the towel, knowing he should say something, but not sure what. There was a paw print next to Bernie's ankle. Ben stared at it, wondering if it had been missed on the first pass. What if he was the only one who saw it? He might need to clean it up himself. His hand reached for the notebook in his shirt pocket. It wasn't there. Where was the notebook? What would happen if he couldn't find it and make a note about the paw print? His head was hurting again. Was it *again*? Had it stopped hurting? He tried to focus on the spot on the floor, because if he looked away without writing it down he would forget and it wouldn't ever get wiped up and if it didn't ever get wiped up then it would—

"You okay, Ben?" Bernie was standing in front of him, looking in his eyes.

"Yeah?" He felt light-headed, off balance, so he steadied himself with a hand on the counter.

"Maybe you should sit down."

Ben looked down at the floor and wasn't sure if sitting there was a good idea. Then he felt a hand on his elbow and he was walking into the living room. The couch. It was a good idea to sit on the couch.

"Let me get you some water."

Bernie handed him a plastic bottle and he drank. Hadn't realized he was so thirsty. It was good.

After half an hour and another bottle of water, Ben seemed to be feeling all right. At least he could answer Bernie's questions with a reasonable amount of clarity. "I didn't eat anything all day, so I think my blood sugar was just off or something. On top of not sleeping and all the stress. It just caught up to me."

Bernie didn't look like he was buying it. "You think you're going to be okay?"

"I am. Thank you, Bernie. I owe you big for this."

"I just hope everything gets worked out."

"After talking to Jennifer and the other detectives today, I think it will."

"You sure you don't want me to stay and help with dinner?"

"No, we're good. You've already done way too much."

Bernie tilted his head and studied Ben for a moment. "You remember when Angie died?" Angie was his first wife. Ben was still in high school when she got sick. "Your mom and dad, they practically lived with us for months. No way would I have made it without them."

Ben wasn't sure why Bernie was bringing that up now.

The question in his expression must have been obvious. "There's no such thing as too much. You understand?"

• • •

It took a while for the aftereffects of the seizure to wane enough that Ben felt relatively normal. He was glad it was still raining so he didn't have to tell Peter that he wasn't up to going for their walk.

He knew it had been a rough day for his father. Bernie told him that everything went smoothly until Sriracha got out in the rain, but Peter seemed more tired than usual, and it was clear he had been worried both about how long Ben had been gone and about his behavior after he got home. They did the *Jeopardy!*-and-medicine routine earlier than usual.

The day had left him drained and exhausted. Bernie called twice to check on him, and after the second call, he took his meds and tried going to bed. It was almost nine. Even though he felt thoroughly beat, there was still too much anxiety roiling in his stomach for him to sleep.

He did twenty-five hundred steps inside to wear the anxiousness down. When he finished in the living room, he laid himself down on the couch and tried to find something on TV that might help him stop thinking for a while. Bill Murray had just punched Ned Ryerson in the face when the phone rang. It had to be Bernie checking in on him again, so he answered it without looking.

"I'm okay, Bernie."

But it wasn't Bernie.

"Ben? Is that you?"

A woman's voice, soft, uncertain. He took the phone away from his ear and looked at the display. The number wasn't one he recognized. Could he be hallucinating? An aftereffect of the seizure?

"Ben," Grace said. "I need help."

TWENTY

Ben couldn't believe it was her. Was this a hallucination? A dream? He looked around the living room. *Groundhog Day* was still playing on the TV. He wasn't light-headed. The moment he heard her voice he'd instantly felt sharp and alert. "It's really you?"

"Yeah," she said, and he knew.

It was her. He really was talking to Grace. "Where are you?"

"I'm in a Target parking lot. I just bought this phone."

"Okay, good." He was glad she wasn't using her own phone. There was a good chance someone would be paying attention to the activity. Becerra, definitely, but Ben wasn't worried about him. It was whoever else was looking for her that concerned him. "I'm going to help. It's going to be all right."

"That cop who got killed at that hotel, that was Rob, wasn't it?" There was genuine fear in her voice. She must have seen the news. They still hadn't released Rob's name.

"Yes, it was." Ben got up from the couch and started toward the office while they talked.

"Oh god." She sounded as if she was starting to panic.

Ben knew he needed to help her calm down as much as he possibly could. "It's going to be all right, Grace. It is."

"I don't see how."

Ben didn't see how, either. Not yet. But if he kept her talking, he might be able to keep her focused on him. When anxiety was facing you down, sometimes the best thing to do was look away from it. He tried to keep his voice calm, to let go the urgency he was feeling. "Where have you been staying?"

"At a friend's apartment. He left to go up to Northern California for a while."

"Is it Kyle's place?"

"You know about Kyle?" There was uncertainty in her voice.

"I've been trying to find you. Amy helped me figure some things out."

When she didn't say anything, he pushed forward. "Does he know you're there?"

"He said it would be okay if I crashed there for a while."

"Nice place?" He felt stupid asking that. What he really wanted to know was if it was safe. But he didn't want her to be any more fearful than she already was.

"It's okay. You can walk down to the water." The tone of her voice was changing. More conversational. Calmer.

"Does anybody else know you're there?"

"No."

"Are you driving your car?"

"No, his. Mine's in the garage."

That's good, Ben thought. No one knew about Kyle except Jennifer, Becerra, and Zepeda, and they all knew that Rob had been investigating other cops from San Bernardino. There was no way they'd let anyone else know. Maybe Kyle's apartment was the best place for her right now. Maybe it was okay to ask. "Do you feel safe there?"

"I did. Then I saw the news about Rob. Now I don't know anymore." The uncertainty was creeping back into her voice.

"Do you want to come here?" He wanted to get her to talk to Zepeda as soon as he could, but she must have been leery of the police or she would have gone to them already. He'd have to work to convince her.

"They know your house." She was right about that. He still thought she'd be safer here, but her feeling secure was important too.

"Who is 'they'?"

"Lopez and Sowers." Lopez. The San Bernardino deputy sheriff who knocked on the door. "I saw that damn car. That's why I ran."

"The red Camaro?"

"You saw it too?"

"Yeah. And Lopez. It's Matthew Lopez, right?"

"Oh god." She was slipping back into the fear.

"Did Rob know where you were staying?"

"Not exactly. We met at a coffee shop a couple of blocks away. He said if I felt safe, it was better if he didn't know exactly where I was." That was good. If Rob didn't have her exact location, then the people who killed him couldn't have gotten it from him.

"It's okay, Grace. I promise we're going to get this all straightened out. I've been talking to some friends of mine with the Long Beach Police. They're investigating Rob's death. They need to talk to you. We can keep you safe."

"Rob said don't talk to any other cops no matter what."

"I know. But he thought he'd be able to watch out for you."

She was quiet on the other end of line.

"I trust them, Grace."

"I promised him. No other cops. That's why I didn't even say anything to you."

That caught him off guard. She had wanted to tell him, but Rob, either directly or indirectly, had stopped her.

"If you don't want me to go to the police, how can I help? I can come right now and—"

"No," she said, her voice firmer now. "You can't leave Peter alone."

"It'll be okay. He hardly ever wakes up in the middle of the night."

"We both know that's not true."

"What can I do?"

"I need money."

• • •

He hadn't wanted to hang up. Only after she promised to keep the phone with her and call him if anything at all alarming, or even just unusual, happened. The plan was to go to the bank as soon as he could in the morning to withdraw as much money as he and Peter could spare, then to meet her at a Starbucks, the same one where she'd met Rob, and deliver the money to her. Then she'd disappear again until Rob's case was closed, hoping that at that point she'd be safe. She made him promise not to tell anyone what he was doing, especially not the police. He couldn't blame her, really. Even though he knew little of her personal history, he knew enough people who'd been cornered into becoming confidential informants that he understood why she didn't trust cops.

He knew he had to change her mind, and he even considered calling Jennifer and taking her with him when he went to meet Grace. If anyone could convince her that the LBPD could be trusted, it would be Jennifer. He'd never worked with anyone who was as good at making empathetic connections with victims as she was. But Grace was on shaky ground in terms of trust. If Jennifer couldn't pull it off, he'd lose Grace's confidence. And if that happened, she'd be completely on her own and in more danger than ever.

There was a kind of selfishness there, too, he had to admit. He didn't think he could bear it if he broke his word to her and she lost her trust in him. It would be too much. He'd been broken too many times. If it happened again, there'd be no putting him back together.

So he decided. He'd meet her and do everything he possibly could to convince her not to run.

It was a very long night and he spent much of it on his feet. By the time the sun came up, he'd already topped ten thousand steps.

• • •

Even though Ben hadn't managed much sleep, he felt a kind of energy that he hadn't since he'd dressed in his detective clothes and flashed his shield. He woke his father a little earlier than usual and was at Wells Fargo at three minutes after nine. Between their two pensions, he and Peter took in almost six thousand dollars a month. Ben had been doing his best to build up their savings in case the time came when Peter could no longer live at home. Grace had asked for a thousand dollars. Ben decided that wasn't enough, so he withdrew three thousand. He would have taken out more, but he was worried that it might be a red flag. The raised eyebrow he got from the teller when he requested all twenties was enough. He'd give her more if she needed it and, in the event that he couldn't convince her to talk to Jennifer, hoped the offer would be enough to keep her from disappearing completely.

It took almost fifty minutes to get from the bank to the Starbucks. The circuitous route he drove before getting on the freeway added to the time. It was worth it, though, to make sure he wasn't being followed. He couldn't remember the last time he had driven over the Vincent Thomas Bridge. It had to be back when he was on the job. In those days, he had reason to cross the bridge much more frequently. There was always some investigation or other that would take him to the harbor, to either the Long Beach port on the east edge of the bay, or its LA sister across the water. He remembered how much he used to enjoy the trip. Every time he drove over the bridge and saw the water and the piers and the cranes below and all the ships out in the harbor waiting to dock, he remembered being a child in the passenger's seat of one his father's previous Volvos, and staring with slack-jawed wonder out the window. How he would imagine the places those freighters and tankers had come from. He never realized his father was manufacturing reasons to travel over the bridge because of how much Ben loved it. "Hey, kiddo," he'd say every couple of weeks, "I need to go to the hardware store in San Pedro. Want to come?" Ben was a teenager before he realized there were a dozen closer hardware stores and that the bridge wasn't even close to the fastest route to the True Value where they always wound up.

The Starbucks he was looking for was on Western, right on the border between San Pedro and Palos Verdes. If Kyle's place was within a few blocks, Grace was in a much more upscale neighborhood than he'd imagined when Amy first mentioned the city to him.

Most people, Ben figured, were like him and didn't imagine the city much beyond the harbor and the downtrodden industrial areas around it. That was good. Even if someone knew to look for Grace in San Pedro, they wouldn't start anywhere near here.

The Starbucks was in a shopping center anchored by an Albertsons and a Rite Aid, but it shared a separate building with a Supercuts, behind Coco's Bakery and across from the Cold Stone Creamery. Ben ordered a venti vanilla latte and took a seat in the corner that allowed him to watch the front door. He was still ten minutes early.

The top of the hour came and went with no sign of Grace.

It's okay, he told himself.

He'd always been a stickler for punctuality, and he'd only gotten worse after his recovery. His invariable anxiety over the possibility of being late usually meant he'd be early, wherever he went. He checked his phone to see if he had missed any calls or messages. He hadn't. At ten after, he sent a text to the number she'd called from last night.

You ok?

He waited a few minutes for a reply, but nothing came. Now he really was worrying and he couldn't rationalize it away anymore. So he called. It rang and rang and then the automated voicemail greeting came up. "It's me," he said, trying to be as vague as he could and still be understood by Grace. It was very unlikely that anyone was listening, but he didn't want to take the chance. "You all right? Let me know."

At half past the hour he called again. "I'm really getting worried. If I don't hear from you soon, I'm going to have to call my friends." Would she even understand that? It was clear who he meant by friends, wasn't it?

His latte was three-quarters gone and so cold it might as well have been iced. It was nearly eleven. She wasn't coming. Ben tried to maintain his composure, but his anxiety was overtaking him. What could have happened? Best-case scenario—she changed her mind. Worst case—he wasn't the only one who came up with the lead on Kyle, and someone else had gotten to her.

What could he do at this point?

He went out and got in the Volvo. He could still see the entrance to Starbucks through the windshield. Something was stopping him from turning the key in the ignition. What if, somehow, she was still coming and he left? She would think he let her down. Could she have gotten the time wrong? Just a few more minutes. He'd wait a little longer. Just to be sure.

But what then?

He'd have to call Jennifer. There weren't any more options. But that would mean breaking his promise to Grace. The latte churned in his stomach.

Then he got an idea. He found the number in the contacts on his phone and made the call.

"Becerra."

"Detective, it's Ben Shepard."

"Hey, how's it going?"

"I need to ask you a question."

"Sure. What do you need?"

"Were you able to do anything with that lead from yesterday? Kyle from San Pedro?"

"As a matter of fact, I was. One of the numbers in Grace's phone records belonged to a Kyle."

"In San Pedro?"

"Yes. I'm not sure there's anything there, though."

"Why not?"

"I visited the billing address this morning," he said. "No one seemed to be there. A neighbor told me that he was out of town for a few weeks."

"What time were you there?"

"Eight thirty. Why?"

"No reason." She could have been in the shower, or maybe still sleeping. But even if she wasn't, she wouldn't open the door to a stranger. Especially not a cop. Becerra would have done everything he could to determine if anyone was inside the apartment. But without knowing the layout, that probably didn't amount to much. How many windows was he able to look in? Would he have been able to hear a shower running, or anything else inside? Until Ben could get a look at the apartment he wouldn't know what to make of it.

Unless she was already outside, though—then, even if Becerra hadn't announced himself, she would know it was a police visit, and at this point, he knew, she wasn't making any distinctions between Long Beach cops and San Bernardino cops. There was a good chance Becerra had spooked her.

Ben needed to know where she was. He could try to reason with Becerra, but he thought he'd try something else first. "What's the address again?"

There was a long pause. "Again?" Becerra said.

"Yeah," Ben said. "I just need to write it down."

"I never gave you the address."

"Of course not. That's why I need it now."

Another pause. "Are you okay, Mr. Shepard?" It was "Mister" now, not "Detective" anymore.

"I need your help," Ben said, his posture collapsing along with his voice.

"What do you need?"

"Kyle's address?"

"Why?"

"I can't say. But I really do need it. I made a promise that I can't break."

"I'm not sure it's a good idea."

Ben wasn't sure either, but that didn't matter, he needed the address. He needed to convince Becerra to give it to him and knew that required a new tactic. Suddenly, surprisingly, he remembered what Becerra had said to him the first time they met, what his lieutenant told him. "Please, Henry. Don't let me down."

TWENTY-ONE

"I don't know if you saw him when he knocked on the door, but he's one of the good guys, Grace," Ben said. She still wasn't answering, so this was the third voicemail. "And he thinks it's a dead end, that no one's there. It's still safe, so go back, okay? Go back and call me."

He was parked across the street from the address Becerra had given him, a nondescript wood-trimmed apartment-and-townhouse complex that looked like it had several dozen units sprawling around central common areas. More than anything, he wanted to investigate, to go inside and look at the apartment for himself, but he decided he wouldn't approach any closer without explicit permission from Grace. He wouldn't make the same mistake that Becerra had.

Ben had been even more cautious this time than he had on his earlier trip to the Starbucks in San Pedro. Before he made lunch for Peter and left home the second time, he'd pulled the Volvo into the garage and dug through boxes until he found the radio-frequency detector he'd purchased online a few years earlier during a paranoid phase. After replacing the batteries, he checked the car thoroughly to be sure no one had planted a GPS tracking device. When he was satisfied, he pulled out into the alley, locked the garage door, and placed a tiny dollop of toothpaste at the edge of the key slot on the bottom of the padlock so he would know if anyone tried to open it.

Now, after he'd exhaustively surveyed Kyle's neighborhood, and sat and watched the building for as long as he dared, he knew it was time to head home. He'd been away from home for nearly three hours already, and he was afraid to leave Peter alone any longer. He'd already be hungry for dinner and probably worried. The thought of calling Bernie had occurred to him, but it worried him, too. There was no doubt in his mind that Bernie had meant what he said the night before—that there was no such thing as too much when it came to helping them. It wasn't abusing his generosity that concerned Ben, it was more that Bernie was already beginning to question Ben's actions, and that was worrisome. He knew that Ben had his shield, and that he'd been using it.

That was Ben's own fault, of course. But he still believed it was the right move—he literally wouldn't be where he was at that moment had he left his badge in the block of Lucite. And honestly, he worried about what Bernie would think of him. Trying to find Grace was one thing, but somebody needed to be taking care of Peter, and Ben was definitely dropping the ball.

He'd left the message for Grace and it was time to go home. But he had little doubt he'd be back.

You don't see the package until you open the patio door, and at first it confuses you. Why would there be a box there? There's no way a delivery person would have left it there. It's not very big. Maybe eight by twelve by three inches. You bend over and pick it up. There's a small card in a pale-blue envelope taped to the top. You pull it off and you can see the package was originally addressed to Grace. The card says, Ben—I found it! I hope you'll let me read it. Love, Grace.

Inside the box, after you dig your way through the inflated plastic pockets of packing material and slip off the tissue-paper wrap, you see it. The familiar back-cover copy and professorial blurbs on the gray-and-blue dust jacket. It's in great shape, almost like new. You flip it over and read the title. Towards Our Distant Rest: World War I and Its Aftermaths. *You run your fingers over your father's name.* Peter Shepard. *It's embossed, just like the title. You remember doing the same thing twenty-five years ago. Why weren't you as impressed then as you are now?*

There's a noise behind you, like the sole of a shoe brushing across concrete. You turn and expect to see Grace outside the studio.

But she's not there. Was she watching? Maybe she ducked inside. You think about going back to say thank you, but look at the book in your hands again, and without another thought, you sit down at the patio table and start reading.

When Ben got home, he found Peter in the kitchen by the coffeepot. He had a wad of wet, brown-soaked paper towels in his hand and was wiping up a puddle on the counter.

"Dad, what happened?"

"I messed up." Peter kept mopping up the spill. When the paper towels were too saturated to soak up any more coffee, he carried them, dripping a trail across the floor, to the wastebasket. Judging by the wet floor tiles, he'd made the trip a few times already.

Ben looked at the coffee maker and the counter around it. The pot was there, as was Peter's favorite coffee cup. Nothing appeared broken. He looked at his father's hands. They seemed all right, no burns or scalding that he could see.

"Can I help clean up?" Ben asked.

Peter carried another wad to the trash. "I can do it," he said.

Ben fought the urge to insist. He knew he could do a better job in a quarter of the time it would take his father. But he also knew it would make Peter feel even worse.

"Okay. I'm just going to go to the bathroom. Just a minute and I'll be back, all right?"

He went into his bedroom and gave Peter a few minutes to manage things for himself. When he thought enough time had passed, he went back into the kitchen. The mess on the counter was pretty much taken care of. He'd need to check it later when Peter wasn't in the room, but it looked like he had done a good job. Apparently, though, he hadn't noticed the half dozen drip lines splashed across the floor from one side of the room to the other.

• • •

"What happened, Dad?" He suspected Peter had tried to get his own coffee because Ben had been away much longer than he had planned to be.

"I was hungry. I'm sorry I messed it up."

"You didn't mess anything up. It was my fault." Ben knew he was right. It was too long to leave his father alone without anything to eat or drink. How could he have been so careless? "I should have been back a lot sooner to help you. I'm the one who's sorry, okay?"

Peter looked away.

"What's wrong?"

"I thought you weren't going to come back."

"Oh, no, Dad. No." Ben put his hands on his father's shoulders and looked him in the eye. "I'm always coming back. No matter what."

"Always?"

"Always." Ben pulled Peter into a hug, and a few seconds later his father raised his arms and hugged him back.

• • •

"Grace," Ben said in the next voicemail, "I need you to call me back. Please. I don't know what to do. If I don't hear back from you soon, I'm going to talk to my friends again. Tell me not to. Just . . . just tell me something."

He stood at the patio door looking out into the gray afternoon, waiting for the rain, and running the tip of his middle finger up and down along the indentation in the back of his head.

• • •

Jennifer had stopped at Steelhead on the way and brought a latte for Ben and a decaf mocha for Peter. She had a cup for herself, too, and Ben tried to remember what she used to drink. In the squad, it was cream and Splenda, but when they were out in the field, she always got something else. No matter how hard he tried, he couldn't remember what it was.

Peter was in the living room watching the last ten minutes of *Steve Harvey* and waiting for *Ellen*. They sat at the table in the dining room. He would have preferred the patio table outside so he wouldn't have to worry about his father hearing something that might upset him, but Weather.com said there was a 95 percent chance of precipitation at three o'clock.

Ben pointed at her cup and asked, "What was it you used to get when we'd go someplace for coffee?"

"All kinds of things. I don't really have a regular. Sometimes chai, sometimes Americano, sometimes just plain tea. Why?"

"I thought there was something you always got. I couldn't remember."

"Well, I always got it with Splenda. Could that be what you're thinking of?"

One corner of his mouth turned up. He hadn't forgotten completely, so he gave himself permission to feel slightly less disappointed with his memory. He tried a sip from his cup. It was still too hot to drink.

"What's up?" she asked.

"Lopez killed Rob."

She raised her eyebrows and tilted her head. "He did?"

"Yeah."

"You sound pretty sure."

"Lopez is the dirty cop he was trying to make the case against in San Bernardino."

"Okay." She leaned in toward him. "Tell me more about it."

"I don't know much more. Did you find any other case notes or files in Rob's room? His briefcase?"

"There was nothing. Whoever killed him even took the safe out of his closet. Used a pry bar or something to rip it right off the shelf so they could open it later."

"That figures."

"You told us you didn't trust Lopez when we talked. What pushed you into the accusation?"

"I talked to Grace."

She was quiet a long time while her eyes drilled into his. Then she said, "Why didn't you—"

"I promised her I wouldn't. That was the only way she'd talk to me." Ben told her about the phone call and everything Grace had told him. "She was supposed to meet me at Starbucks this morning so I could give her the money."

"Supposed to?"

"She didn't show up."

"You think Lopez got to her?"

"No, I think Becerra spooked her when he knocked on the door."

Her eyes widened. Ben couldn't tell if she was surprised about Becerra's visit itself or the fact that he knew about it. "I called him. He told me about it. One of the neighbors told him Kyle was out of town, so he thought it seemed like a dead end."

"But the neighbor didn't say anything about Grace?"

Ben shook his head. "I figure she's keeping a low profile."

"Did you tell Becerra any of this?"

"No. I've been leaving her voicemail messages, telling her it's safe to go back. Thought if he didn't think she was there, it might be."

"You don't trust him?"

"I do, but she doesn't."

"Why are you telling me all this now? You think Lopez got to her?"

"That's part of it."

"What's the rest?"

"If he hasn't found her yet and you guys can't find anything solid on him, she really is going to have to disappear."

• • •

Ben still felt bad about what happened with his father earlier in the day, so he watched the second half hour of *Ellen* with him. There was a mother of quadruplets who'd made a video of herself hiding from them in her pantry. When she held the camera down to the bottom of the door and showed one of the toddlers peeking underneath and saying "Hi!" Peter laughed out loud, and for a minute Ben smiled, too.

When the show was over, Ben helped his father with a load of laundry and reminded him to do his floor exercises.

He paid close attention to Peter. Ben was self-aware enough to understand he wasn't just trying to make up for his neglect that morning, but also trying to distract himself from everything weighing on him. Every minute he focused on his father was one he didn't focus on his phone and worry about Grace.

When he was done with his last stretch, Peter rolled up his exercise mat and stashed it in its regular spot behind his chair. "Can we walk today?"

"I'm not sure," Ben said. "Is it still raining?"

Peter peeked out through the shutter on the front window and nodded sadly. "Yeah."

"I'm sorry, Dad. We'll walk tomorrow, okay?"

The corners of his mouth turned down in disappointment. "Okay."

And then Ben's phone finally rang. It startled him so much that he dropped it trying to get it out of his pocket.

"I need the money," Grace said.

Ben convinced her that the safest place to be right now was still in Kyle's apartment. He said he would bring it to her as soon as Peter went to bed. She didn't want Ben to leave him alone at night. She said she would be all right until the morning.

Peter realized that Ben was talking about him and said loudly, "I'll be okay. You can go."

"Did you hear that?" Ben asked her.

Her voice softened. "Is that him?"

"Yeah."

"Can I . . ."

Ben went back into the living room and held the phone out to his father. "Dad, it's Grace. She wants to say hi."

"Grace?" He looked unsure as he held the phone tentatively up to his ear. "Hello?"

Leaning his head in close to his father's, Ben was just barely able to make out her voice.

"Hi, Pete! I miss you."

He looked confused. Ben wondered if he knew who she was.

She went on. "Have you been having coffee on the patio without me?"

His face brightened with recognition. "No, it's been raining every day. Are you coming home?"

There was a moment of silence before she spoke again. "I hope so. I really do." To Ben's ear, it sounded like she meant it.

"Do you need some money?" Before she could reply, he turned to Ben. "I have money, don't I?"

Ben nodded. "I already told her we would give her some."

His father smiled. "Did you hear?"

"Yes. Thank you. You guys are always really nice to me."

"Because you're nice. When you get it, you'll come home?"

"I hope so," she said again. "It's really good to hear your voice, Pete."

"You too, you too."

"I'll talk to you again soon, okay?"

Peter nodded and handed the phone back to Ben. "He's nodding yes. Thank you for talking to him."

She didn't say anything.

"You sure you don't want me to come tonight?"

"I'll see you in the morning. Take good care of him, okay?"

"I will," he said, hoping she'd never find out how much he'd been screwing up in the last few days. "You call me if you need to. If you see or hear anything or you get scared. Even if you just can't sleep. Promise me."

Her voice was almost a whisper. "Cross my heart."

Of all the things that were keeping him awake when he went to bed and tried to sleep that night, the one he obsessed over the most was the note he wrote in his journal shortly after finishing the phone call. He couldn't remember or even imagine what he'd been thinking.

Cross my heart
And hope to die
Stick a needle in my eye

TWENTY-TWO

"You said if I couldn't sleep I should call."

The clock on the nightstand read 3:50. "I'm glad you did. I'm not sleeping, either."

"Really?" He thought he could hear a smirk in her voice. "'Cause you sound like you were asleep."

"I just nodded off for a second. Really. I've been tossing and turning all night."

"I hope that's true."

"Thanks." He chuckled.

"No, because I won't feel so bad for waking you up."

"It's okay, Grace. Really."

They were silent for a few moments.

"I don't know what to say," she said.

"Tell me a story."

"I don't know any."

"Tell me *the* story."

She did.

• • •

Of course it was a guy. How else could something like that happen?

And she hated herself for not seeing through him sooner. Her best friend, Lisa, knew right away. "Dude," she'd said to Grace the night she met him, "Isn't the first rule of grad school like *Don't date the douchebros in the MFA program?*"

If it was, nobody told her. It was her first quarter working on her master's in art history at UC Riverside, and she met him at the first gallery show she'd gone to.

"And what the hell kind of name is Steph for a guy, anyway?" Lisa continued. "I'll bet you a thousand dollars his name was Steve until that basketball guy got famous. What kind of art does he do? And do not fucking say 'digital media.'"

She already felt too embarrassed to say anything. There was no way she was going to admit that he'd had a video installation at that first show.

Why hadn't she listened to Lisa?

•　•　•

They'd been undergrads together at Cal State San Bernardino. When she got into the UCR grad program, Lisa got a job in an arts nonprofit and they found a small two-bedroom that was only like a twenty-minute drive north of campus.

Things were great as long as she was able to keep Lisa away from Steph. That got harder as the weeks went on and she was seeing more and more of him. Then, after he told her his car had been stolen, it seemed like they were together more often than not. He even started leaving her alone at his place while he borrowed her Corolla. More and more, she'd wind up staying for a day or two at a time. The thought of moving in together had occurred to her, but she dismissed it. Mostly because she didn't think Lisa would approve, and she was already feeling like they didn't spend enough time together anymore.

• • •

He'd borrowed the car again the day she got pulled over on her way back to the apartment. The flashing lights appeared in her rearview mirror as she was driving north on the 215. She was pretty sure she hadn't been speeding. Or at least not going more than a few miles an hour over the speed limit like everybody else. She had been in one of the middle lanes and cars were zooming past on her left. So it couldn't be speeding. Maybe she had a taillight out or something. As she started to pull onto the shoulder she heard the loudspeaker behind her. "EXIT THE FREEWAY." How loud did it have to be for her to hear it with her windows rolled up? She did as she was told. The next off-ramp was maybe half a mile away. She was getting more and more nervous. But it couldn't be anything bad. She was a good driver. Never had an accident or a moving violation. There was nothing to worry about.

A hundred yards or so from the exit, she pulled over to the side of the road. It was a good spot. There wasn't much traffic and it was still a ways to the shopping center ahead. She rolled down the window and waited for the officer, but no one approached her. In the mirror, she saw one officer on each side of the patrol car, standing behind their open doors.

Something was wrong. It wasn't supposed to go like this.

"DRIVER, WITH YOUR LEFT HAND TURN OFF THE VEHICLE AND DROP THE KEYS ON THE GROUND OUTSIDE THE VEHICLE."

Oh god. Something was really wrong.

"DRIVER, WITH YOUR LEFT HAND ONLY, UNFASTEN YOUR SEAT BELT."

It was going to be okay. There was obviously some mistake. She struggled to undo the buckle.

"DRIVER, WITH YOUR RIGHT HAND OPEN THE CAR DOOR WITH THE OUTSIDE HANDLE."

If she stayed calm and did exactly what they told her to, it would be okay. It would. It would be okay. She reached out the window and opened the door.

"WITH YOUR ARMS ABOVE YOUR HEAD, SLOWLY EXIT THE VEHICLE AND FACE AWAY FROM US."

She took a deep breath, not sure if she even could get out without using her hands. But she could. And she did.

"TAKE TWO STEPS TO YOUR LEFT AND CLOSE THE DOOR."

She did.

"KEEPING YOUR HANDS ABOVE YOUR HEAD, WALK BACKWARD TOWARD US."

She did.

"STOP. KEEPING YOUR HANDS ABOVE YOUR HEAD, TURN IN A CIRCLE UNTIL INSTRUCTED TO STOP."

When she'd turned halfway around, she was startled to see the officer on the passenger's side of the patrol was pointing his gun at her. But she kept turning until she was facing away from them again.

"STOP. KEEPING YOUR HANDS ABOVE YOUR HEAD, WALK BACKWARD TOWARD US UNTIL INSTRUCTED TO STOP."

She counted off eight steps.

"STOP."

She heard one of the officers approaching her, but still she was surprised to hear his unamplified voice.

"Do you have any weapons or anything that might be used as a weapon?"

"No."

"Guns, knives, needles, tools of any kind?"

"No."

"Place your hands behind your head."

She had been very nervous up to that point, but the real fear set in when she felt his hands on her. First his left hand, grabbing her wrists and pinning them together behind her head, then his right, starting with each of her wrists and working its way down each arm, around her neck, her chest, under her breasts, around her waist, down each leg, and finally her crotch. She felt something catch in her throat and she knew she had been wrong. This wasn't going to be okay at all.

• • •

Handcuffed and locked in the back of the squad car, she watched them searching her car, thinking, *They can't do that, can they?* One of them was going through the trunk, tossing all her stuff on the ground, lifting the floor panel, moving the spare tire. He pulled out a plastic bag. Looked inside. Called his partner over. The partner looked inside. Then in unison they both turned their heads and stared at her trapped in the back seat.

• • •

She sat at a dirty gray table in a small room with dirty gray walls. She couldn't see it, but the chair was probably dirty and gray too. Matthew Lopez was sitting across from her, had been for what seemed like hours. He kept asking her the same questions over and over again. Where'd she get the Oxy? Who was she going to sell it to? Who was she working with? How'd she get started dealing? He did that thing she'd seen on TV where he was super friendly, as nice as he could possibly be. *Can I get you something to drink? Are you hungry? I get how hard it is, how expensive tuition is, especially for grad school. Art history? Wow. Who's your favorite artist? I saw this Picasso at LACMA once, The Crying Lady, you ever see that one? It's really something. Where'd you get the Oxy?*

There was only one person who could have stashed it in her car. She couldn't believe it, didn't want to believe it, but it had to be true. There was no other way the bag could have gotten in her trunk. It had to be the biggest shock, the biggest betrayal she'd ever experienced. She knew he liked weed, but Oxy? And dealing it? That was more than she could take in.

Later, after they'd gone through the cycle several more times, after she'd caved and accepted a can of Sprite from him, after the shock had faded to numbness, she said, "Don't I get a lawyer or something?"

One corner of Lopez's mouth curled up and he said, "If that's the road you want to go down, sure, we can get you a lawyer."

What other road was there?

•   •   •

The other road was a four-page confidential-informant contract that promised to drop the charges against her if she agreed to help Lopez and his colleagues gather enough evidence against both Steph and his supplier to convict them. If she did that, she was off the hook.

She didn't know what to do. Surely they couldn't convict her for drug trafficking, could they? Lopez made it sound like a slam dunk. Like it didn't matter that there was nothing else besides the bag of Oxy in her trunk, that just the fact that they found it in the back of her car was more than enough for her to go to jail for a very long time. But she had to choose. Of course she could talk to an attorney, that was her constitutional right, but the CI deal would be off the table if she did. It sucked, he said, that it had to be like that, but he knew from experience that CI operations only worked if they really were confidential. As soon as someone outside the team was involved, things always started to fall apart. He couldn't let that happen, he said, couldn't let her be in that kind of danger. By that point, after hours in the tiny room, she was so tired she had actually started to believe him.

•   •   •

When they let her go, she went back to Steph's place like they told her to. But she knew it was wrong as soon as she went inside. She checked the closet. His big duffel bag was gone. So were half of his clothes. His toothbrush and razor. Even his Xbox One.

Somehow Steph had found out.

She knew he was gone for good.

• • •

Lopez was waiting for her at the Pick Up Stix, just as he'd said he would be. He introduced her to his partner, Brett Sowers. He looked kind of like Lopez, but younger and slimmer, with a toady sheen and eyes that were too small for his face.

She told them Steph was gone.

"That's too bad," Lopez said. "But you still owe us two convictions."

• • •

It was easier than she could have imagined. In an academic department where all-nighters in the studios and media labs were the norm, Addy was everywhere. She barely even had to ask. It only took a sheepish grin and an "Anything stronger?" to move up to the majors. Only halfway through the quarter and she had already made two buys for Lopez. Didn't even have to wear a wire. He just gave her a smartphone with some app or something that she kept in her pocket to record everything. The art department was so big that no one seemed to notice.

"So we're done, right?" she asked.

Lopez finished chewing his crispy honey chicken and took his time wiping the glaze from his mouth with a napkin. "The deal was for a dealer *and* a supplier."

Sowers grinned and popped another cream-cheese wonton into his mouth.

• • •

The grad-student lounge was really just an extra office, but instead of being stuffed full of faculty desks, it had a couch and a little round conference table and a microwave and a minifridge. It was one of those rare moments that she had the room all to herself. There was frozen vegetarian lasagna heating up in the microwave when the big guy with the mustache came in.

She figured he must be a professor from another department or something, because he sure didn't look art school to her.

"Hi," she said. "Can I help you?"

"No." He slipped a wallet from his coat pocket and flashed his badge, quickly and subtly, as if concerned that someone coming in or passing the door might see. "But I might be able to help you."

• • •

They went to a pizza place a few blocks from campus and found a table in the back that offered a bit of privacy. At three thirty on a Tuesday, the place was fairly empty.

Rob explained who he was and filled her in on his investigation of Lopez and Sowers and the rest of the Narcotics team they worked with. Internal Affairs had been tipped off that they were running their CIs fast and loose and keeping sketchy records so they could skim both drugs and money.

She told him what she'd purchased at their behest. One of the buys hadn't even been officially reported, and on the other, less than half of what she'd bought had been logged into evidence.

He asked if she'd be willing to help with his investigation. There were risks, he said, but he'd do everything he could to minimize them. If she didn't want to, she could walk away right now and that would be the end of it.

"What about the drugs they found in my car? Will I go to jail?"

"No. That ex of yours, Stephen?"

"Steph," she said.

"He had priors and was heading downhill fast. The reason your car was flagged was because someone fitting his description was seen driving it away from a buy. If Lopez hadn't stuck his nose in, they would have tested the bag, found his fingerprints and not yours, and you wouldn't have had anything to worry about."

"Except my boyfriend being a piece of shit."

Rob chuckled. "We'd appreciate it if you would help us out, but I understand if you don't want to."

She thought about it, made up her mind. "Fuck Matthew Lopez."

• • •

There were two more buys like the ones before. Small. Undergrad students from other departments, so it would be less likely that anyone might connect them to her. Then Rob told her they were ready to make their case and take Lopez down.

• • •

She had no idea how it all fell apart. Late one night, Rob called and said it would be best if she went away for a while. He had everything set up for her. A good place to stay.

"How long?" she asked.

"A while."

"What about school?"

"You might need to do a leave of absence."

"What's happening?"

"We're minimizing risks."

She hung up the phone and heard Lisa knocking on her bedroom door. When she opened the door, Grace was crying.

"What's wrong?" Lisa asked, pulling her into a hug.

She'd been careful about what she said, though Lisa did know about Steph and how he'd gotten her into trouble. But she had held back most of the details about what she was trying to do to get herself out of it. Now it all just came pouring out.

"Oh my god," Lisa said. "I was scared for you before, but now I'm fucking terrified."

"Me too," she said. "Me too."

• • •

All that time, Ben thought, she had been carrying so much. And he'd had no idea. Could he have done something to help her sooner if he had known?

"The sun's going to be coming up soon," she said. "I'm sorry I kept you up all night."

"You have nothing to be sorry for." He hoped she believed him. "And Grace?"

"Yeah?"

"It's going to be all right."

TWENTY-THREE

After breakfast, Peter's stomach was bothering him more than usual, so he went back into his bedroom to lie down for a while. "Not for very long, just a minute," he said. "Then I'll get going."

"Sure, Dad. There's no rush. Just try to relax so you'll feel better."

Peter eased his head down onto the pillow. "I'll get going in just a minute."

Ben was anxious to go see Grace, so he went into his bathroom and got in the shower. He hadn't realized how tight the muscles in his neck and shoulders had been until the hot water began to wash away the tension. After several minutes, he started to worry about how long he was taking. He intended to keep the shower short, so he could be ready to go as soon as his father was up and feeling better. *Just a few more minutes,* he thought. Grace was waiting for him, but the more centered and focused he was, the more likely he'd be able to talk her into trusting the LBPD.

As he toweled off, he heard his father's voice outside his bedroom door. "Ben?" His voice was weak, almost a whimper.

The calm Ben had been so earnestly cultivating in the shower crumbled and he felt something snap in his head. "What now?" he yelled, coming out of the bathroom to see his father shrinking away from the open bedroom door.

Peter's eyes widened, then his lips began to tremble as he said, "Nothing. I'm sorry." He wrung his hands and shuffled away toward the back of the house.

"Fuck!" Ben snarled as he clumsily put on the dirty shorts he'd taken off before getting in the shower. What was wrong now? What was . . . what was his father wearing? He'd only had on his undershirt and boxers. Peter never came out of his room like that.

Guilt washed over Ben now as he hurried back to his father's bedroom.

"Dad?" he said through the closed door. "I'm so sorry. I shouldn't have snapped. I'm really, really sorry." He turned the knob, opened the door halfway, and leaned in. "Dad?"

Sometimes the Miralax worked too well.

There was a brown puddle in the middle of Peter's bed. The diarrhea had gotten all over the sheets. His father was hunched over and using a baby wipe, trying to clean up the footprints that trailed across the hardwood floor into the bathroom. It must have run down his legs as he was rushing to the toilet.

"Oh no," Ben whispered.

Peter looked up at him, holding the empty wipe package in one hand, eyes wet with humiliation, and said, "Is there more of these?"

• • •

After he got Peter showered and dressed, the sheets in the wash, and the floor cleaned up, Ben called Grace and told her he was running late but would be on the way soon.

"It's a good thing I was too lazy to take that plastic liner off your bed after the last surgery," Ben said.

"You're not lazy," Peter said as he spooned another bit of yogurt into his mouth.

Ben put a hand on his shoulder.

"I know you have to go now." He didn't look up from his snack.

"I do," Ben said, trying hard not to let the guilt and shame he felt slip into his tone.

"It's okay."

"You want to come with me?"

Half an hour later, they were crossing Terminal Island with the Vincent Thomas Bridge rising in front of them. Peter stared at it through the windshield. "We used to come this way," he said.

"That's right, Dad, we did."

"You were such a good boy."

Ben wiped at the corner of his eye and felt his father's hand squeeze his knee.

"And you still are."

●   ●   ●

"Pete," Grace squealed, throwing her arms around him. "It's so good to see you. What are you doing here?"

He returned her enthusiastic hug, grinning and looking happier than Ben had seen him since all of this had started. "I shit the bed," he said seriously.

Grace looked at him, at Ben, then back at him and started laughing, then Peter joined in. Ben couldn't quite go that far, but he managed a half-hearted grin.

She led Peter over to the sofa and sat next to him. "How have you been?"

"Hanging in there," he said, staring at her.

"Well, that's good."

"Are you coming home?" he asked with hopeful eagerness.

She shot Ben a glance before she answered. "I don't know yet. I hope so."

"Me too. We miss you."

"I miss you, too."

There was a long silence. It felt awkward to Ben, but Peter didn't seem to mind it. He couldn't read Grace's expression well enough to guess how she was feeling.

Peter looked at the TV across the room. "Want to watch *Ellen*?"

The question surprised Ben. His father hadn't been able to remember the name of the show in a long time. Ben couldn't recall him doing that since the last time he came home from the hospital.

"I'd love to," she said, "but I don't have it recorded like you guys do. If I'd have known you were coming . . ." She shot Ben another glance. He should have told her he was bringing his father. It was a dick move to surprise her, especially with how much stress she'd been under. He just didn't feel like he'd had another choice. Not that morning.

"Can I go to the bathroom?" Peter asked.

Grace took his arm, helped him up, and led him down the short hallway. She reached into the door on the right and turned on the light. "Here you go."

Peter went inside and looked around for a few seconds to get his bearings.

"You need some help?"

"I'm okay," he said, carefully closing the door.

She returned to the living room and sat back down on the sofa. "That was a surprise."

"I'm sorry," Ben said. "Things took a rough turn this morning."

"It's okay. It really is good to see him."

"You changed your hair." Her dark shoulder-length curls were gone. The new cut was short and kind of shaggy, maybe two shades lighter.

She seemed surprised that he noticed. "I saw the Supercuts and thought it would be a good idea."

"It was." From a distance he might have had to look twice to recognize her.

Ben didn't know what else to say, so he leaned forward and took the three bank envelopes out of his back pocket and put them on the coffee table in front of her. "There's a thousand in each one, all twenties, so they'll be easier to spend."

"Three thousand? That's—"

"Not enough," Ben said. "I know you don't trust the police. That's completely understandable. But trust me. Let me talk to my friends again before you go. See where they're at with Rob's case. Maybe you won't have to run at all."

"I don't know, Ben." She bit her lower lip. "Disappearing seems like the best thing."

"Maybe it is. If my friends can't get Lopez, you might have to. But I think they can, especially if you—"

"I won't agree to testify again. I never should have done that in the first place."

"That's fine. But will you talk to them?"

"I don't know."

"Just think about it, okay?"

They heard the toilet flush.

She nodded. "I will."

●   ●   ●

Peter hadn't wanted to leave, so Grace turned on the TV, flipped through the channels, and found a movie with Tom Hanks where he's an older guy who goes back to community college where Julia Roberts is a professor. One of the classroom scenes caught Peter's attention and he leaned in to see it better.

Ben looked at Grace. She was watching Peter with an expression Ben couldn't quite read. Wistfulness, maybe.

When he guessed there was maybe twenty minutes of the movie left, Ben excused himself, saying he needed to get something out of the car, and went outside. The apartment was on the lower floor, and it was one of those complexes that had been popular in the eighties when he was a kid, with recessed and staggered entryways to each unit to maximize privacy. He walked around the perimeter of the building looking for anything out of place, a car or person that didn't seem to belong, searching for a place where someone might hide or watch. He looked for cars with people sitting in them, delivery trucks or utility vans that didn't to seem to belong to someone working nearby. He asked himself how he would set up surveillance on Kyle's apartment and checked out every possible angle he could think of. There was nothing he saw that seemed out of place or as if it might be part of a stakeout operation. When he was satisfied that the only way someone could be watching Grace was if they'd moved into one of the other units, which seemed highly unlikely given the time frame and other constraints Lopez would have to work against, he went to the Volvo in the guest parking area, got the canvas tote bag out of the trunk, and went back to join Grace and Peter.

"That took a while," she said.

"I wanted to take a look around."

"And?"

"Everything looks good."

When the movie ended, Peter said, "That was a good one, wasn't it?"

"Yeah, it was," Grace said. Then she looked at Ben and tilted her head toward his father. "Too bad you missed it."

"Hey, Dad," he said. "Maybe we could watch it again at home. Would you like that?"

Peter nodded. "That was a good one."

"Let's get you home for some lunch."

Graced hugged them both again, and as they got to the door, Ben said, "Dad, would you wait on the porch for just a minute?"

When his father was outside, he pushed the door almost closed, walked over to the dining nook, and put the tote bag down on the table. Inside were two objects wrapped in kitchen towels.

"What's that?" she asked.

"Have you ever shot a gun?"

Her eyes widened. "No."

"I'm sure you won't need this," he said, unwrapping the Glock. The magazine was in the other towel. He checked the chamber to make sure it was empty and handed the pistol to her. "Just in case."

He showed her how to work the slide, checked the chamber again, and had her point the muzzle at the floor and dry fire it to get the feel of the trigger. Then he slid the magazine into the well in the grip and gave it back to her.

"Remember," he said. "Keep your finger out of the trigger guard until you're ready to shoot, and never, ever point it at anything you're not willing to kill."

Ben could see the weight of it, not just in her hand but in her eyes as well. He hoped he had made the right call. "Promise you won't go without calling me first."

She nodded, but didn't say anything until he was back out on the porch with his father, and then she spoke quietly, her voice almost a whisper. "Thank you, Ben. For everything."

He hoped that wasn't a goodbye.

●   ●   ●

Peter was in a good mood when they got home. Seeing Grace had either wiped the memories of the difficult morning away or been enough to raise his spirits in spite of them. Either way, Ben was relieved. Hoping to maintain his father's state of mind, he asked Bernie to hang out with Peter while he took care of some business that he needed to attend to.

There was some trepidation on Bernie's part, not about looking after Peter, but rather about just what business it was that Ben needed to take care of. When he told him he had to go to the police station, Bernie's sense of relief was palpable even over the phone.

●   ●   ●

Only Jennifer and Zepeda were there. Ben didn't know where Becerra was and he didn't ask. He didn't want to be the one who had to tell the younger detective that he'd knocked on Grace's door and left convinced that it was a dead end.

"We should just go talk to her," Zepeda said.

"Not if you want her to cooperate," Ben said.

Zepeda didn't like that. "You're saying if we go pick her up, she won't talk to us?"

"No, she won't." Ben was beginning to think that maybe Grace was right. "Can you blame her?"

Jennifer apparently saw where the two men were headed and said, "What does she need from us in order to cooperate?"

"She needs to feel safe," Ben said. "She hasn't felt that way in a long time."

Zepeda grumbled. "How are we supposed to do that?"

"I don't know," Ben said. "Maybe start with some official protection?"

"Yeah, right. Half the time we can't even get that approved when shot callers are putting up open bounties on trial witnesses. Get her in here to talk and if she gives us something solid, I mean really solid, we might be able to get someone to consider the request. Even then, though, it's a long shot."

Ben looked at Jennifer. "Do you have anything at all on Lopez?"

"San Bernardino IA won't release any of Rob's reports or files. They're saying it's too sensitive. And whoever killed Rob took anything he had with him."

"So there's nothing?"

"We did ID one relevant set of prints at the scene. Took the techs a long time to sort through everything."

Ben remembered how hard it was to get useful prints in a hotel room. They were rarely, if ever, cleaned thoroughly enough to erase the evidence of the hundreds of people who passed through them. "Whose were they?"

Zepeda said, "Brett Sowers. One of Lopez's crew."

"Well, that's a start."

Zepeda shook his head.

"Why not?"

"There's evidence that he was in the room prior to the crime."

"What evidence?" Ben asked.

Zepeda raised his eyebrows, opened the cover of the iPad on the table in front of him, tapped and swiped the screen, then turned it around for Ben to see. It was Sowers's SB Sheriff's Department ID. His face looked familiar, but Ben couldn't quite place it.

"You don't recognize him?" Zepeda asked.

"I think I've seen him somewhere, but I can't say for sure."

Zepeda snorted and turned the tablet back toward himself. He swiped the screen a few more times and then showed it to Ben again.

It was the swollen and bloodied face of the stranger drooling on the carpet in Rob's room.

Ben nearly said they had him for B&E and assault, when he realized the only witness to those crimes was someone who'd committed them himself. And honestly, Ben was the only person who'd really committed assault in that room, wasn't he?

"What are you going to do?" Ben asked.

Zepeda looked at Jennifer.

"Our lieutenant is pressing San Bernardino to release whatever Rob gave them on Lopez. We'll go higher up the chain if we have to. We're not going to let it go. For the time being, though, all we really have is Grace's word."

"Fuck," Zepeda said, sighing the word as much as speaking it. "We don't even have that. All we have is you telling us what she said."

• • •

"I know that's not what you were hoping to hear," Jennifer said when she was walking him out to the parking lot. "But we're going to stay on it. San Bernardino will come through with Rob's reports. We'll make the case."

"You don't think they'd let a case go cold to cover their asses?"

"No," she said. "Think about it. It's Internal Affairs. They live for this kind of shit. Taking down a cop who killed another cop? That's like the Super Bowl for them."

"Maybe," Ben said. "But do you think they'll let Long Beach win it?"

Fortunately for him, he was too angry to remember what happened the last time he left the visitors' parking lot.

• • •

Instead of turning on Bixby Road and going home, Ben continued north on Cherry. He didn't have to go too far to get to the Public Storage facility. Just a few blocks north of Carson Street, he stopped at the gate and fumbled through his wallet until he found the slip of paper with the gate code. He punched the number in and drove around back to the east side of the building. They had an outside ten-by-fifteen unit with drive-up access.

He parked the Volvo, unlocked the door, and heaved it open. Usually he'd get lost in nostalgia every time he'd visit. Seeing all the old furniture—most of which they'd moved out to make room for him when he was released from the rehab center—and so many of his mother's old possessions was comforting, and he'd spend an hour or two just going through things and trying to remember. In those early days, before Peter's first emergency surgery, they would visit every two or three months. He felt a pang thinking about the time when his father could remember more than he could himself, and he couldn't help wondering what would happen if he brought Peter back here now. Some of the things might trigger memories. It might be good for him.

Bring dad to storage unit, he scribbled in his book.

He didn't have time to linger today, though—he knew exactly why he was here. He worked his way to the back of the unit, past the rocking chair and the love seat and the bookcases and the plastic storage boxes to the small safe in the corner. He squatted down in front of it and entered the combination—his father's birthday, 7-25-34—and opened the door.

There was only one thing inside. A brown suede pistol rug. He took it out and unzipped it, laying it flat on top of the safe. The Smith & Wesson Model 65LS looked as clean and well maintained as it had the day he'd last locked it up inside, a few weeks after her funeral. It had been her carry gun when she first made detective, and it stayed with her through every subsequent plainclothes assignment of her career.

When he came home from the hospital, they told him it would be better if he didn't have access to firearms. Of course he found that insulting, but he also knew it was true. The department had already confiscated his duty weapon as part of the investigation of his shooting. So he sold his other two pistols, a Sig P229 that he sometimes carried off duty and the Ruger SP101 he used as a backup. But he'd forgotten about his mom's gun. Peter had moved the safe into the storage unit with all the other things and not mentioned it to Ben.

He picked up the revolver, checked the cylinder to be sure it wasn't loaded, pointed the muzzle at the concrete floor, and dry fired it a few times. Just as smooth as it had been decades ago when she taught him to shoot with it.

With the pistol rug on the passenger's seat, he drove down Cherry past his house one more time, turned left on Willow, and parked in front of Turner's Outdoorsman. Inside, he bought two boxes of .38 Special +P Hollow Points, and then, finally, went home.

TWENTY-FOUR

There was a towel in the back seat. He'd brought it out with him one day when the rain was particularly heavy, and since it hadn't cleared up for more than a few days at a time in the last few weeks, he left it there. Just in case he might need it.

He wrapped the case and the boxes of ammunition in it and went inside, hoping he could get them into his room without Bernie or his father asking about them. They were both in the living room watching a home-renovation show that Ben didn't recognize.

"Hey, guys," he said. "How's it going?"

Sriracha bounded over to him and wagged her tail. He reached down and scratched her head.

"Good," Bernie said. "How about you? Everything go okay downtown?"

"Yeah," Ben lied. "I think things are going to get cleared up pretty soon."

"That's good news."

Ben nodded. "How you doing, Dad?"

"Hanging in there," he said, watching the dog. He clapped his hands together lightly and she jogged back over to him. He leaned forward in his chair to pet her, then she jumped up into his lap.

Ben took that as his cue to disappear into the bedroom, closing the door behind him.

He put the bundled towel down on the bed and unfolded it. How long was it since he'd fired the revolver? Twenty-five years? More? He picked up the gun, felt its familiar heft, looked at the etched *Lady Smith* on the right side of the frame below the cylinder, remembered how lame he thought it was when he was thirteen. Only after his mother told him she'd taught his father to shoot with the same revolver did he finally agree that maybe a girl's gun wouldn't be so bad. A few years later, when she realized he was serious about following her career path, she'd taken him back to the range. It became a regular weekend routine.

Why had he bought two boxes of ammo? One would have been plenty. Even just six rounds. If Lopez came for them and they wound up needing the gun, they'd have two or three shots at most. There wouldn't be any reloading.

He pushed the cylinder release, slipped a round into each chamber, and clicked it back into place. Then he extended his arm, pointed the muzzle at the pillow on his bed, and focused on the front sight notched perfectly in the rear. Could he pull the trigger if he needed to? When he was still a cop, he'd occasionally pondered that question. The answer then was always yes.

There was a knock on the bedroom door, then his father's voice. "You okay?"

Ben moved to put the revolver in the top drawer in the nightstand, exactly where the Glock had been until he gave it to Grace, but the door opened when his hand was still two feet away, startling him. He tossed the gun in the drawer and pushed it closed.

"Did I scare you?"

"A little, yeah."

"I'm sorry."

Ben studied his father's face for a sign that he'd seen the gun. It didn't look like he had. "Yeah, I'm good. What's up?"

"Can we go outside?" Sriracha was rubbing herself against his leg.

"Just make sure the grass isn't still wet."

Peter nodded and headed for the patio door.

Bernie was still on the couch, watching a big guy in overalls point-ing at an exposed ceiling beam and explaining how somebody had really screwed it up.

"How'd it go with the cops?" he said.

"Not exactly what I was hoping for, but I think it's going to be okay."

"Good."

"You still rent out the cabin in Julian?"

"Sometimes, yeah."

"Anybody using it now?"

"No. Why?"

• • •

"Where is that?" Grace asked. "By Big Bear?"

"It's down south, inland from San Diego."

"Is that far enough away?"

"For now, I think it is. If Long Beach or San Bernardino don't get Lopez soon, we'll make other plans. Right now, though, it might be good if you're not completely cut off. I can let you know what's going on. When it's safe to come back."

"If. If it's safe to come back."

"Yeah," Ben said. "If."

• • •

The plan was simple enough. Grace would pack up, Ben would meet her at Kyle's place, bring her home so she could get the rest of her things from the studio, and then, early enough in the morning to beat the traf-fic, they would all head south to Bernie's cabin in Julian. Ben and Peter would stay with her for a day or two until she got settled, and then head back. It wasn't perfect, but he believed it was their best option. Even if Zepeda and Jennifer couldn't make the case against Lopez, and even if San Bernardino stonewalled them, the investigation would surely curtail and limit his actions. He had to know he was a suspect. There would be no direct link between Grace and Bernie, no electronic or paper records to track down to provide a trail. The only possible way Lopez could find out where Grace was going would be if he already had Ben under surveillance and followed them. There had been no indication that anyone had been watching, and Ben had exercised great caution. He was confident that they could make the trip undetected.

It was a good plan. It would work. Grace would be safe and she wouldn't walk away from her life and become someone else.

It was a good plan.

You're surprised at how angry you feel. The way she blindsided you. And how could she have done that to you? How could he have betrayed you like that? You want to scream, to throw something, to lash out.

"Oh no," Grace says. "I'm so sorry. I didn't mean to upset you."

Of course she's sorry. She didn't know. How could she possibly know? Your father couldn't tell her, any more than he could have betrayed you. He was just showing her photos in an album. All she said was that she didn't know you were married. Asked your wife's name.

The person you should be angry with is yourself. If you didn't want anyone to see the photos, you should have just taken them out of the album. But you didn't do that, did you? No. You were too worried about making yourself uncomfortable to look at them before you gave the book to your father. And you didn't even do that right, did you? If you really wanted to protect yourself you should have just thrown those photos out at the same time you dumped the wedding album in the garbage. But did you do that? No. Because you were too much of a pussy to even—

"Ben," she says softly, calmly, "I'm sorry."

"It's . . ." You try to get the words out, but they catch in your throat. "I try not to think about it." But you are thinking about it now. You can't stop thinking about it. About her.

They were in the living room, your father and Grace, sitting on the couch. Peter had the album in his lap and he was slowly turning the pages. You were watching from the dining room. They didn't seem to know you were there. He wasn't saying much. Occasionally he'd point out you or your mom, but mostly he was just looking. Grace was watching him as much as she was looking at the pictures. Mostly, he didn't seem to know what he was looking at, but every page or two he would see something that made his face light up, and she'd smile, too. When they got about two-thirds of the way through, Peter stopped, a sad look on his face. "What's wrong, Pete?"

she asked. He looked at her and whispered, "Kate." Whatever you did or said, you can't remember, but they both looked up at you with surprise and concern in their faces. Then you stormed out the patio door.

"It's okay," she says. "You don't have to talk about it. You want to go back inside?"

You do want to. You want to go back inside and forget this happened. But instead you sit down at the patio table. Grace sits next to you.

"Kate and I were married for nine years."

She doesn't say anything, but you can see the question in her eyes.

"Do you remember when I told you about the hole?"

She looks puzzled.

"The time I can't remember, all those months I lost around the time that I was shot?"

"Yes."

"Kate left me a little over a month before it happened."

Grace's eyes widen. "And you don't remember it?"

"Not at all. The last thing I remember, we were happily married." You don't want to think about it, but you can't help it. "The edges of the hole are hazy, you know? Kind of like when you can't quite remember a dream? The last clear memory of us together is here, having dinner with my dad." You close your eyes, remember standing next to her in the kitchen, helping with the dishes, sneaking a kiss when your father stepped out of the room. "We did that after my mom died. Tried to see him more often. That was Kate. She worried about him."

You're quiet for a long time. Not wanting to say what comes next.

"Next thing I remember, she's by my bed in the hospital, crying, trying to explain. She shows me the divorce papers I signed before everything went down. She'd told me before, but I didn't believe her, thought it was some kind of cruel joke. That's why she had the papers with her. Why, I asked her, why?" You can't bring yourself to repeat her words.

"What did she say?" she asks.

"That I fucked someone else."

You watch her reaction. Is there a flash of revulsion in the narrowing of her eyes and the turned-down corners of her mouth? If there is, it vanishes as quickly as it appeared.

"I told her that wasn't true. That I'd never do something like that. She said, 'You really believe that, don't you?' I did believe it. More than I believed anything. Somehow I think that hurt her even more."

Grace can see where you're headed, and you're glad that you don't have to explain it. "Who was it?"

"A patrol sergeant from North Division. It was a one-time thing. We both drank too much at a retirement party. She seemed almost as hurt as Kate that I couldn't remember. I interviewed her like a witness. Wrote everything down in my little notebook like it happened to someone else. Even now, it still feels like that."

"And you have no memory of any of it?"

You shake your head. "I still can't believe I did it, that I was even capable of that."

Grace's face is clouded. Is she disappointed in you? How could she not be? You loved Kate more than anything. You can't remember a time when you ever even thought about betraying her, when you'd ever even consider it. Yet you did. You're not just disappointed, you're ashamed.

"Sometimes," Grace says, putting her hand on top of yours, "I don't think we really know any more about who we were than about who we're going to be."

She squeezes your hand, stands up, and walks across the lawn toward her door without looking back.

After his father was in bed, Ben let Bernie in. "Where's Sriracha?"

"Left her home. She'd just make noise and keep your dad up."

"Thanks for doing this. We should be back in two hours or so."

"No worries," Bernie said, sitting down on the couch and flipping the channels around until he found the DIY Network.

Ben went out the front door and walked the street from one end of the block to the other, looking for cars he didn't recognize or anything else out of place, then turned the corner and did the same in the alley.

When he was satisfied that no one was watching, he went through the gate and checked the keyhole on the knob of the back door of the garage. The tiny dab of toothpaste was still there. The one on the padlock in front was still there, too, until he picked it off with his fingernail and opened the door. No one else had been in the garage. Still, to be cautious, he checked the Volvo with the RF-signal detector one more time. It was clean.

With the garage locked and a fresh dot of toothpaste on the padlock, Ben turned right out of the alley and, following protocol, did a series of stair-step right and left turns through California Heights, then complete laps around two separate blocks. When he was absolutely certain no one was following him, he got on the freeway. After exiting in Harbor City, he repeated the process. He knew it was overkill, but he wasn't going to take any chances.

• • •

"When is Kyle coming back?" Ben asked.

"Two weeks or so, he said." Grace had packed everything into her suitcase and backpack. She hadn't brought much with her.

"We're going to need to borrow his car for a while. Yours can stay in his garage."

"I'm not sure about that," she said.

"Don't worry. I'll make sure it gets back here before he does. Taking your car isn't a good idea."

"Because they might spot it."

"Right," he said. "You want to take one more look around to make sure you have everything?"

Grace shook her head. "I had everything ten minutes after you called."

"What's the plan?" Ben asked.

"You follow me back to the house. I park in the alley by the garage and wait for you to do a lap around the block to check things out, then we park both cars inside."

"That's it. You ready?"

She sighed. "I haven't been ready for anything since they found Steph's shit in my trunk."

• • •

It was raining again by the time they loaded her things into the back of Kyle's Kia Soul, but otherwise everything went according to plan.

"Hi, Bernie," Grace said, entering the living room.

He stood up and gave her a hug she wasn't expecting.

"Ben told me everything you've done to help. Thank you."

"No problem."

"Is Julian as nice as Ben says?"

"You like apple pie?"

"Doesn't everybody?"

"How about snow?"

She raised her eyebrows. "There's snow?"

"Yeah, with all the storms, they just got a bunch."

"I haven't seen snow in a long time."

"Looks like it's going to be a white Groundhog Day."

Ben had an odd sense of déjà vu but couldn't figure out why. He held the manila envelope Bernie had given him earlier, with the keys to the cabin and two pages of instructions on how to manage everything from the kitchen appliances to the furnace to the toilets.

"Did you see the weather for tomorrow?" Bernie asked.

Ben had been checking regularly, but the day had gotten away from him. "Not for the last day or two," he said.

"Supposed to be coming down hard tomorrow. Like real hard."

Shit. Ben had been so on top of everything. Why hadn't he thought to check that? "I'll take a look. Unless it's crazy bad, I think we'll still probably head out."

"Okay, you let me know if you need anything."

"We will."

Bernie looked at Grace. "You got my number, right?"

She shook her head.

"I'll make sure she has it before we take off. And remember, I won't have my regular phone."

"Yeah, I have the other number." He grinned. "That's a burner, right, like they talk about on TV?"

Ben nodded. "Yeah."

Bernie seemed to love that. On the front porch he said, "It's already starting to come down. I should have brought my umbrella."

"You want to borrow one?" Ben asked.

"Nah. You'll need it in the morning." He flipped his hood up over his head and jogged up the street to his house.

Ben shut the door and locked the deadbolt. When he turned around he saw Grace standing by the patio door and looking out into the darkness.

The plan had been to pack up the rest of her things before bed so they could be ready to go first thing in the morning. He and Peter were both already set with food and meds and a few changes of clothes. But as he watched her, he reconsidered. She hadn't left much in the studio, and he'd already moved a few empty boxes in from the garage for her to use. They'd only need an extra half hour or so to do it after they woke up.

He took a few steps toward her and she turned to him. She was trying to be calm and nonchalant, but he could see the tension in her neck and shoulders.

"Do you think maybe—"

Ben cut her off. "You're going to take my bed tonight. I'm okay on the couch. Been sleeping there as often as not the last few weeks anyway."

"You sure?" she said. "I really don't mind."

"I'm sure." He didn't tell her he wasn't expecting to sleep much, and if he did manage to nod off for a while he wanted to be in the living room, closer to the center of the house, just in case, to maintain better situational awareness.

While she took a shower, he changed the sheets on the bed and got the revolver out of the nightstand. He stashed it under one of the pillows on the sofa. It occurred to him to ask her about the Glock, but he didn't want her trying to go to sleep thinking about the gun. One person in the house worrying about that would be plenty.

She came out of the bathroom wearing pajama bottoms and a T-shirt that said *Pussy Grabs Back*.

"Sorry you missed the Women's March today," he said.

"I watched it on TV," she said.

"It's going to get better."

She smiled at him, but he didn't believe her.

• • •

1/21 11:15 pm
~~Evening Meds~~
Anxious about tomorrow (ONE lorazepam only—Need to be able
to wake up, just in case)
Weather says a lot of rain, worried too much to go
Is it safe?

• • •

It was almost midnight when Amy called to tell him a cop had come to the restaurant asking about Grace.

"Did you get his name?" he asked.

"No."

He described Lopez to her. "That sounds like him," she said. "Talked to a few different people. It didn't seem like he knew that Grace and I were friends."

"That's good. What did he ask you?"

"Just basic stuff, like how well I knew her. I lied. Said I only knew her at work. Was that the right thing to do?"

"Yes, it was. Did he ask anything else?"

"Just if she had ever said anything about where she came from, and if I knew her boyfriend."

"Did he say that? Boyfriend? Did he say Kyle's name?"

"He didn't. It didn't sound like he knew anything about him for sure."

"That's good, Amy. Thank you for calling. This helps a lot."

"Do you think you'll be able to find her before he does?"

He wanted to tell her that he already had, but he knew they would all be safer if he didn't. "I do, yeah."

After she hung up, Ben sat at the computer for almost an hour, logged in to Weather.com and watching the overnight Doppler radar projections for Long Beach. The yellow-and-orange blob indicating heavy precipitation twisted and whirled across the map for the foreseeable future. He didn't know how Lopez had found his way to the Attic. Maybe he had followed the same trail of breadcrumbs from Rob's notes that Ben himself had. It didn't really matter. What mattered was that Lopez was getting closer. Ben thought they would be all right holed up here during the rain. There were no hidden transmitters of any kind, and up until that point, no one was watching, of that he was confident. Lopez would still have no way of knowing she was here. Even if he did, Ben couldn't imagine him thinking there was a solid tactical approach without a full team backing him up. Could that be within his capabilities? It didn't seem likely. Not in another jurisdiction where he was already a suspect in a murder investigation.

The more he thought about it, though, the more he worried. They would leave in the morning, no matter how hard the rain was falling.

With nothing else to do other than wait, Ben put the revolver on the coffee table, covering it with a kitchen towel in case anyone came into the living room, stretched out on the sofa under a fleece blanket, and watched the talking heads on cable news mutter under the endless footage of millions of women who had turned out to march, all over the country, because of their hopeful belief that no matter how frightening things had become, they didn't have to stay that way.

Ben slept more than he had expected to. Maybe three and a half hours when all the tossing, turning, and bathroom time was subtracted. But by a quarter after four, he knew he was done and no more rest was in the cards.

He made himself toast and coffee and sat back down on the couch. The local news was beginning its early-morning broadcast in full *Stormwatch!* mode and saying it looked like some new Southern California rainfall records would be set in the coming hours.

With his hopes dimmed and nothing else to do, he checked his Fitbit. Six hundred eighty-seven steps since midnight. It would be a few hours before anyone else got up, so he started in on the living-room-dining-table-kitchen circuit. If he paced himself and didn't get distracted, he might be able to hit ten thousand before sunrise.

TWENTY-FIVE

Grace was the first one up, less than half an hour after Ben had written *11,227* in his notebook.

"How'd you sleep?" Ben asked.

"Better than I expected to," she said. "It was nice not to be the only one in the house for a change."

"Breakfast? I'm sorry, I didn't think to go shopping, so we don't have much."

"You've got yogurt and oatmeal, right?"

"That we do." He filled the kettle and put it on the stove to boil. While he waited, he poured her a cup of coffee.

"It's really coming down out there, isn't it?" she said.

It was. Ben was surprised the sound of the rain hitting the roof and splashing down onto the patio hadn't awakened his father. "Yeah. I've been watching on TV and the computer. It's not as bad down south, but we should probably see what happens for a while before we leave."

"Okay." She took a sip of her coffee. If she was concerned about the delay, Ben couldn't see it.

The kettle whistled and he poured a quarter cup of hot water into the bowl with the instant oatmeal and stirred it up. He put it and the sugar bowl on the counter in front of Grace.

"Do you have any cinnamon?" she asked.

He opened the cupboard and, after moving a few dozen unused spice containers out of the way, found a red-and-white can in the back. He looked at it closely, trying to find an expiration date.

"It's okay, I don't think it goes bad," she said.

"You sure?"

"I'll risk it. I'm feeling pretty daring these days." There was a smile on her face of a kind he hadn't seen in a long time.

He was happy to see her in a good mood, but couldn't help worrying that it might be premature.

After a long shower, he came out in fresh clothes and found her in the living room sitting on the couch, with a cup of coffee in one hand and the remote in the other. She looked at him and said, "Boy, you've got a lot of cop shows in your Netflix queue."

Ben chuckled. "I like to watch them and complain about how they get all the police stuff wrong."

"Who do you complain to?"

"Just myself, mostly."

"Are you trying to make me sad?"

Ben gestured for her to hand him the remote. She did and he thumbed through his list until he found what he was looking for. He hit "Play" and handed the controller back to her. That was when he realized he'd left the towel-covered revolver on the coffee table. Trying to be nonchalant, he grabbed the gun through the fabric one-handed and picked up the whole bundle.

"What's that?" Grace asked.

With his other hand, he unwrapped just enough of it so she could see the walnut grip.

In his bedroom, he put the gun in the nightstand, and he slid the drawer shut just as the theme song to *Unbreakable Kimmy Schmidt* began playing in the other room.

• • •

"Is it time to go?" Peter asked, shuffling into the kitchen.

"Not yet, Dad," Ben said. "It's raining too hard. We're going to wait a while, until it lets up a bit."

He looked out the window. "It's a lot," he said, sitting down at the counter to his oatmeal and Boost/coffee.

The storm was showing no signs of slowing. It was actually coming down even harder. He didn't even need to check outside. The muffled thrum of the rainfall on the roof told him everything he needed to know.

Not long after Peter finished eating, Grace had changed into jeans and a green hooded jacket that looked like it had its work cut out for it with the deluge outside. "I'm going to go out to the studio and get my stuff packed up."

"Let me just change my shoes and grab an umbrella," Ben said.

"That's okay. I've got my key."

"Wait just a second," he said, unsure whether he was being patronizing or condescending. Maybe it was both? "Let me check it out. I'll feel better."

"Sure," she said, seeming unconcerned by Ben's caution. He went into his bedroom and slipped on a pair of waterproof Rockports. In the coat closet he found the big umbrella and met Grace by the patio door.

Outside it was much louder. The water rushed off the edge of the patio roof like a waterfall. The lawn was saturated, and the small concrete walkway between the grass and the planter along the wall of the house looked like a floating bridge on a swamp. If the storm didn't ease up, it would soon be submerged. With Grace huddled close, he opened the umbrella and they started back.

Ben had expected cold, but ten steps off the patio, he was already beginning to shiver. The covered porch outside the studio door was much smaller, but there was enough room for both of them to get out of the rain. Grace unlocked the door and stepped inside while Ben closed the umbrella and propped it up against the frame. He shook as much water as he could off of his shoes and followed her.

He gestured to the five packing boxes he'd brought in from the garage. "I thought you could use these."

"I missed this place," she said, not looking at him.

"Well, hopefully you'll be able to come back soon."

When she turned to him, her eyes looked faraway and he waited for her to say something. She didn't.

Ben adjusted the thermostat, surprised that he could hear the furnace click on with the noise of the rain outside. "Do you want some help?"

"No," she said.

"All right. I'll let you get to it, then." He stood there. "I, uh, turned the heat way up, so if it gets too—"

"Thanks." She smiled at him for the first time since they'd come inside. "I'll just be a few minutes."

Outside, Ben went around the corner to check the lock on the gate. It was still secured. With the storm raging, he didn't expect to find the toothpaste on the keyhole. He was right. The rain had washed it away.

Halfway back on the walkway, he saw Peter standing at the edge of the patio in his bare feet, watching him.

"Dad, your feet! What are you doing?"

"I didn't want to get my slippers wet."

• • •

After Ben got his father's feet dried off, warmed up, and reslippered, he checked his phone and realized Jennifer had called while he was out in the studio with Grace. He called her back.

"What's up?" he asked.

"Sowers is dead. He killed himself."

Ben was silent.

Jennifer went on. "GSW to the right temple. He drove his red Camaro off to the side of the road in Twentynine Palms and pulled the trigger."

"You sure it was suicide? He didn't have any help?"

"He left a note."

"What did it say?"

"He confessed to killing Rob. Said he was the one skimming the drugs and money. Exonerated the rest of the team."

"Lopez too?"

"Everyone. Said he acted alone."

"Are they sure he wrote it?"

"It was in his own handwriting."

Ben tried to remember everything Grace had told him. Was it possible that it was all Sowers? Maybe. According to what she'd said, the only thing she knew for sure about Lopez was that he'd violated the terms of their confidential-informant contract and kept stringing her along to make more buys and arrests. That was a shitty thing to do, but not at all uncommon with CIs, especially when they were working Narcotics. And it was a long way from murder. All he really had on Lopez came from the few vague hints Rob had dropped.

"Rob seemed confident that Lopez was calling the shots," he said.

"It doesn't look like that," Jennifer said. "Zepeda's going to call it on the murder case. He's got a signed confession. You can let Grace know she's in the clear."

Ben felt light-headed. Could it really be over? He hurried to the door and put his boots back on.

"What is it?" Peter asked.

"Good news, Dad, very good news."

Peter smiled at him as he grabbed the umbrella and hurried out into the rain. He knocked on the door, but couldn't wait for a response before turning the knob.

As soon as the door opened, he heard Grace yell, "Ben, no!"

He never even saw the pistol as it whipped across his temple and he collapsed to the floor.

TWENTY-SIX

The next thing Ben knew, he was being dragged across the room. His head felt like it was on fire and his vision was blurry. He didn't know what had happened, why he had fallen, who was pulling him by the collar. Then his face hit something, bounced, and he was prone on the floor. He rolled over, realized he was next to a couch. No. It was a sofa bed. Grace's sofa bed. Folded closed. In the studio. And there was Grace, leaning over him, helping him sit up, asking, "Are you all right?" Why was she wearing handcuffs? He couldn't focus.

"Shit, man, I wish you'd stayed in the house. This fucking rain, you wouldn't have even heard anything." It was Lopez, standing by the door, pointing a pistol at them. Was it a Sig? Ben thought it looked like a Sig.

"How much does the old man know?"

Ben felt something flare inside his head.

Grace said, "He has dementia. He doesn't know anything."

There was a hardness in her voice Ben had never heard before. *Focus,* he told himself. *Breathe.* He did, in through the nose, out through the mouth. The pressure between his temples seemed to be bleeding out. A few more seconds, he needed a few more seconds. "How'd you do it?" he asked Lopez.

"What?"

Still on the floor, Ben got his arm up on the seat cushion, hoisted himself up a little more, propped his shoulder against the arm of the sofa. "Get Sowers to write the confession before he blew his brains out?"

"Easy. Brett went home two nights ago, his wife and baby weren't there. He decided he didn't want anything bad to happen to them."

Then Ben saw it. A long shot, but so what? Lopez was going to shoot them both anyway. Then maybe kill his father just in case. He only needed to move his foot a couple of inches. "And what about Rob?"

"What about him? You don't already understand that, then you're just shit out of—"

Ben brought both knees up to his chest and drove the heels of his boots into the edge of the coffee table with all his strength.

Lopez tried to raise the Sig and aim, but the opposite edge of the table impacted his shins with enough force to knock his feet out from under him and topple him. The pistol shot went high and wide as he landed on the tabletop and rolled off to end facedown on the other side.

Ears ringing, Ben scrambled onto his knees and lunged over the table onto Lopez, wrapping both hands around his right wrist, trying to control the weapon. With one knee between the shoulder blades and the other on the elbow, Ben was able to twist the pistol out of Lopez's grip. He thought he felt the trigger finger snap as he yanked it free.

Grace was on her feet and yelling something, but Ben still could barely hear her.

"What?" he shouted.

Then Lopez bucked and sent Ben back to the floor, the Sig skittering out of his hand and across the tile of the kitchenette.

Lopez swung a wild backhand that caught Grace square in the jaw and dropped her, then he charged toward Ben, who was up on his hands and knees, making his abdomen a perfect target.

Ben saw the kick coming, tried to roll away from it, but was too slow. Lopez's steel-toed oxford caught him in the ribs and he was on his back again, gasping desperately to fill his lungs with air.

When he could focus, Ben looked up into the muzzle of the Sig. He had survived one bullet in the head only to die by a second.

Lopez was standing a few feet off to his right, just far enough away that Ben would not be able to get to him before he could pull the trigger. He was holding the pistol in both hands, his left index finger in the trigger guard.

At least I managed that, Ben thought as he heard the gun go off.

TWENTY-SEVEN

After you tell her about Kate, you make a point of not joining them for coffee the next few mornings. You fix Peter's breakfast and then go back and hide in your room or take a shower. Maybe you peek out the window and watch them for a minute or two, maybe you don't.

You ask yourself over and over why you told her, why you opened up the old wound after you'd spent so much time and effort burying it in layer after layer of scar tissue.

She says, "Hey, Ben," but her voice sounds different. At least you imagine that it does.

You say, "Hey" but turn your eyes away and offer nothing else.

It goes on like that for a while. The awkwardness begins to feel normal. Like this is how it's supposed to be, like what came before was the aberration.

Then the mailman leaves three green plastic shipping bags from L.L. Bean on the porch and you remember it's almost Christmas. You go out into the garage and get a couple of boxes to use to wrap up your father's new pants and shirts. For the last few years, you've told yourself you're not going to bother with the decorations anymore because your father doesn't really seem to notice and it just makes you sad, but then you reach up to the top shelf and take down the box with the little pre-lit tabletop Christmas tree and bring it inside and set it up on the end table in the living room anyway.

"It's time?" Peter says as you plug it in and hang a few of your mother's old ornaments on the plastic branches.

"Yeah, Dad, it is."

"What about for her?"

You know who he means, but you say it anyway. "For who?"

"For Grace."

He remembers her name.

• • •

You don't see her at all on Christmas Eve. In the morning, you make the breakfast your father always made for you before you opened presents, scrambled eggs and silver-dollar pancakes. He insists on bundling up and eating on the patio and is clearly disappointed when she doesn't join you.

"Can we ask her?" he says.

You'd rather not, but his sad eyes are too much for you to bear, so the two of you walk back to the studio and knock on the door.

She's been crying.

You don't know what to say.

Your father does. "We have pancakes."

• • •

She opens the box of See's Candies. It was Peter's idea. The one thing your mother got you every year. Your very own box. All creams. When you tell her about it, she starts to tear up again.

"What's wrong?" Peter asks.

"I miss my mom."

"You can go see her," he says. Then he turns to you. "Can we take her?"

You're not sure what to say, but she speaks first. "She died, Pete. This is only my second Christmas without her."

Peter moves over to the sofa, sits next to her, and pats her leg. Then he looks at you. "How many for us?" he says.

You have to think about it before you answer. "Eight," you finally say.

Later, after you've all watched Elf, *she asks you to walk her back to the studio.*

At the door, she hugs you and says, "Thank you for today."

Then she looks you in the eyes. She sees that there's something you want to say but can't, so she speaks instead. "It doesn't matter who we used to be, Ben. All that matters is who we are now."

She says it with such simple certainty that you almost believe her.

TWENTY-EIGHT

Ben knew he shouldn't have heard the gun at all.

He should have been dead.

Lopez seemed surprised, too. Then they heard the second shot and he spun toward the door.

He was still moving when the third shot caught him just in front of the ear and half his face disappeared. His body collapsed to the floor. Shot four hit him in the shoulder as he rolled over onto his back. Five and six were center mass in the middle of his chest.

Ben turned toward Grace. She must have had the Glock hidden somewhere. But no, she was staring at Lopez with the same shocked amazement that Ben himself had.

Simultaneously they both turned their heads toward the door.

Peter stood there, soaking wet, shivering, still pointing the revolver at Lopez's body and pulling the trigger, the hammer falling again and again on the spent cartridges.

As Ben struggled to his feet, his father looked at him and lowered the gun. Ben was unsteady and felt unbalanced. He had to put a hand on the wall to stop himself from falling.

Grace was already up and next to Peter. Hands still cuffed, she delicately took the revolver from Peter's hands and dropped it onto the sofa cushion. She was saying something to him, but Ben couldn't hear. His ears were still ringing. Or they were ringing again. He wasn't sure.

Could he hear the rain pounding on the roof or was that something else? As he got closer to them he could see his father was saying something to Grace over and over. She was shaking her head.

The light began to brighten outside, silhouetting them in the doorway.

He smelled something burning.

The ringing faded.

The last thing he heard before the seizure took him was his father's voice, thick with fear.

"Did I do something bad?"

TWENTY-NINE

When he came to, Ben was strapped to a gurney in the back of an ambulance. An EMT was next to him, saying, "Mr. Shepard? Can you hear me?" She looked very young.

Ben nodded. "Yes." His voice felt sticky in his mouth. He could taste blood.

"You may have a concussion." She released the buckle on the strap across his chest. "Do you know what day it is?"

"Where's my father?"

"He's okay. What day is it?"

"Sunday. Where's Grace?"

"She's okay, too. I need you to follow my finger with your eyes, okay?" She held up her index finger and moved it slowly back and forth across his field of vision. Ben only wanted to get up, to go to Peter and Grace, so he did his best to comply. When she seemed satisfied, she said, "Who's the president?"

He remembered Grace's T-shirt. "If you're evaluating trauma, you probably shouldn't ask that anymore."

"I'm just going to put down that you got that one right."

Ben couldn't stay there much longer or he'd snap. "Please, I need to go see my father."

"We need to take you to the ER for some more tests."

"Please," he said. "I need to know he's okay. He has dementia and he needs help. Just let me check on him and I'll·go with you."

"Let me talk to somebody. I'll see what we can do."

She opened the door, went outside, and closed it. Ben only got a quick glimpse, but it was enough for him to see that the rain was still coming down and the ambulance was parked in the alley, not more than thirty feet from Grace's door.

It seemed to take forever.

Ben was feeling groggy and his head hurt. His whole body hurt. When he shifted on the gurney, there was a sharp, stabbing pain on his right side where Lopez had kicked him. Probably a broken rib.

What was taking so long? His mind began to race when he realized the ambulance meant the police were there, too. How long had he been unconscious? Was Homicide here yet? Were they questioning his father?

He remembered the last words his father had said before the seizure hit. "Did I do something bad?" If Homicide was interrogating him, they'd go over it and over it again and again. It would stay with him. Maybe not the details, but the accusations and implications.

Shit, what if it was Zepeda? That withered old bastard had all the sensitivity of a concrete block. The questions could be even more agitating and traumatizing than the shooting itself. Ben sat up, his ribs screaming, and leaned forward to unstrap his legs.

What was taking so damn long?

Somebody pounded on the door. Loud, so it would be heard over the drumming on the roof. He heard the latch click, and the door swung open. A head in a dripping hood popped inside. Ben recognized the face.

"Detective Shepard? I'm Dan—"

"I know who you are," Ben said, swinging his legs to the side and planting his feet on the floor. "Jennifer's partner."

"I was. We need you to—"

"Who caught the case?" Ben was dizzy when he stood. Nearly hit his head on the roof. "Are you the primary?"

"No," he said. "Because of the connection to the other—"

"It's Zepeda?" Ben was at the door, trying to push his way past the detective, who had his arms spread and a hand holding on to each edge of the door frame.

"You really need to sit back down."

"What I need is to see my father. I'm his legal guardian and I have power of attorney. No one is saying another word until we have our attorney here."

The detective had a puzzled look on his face, but stepped to the side so Ben could climb down out of the ambulance.

Before he even had both feet on the ground, the icy rain was pounding him, soaking though his thin shirt and cutting to the bone. Ben started for the gate, but the detective grabbed his elbow.

"Crime scene," he said. "Have to go that way." He pointed to the other gate on the far side of the garage.

Before he even finished the sentence, Ben was halfway there. He ran along the side of the garage, ignoring the flood of rain sheeting off the edge of the roof. By the time he reached the kitchen, he was soaked through. He couldn't have gotten any wetter.

There was a uniform inside by the sink. Ben shouted, "Where's Zepeda?"

Eyes wide, the officer said, "With the shooter," and hooked a thumb toward the front bedroom. Ben's room.

He hurried through the dining room and charged toward the closed bedroom door.

But something caught his eye and stopped him where he stood.

Peter.

Sitting by himself in the middle of the sofa, hugging himself and slowly rocking forward and back. Another uniform stood watch in the corner.

Ben sat next to him, put his arms around his shoulders. His father leaned in to him and whispered, "She told me not to say anything to anybody."

Only then did Ben begin to understand what Grace was doing in the other room.

• • •

The rain kept coming. It only started to ease as evening came and Zepeda finally cleared out with the rest of the cops. The floors were covered in puddles and splotches of mud throughout the house, and everything felt contaminated by the throngs of strangers that had invaded their home.

Ben used to feel comfortable around cops, at ease, a part of the family. The way that comfort had transformed into awkwardness after he was shot was one of his most overpowering regrets. Now, though, all he felt was disdain.

Earlier, after Zepeda had finished with Grace, he immediately called Ben into his own bedroom. It was one of the first rules—keep the witnesses apart, never let them have a chance to get their stories synched.

"Have a seat," Zepeda said, gesturing to the bed.

"Should I make myself at home?" Ben regretted the snark before he'd even completed the sentence.

"I know this is rough." There was more compassion in his voice than Ben had expected. "Is your dad holding up okay?"

"As well as can be expected."

"We'll try to make this as quick as we can."

Grace had been in here with him for an hour and a half. "Thanks."

"What happened?"

Ben thought carefully about his words. He had a strong suspicion of what Grace had told him, but he couldn't be sure. There was only one way to back her play without being certain of what it was. "I don't remember."

Of course, it wasn't that easy. With Zepeda's probing, Ben led him through the last twenty-four hours. From the planning of the escape to Julian, through the long night, into the morning's rain delay and the call from Jennifer.

"Then what?"

"I went back to the studio to tell Grace the good news. Opened up the door, stepped inside, got hit in the head." Ben turned his head so Zepeda could get a good look at the contusion and swelling where Lopez had pistol-whipped him.

"That's the last thing you remember?"

"Yeah."

And that was it. Zepeda made him go through it all three more times. With each retelling, the lie got easier. Maybe, with a little luck, he really would be able to forget the truth.

Now they were gone, but they'd left their mark. The studio and the entire yard, from the patio back, were cordoned off with yellow crime-scene tape, the floors covered in wet and muddy footprints, the back lawn swamped by the storm and torn and rutted by the dozens of strangers and their thousands of steps.

Ben sat down on the sofa next to his father and Grace.

"What did you tell them?" he asked her.

"That Lopez was going to kill you and I shot him," she said. There was more, Ben knew, much more, but he didn't need to hear anything else. She had spared his father from the investigation. She knew what it would do to him, the relentless questioning, having to go over it again and again, maybe even a trial. He might not remember the details. But no matter what the outcome of the investigation was, after having the details of the shooting drilled into him over and over, the shadow would engulf him. And no matter what they told him, he would never believe he hadn't done a bad thing. They still might not be able to convince him that he'd saved their lives, that what he'd done was something good. But at least now there would be a chance of that. So Ben didn't need to hear anything else. Not then, at least.

Peter was quiet and his eyes were faraway. Ben put his arm around him and felt him shivering. The fleece blanket Ben had used, sleeping there the night before, was folded on the ottoman. He reached over and spread it across his father's lap, pulling the edge up over his abdomen and tucking it under his arms. Then he leaned in and kissed him on the cheek.

"You saved our lives, Dad."

Peter turned toward him and said, "I did?"

"Yeah. You did a good thing."

THIRTY

Ben decided to replace the whole floor in the studio. The blood had seeped too deeply into the wood for it to be refinished. The contractor said he could just replace the damaged slats and that the patch job would only be noticeable if you knew what you were for looking for, but that wouldn't work. Ben would always know.

He showed Grace some samples and she chose a nice blond-streaked bamboo. And since they'd need to move everything out anyway, why not have the place painted, too?

For Ben, it was a good distraction from the continuing investigation. He'd spent four long days downtown repeating the story of the shooting and what had led up to it for different groups of suits from Long Beach and San Bernardino. Grace had been there even more than he had. Peter only had to do one brief interview that Zepeda recorded on video. The old detective was surprisingly gentle with him and didn't even press when the answers didn't seem to add up into a coherent narrative.

By the time the renovation was completed, there were all-new furniture, an upgraded refrigerator in the kitchenette, and retractable shades on all the windows. Grace had been uncomfortable making so many of the choices when she wasn't sure of her plans, but Ben wouldn't take no for an answer.

• • •

"How's your dad doing?" Jennifer asked. They were sitting on the patio. The sun was shining and the air was clear and cold. It had been eleven days.

"Not too bad."

She studied him. He wondered if she suspected what had really happened. If she did, would she understand why Grace lied and why he went along with it? She would, he thought, but understanding probably wouldn't be enough for her to let it go. Unless she'd changed in the years since they'd worked together. She'd always been by the book, and he had always respected her integrity. But that was the old Ben Shepard. Now he wasn't sure that integrity meant the same thing to him it once had.

"Have they made the call yet?"

"It's complicated. Dead cops and multiple jurisdictions and everything. But Zepeda's calling what happened here justified."

"Is he getting pushback?"

"Nothing strong enough to worry about. Just a lot of red tape before they close it."

"That's good," Ben said. "They figure out how Lopez knew she was here?" That question had been keeping him up at night. He couldn't stop worrying that he'd screwed up, that he'd missed something, that it was his fault.

"That's one of the things I wanted to show you." She slid her iPad out of its case, flipped open the cover, and started tapping and swiping. When she turned it around, he saw a picture of a house taken from overhead. It took a second for it to register that he was looking at his own home. He swiped through ten or twelve more pictures taken at different times of day and in different weather conditions, and he realized.

Tim over on Gardenia wasn't the only one with a drone.

"I didn't know you could fly those in the rain."

"Some of the high-end ones you can. Nothing but the best for the narcs."

"I tried to be careful. To make sure no one was watching."

"You did good, Ben. I wouldn't have thought to watch out for something like this, and I'm supposed to be on top of this kind of stuff. Drones weren't even a thing the last time you wore your shield. How could you know?"

He felt a pang of guilt for all the things he was holding back from her. But he managed it. He had one more question for her. "Can I get my mother's gun back?"

"We can probably swing that if it goes down the way it looks like it will."

He walked her out to her car. "Lunch soon?"

She smiled at him. "I'd like that."

•   •   •

Two days after they'd gotten the official word that Lopez's shooting had been ruled justifiable homicide, the electrician finished hanging the new ceiling fan and they went inside.

"Wow," Grace said. "This doesn't even look like the same place."

It was true. The room his mother had decorated so long ago was gone. For Ben, though, that room had disappeared the moment Lopez had stepped inside. Now, the room where he died was gone, too.

"What do you think?" Ben said, rubbing the back of his head. "Want to give it a try?"

Grace nodded. "I think so. Yeah."

"Does it feel weird, with what happened?"

"No," she said. "It ended here. It feels safe."

•   •   •

It had been three and a half weeks since the last seizure, on the day of the storm. He didn't mention it when they did the CAT scan the next day. Somehow, the results came back negative, no concussion. If he had another one before his neuro consult, he'd report it. He couldn't risk a mandatory DMV suspension of his license. How would he take care of Peter if he couldn't drive? Besides, he was doing better than he had in a long time.

They all were. He'd been worried about his father, but the nightmares that came every night the first week were fading. It had been six days since the last one. And Grace was checking out the grad program at Cal State Long Beach. Maybe she wouldn't go back to Riverside after all.

After the storm flooded Long Beach with more rain than any other ever had, even the rain seemed to be moving on.

On their evening walk, Peter looked disappointed when Sriracha bounded up to them and greeted Grace before she greeted him. But then the sound of a small plane rose in the distance and he looked up to search the sky for it.

Ben saw it before his father did, one of the training flights, passing from behind the cover of the trees into view, and banking north to continue its loop. "There it is," he said, pointing up at the plane so his father could see.

Peter's hand shot up high over his head and he waved it back and forth.

Then it happened. The plane dipped its wing toward them.

Peter stopped waving, turned quickly to Ben, as if he couldn't believe what he had just seen. Ben nodded, and Peter turned back to the plane and waved even more enthusiastically than before.

The plane dipped its wing again.

Peter kept waving as it flew past them, then turned to Ben, his eyes alight with joyful wonder. "Did they really?"

"Yeah, they really did, Dad." Ben felt something catch in his throat. "They waved back. They saw us."

Photo © 2012 Nicole Gharda

Tyler Dilts received his BA in theater from Cal State Long Beach and performed in more than sixty plays before turning his focus to writing. His work has appeared in the *Los Angeles Times*, the *Los Angeles Review of Books*, and *The Best American Mystery Stories*. He is also the author of the Long Beach Homicide series of detective novels: *A King of Infinite Space*, *The Pain Scale*, *A Cold and Broken Hallelujah* (an Amazon #1 bestseller) and, most recently, the Edgar Award–nominated *Come Twilight*. In 2014, he was the Writer-in-Residence at John Cabot University in Rome, and in 2015 he joined the teaching staff of the Community of Writers at Squaw Valley. He currently teaches English at his alma mater, where his specialties include creative writing, crime fiction, and literary theory. He lives with his wife in Long Beach, California. Contact Tyler at www.facebook.com/tylerdiltsbooks.